Also by Stephen Blackmoore:
CITY OF THE LOST

DEAD THINGS

STEPHEN BLACKMOORE

DAW BOOKS, INC.

DONALD A. WOLLHEIM, FOUNDER

375 Hudson Street, New York, NY 10014

ELIZABETH R. WOLLHEIM

SHEILA E. GILBERT

PUBLISHERS

http://www.dawbooks.com

First Printing, February 2013

ACKNOWLEDGMENTS

Writing is hard.

Not ditch-digging hard. Not cancer-curing hard. But there's a lot to juggle, a lot to keep track of. It'll eat your brain like it's a Little Debbie snack cake if you're not careful. Mmmmm. Munch-munch. Braaaaains. Just like that. And if you don't have people in your corner, people rooting for you, helping you out, you're screwed. I've been lucky to have some amazing people in my corner.

Many thanks to all of the friends who have helped make this book what it is. People like Chuck Wendig, John Hornor Jacobs, Chris Holm and other people too numerous to count. Your input and support has meant a tremendous amount to me. Brett Battles, who beat me up in one of his books so many years ago; I've returned the favor. A special shout out to Wenhsiu Hassan, who gave me the title for the last book when the one it had just wouldn't do. My agent, Allan Guthrie, who helped me hammer the hell out of this thing until it looked something like a book. To my editor Betsy Wollheim and the superhero team at DAW. They make me look good. A Herculean task at the best of times.

Most importantly, my wife, Kari, without whom this whole strange writing trip wouldn't have even happened. Thank you, darlin', for asking me if I wanted to write a book all those years ago.

Chapter 1

When I pull up to the bar, the truck kicking up dust and gravel behind me, I know it's already too late to help anyone. Of the eight or nine cars in the parking lot, two of them are Texas State Troopers', their roof racks still flashing.

The car I'm looking for, a '73 Cadillac Eldorado convertible I've been following since Miami, sits parked neatly in the dirt lot next to a couple of F-150s with gun racks and mud flaps decorated with chrome women.

I check to make sure I have my gear on me, making the sign of the cross as I touch each thing. Like that old joke: spectacles, testicles, wallet and watch.

Only this is a smudge of graveyard dirt on my forehead, my belt buckle (an intricate weave of braided iron to ward off the Evil Eye), a straight razor I stole from the man it'd been buried with, and yes, a watch. An Illinois Sangamo Special from 1919. Railroad grade. Keeps great time.

I hope I don't have to use it.

Next comes the knapsack. I've looked inside fifteen times since I woke up this morning, but it pays to know where your shit is.

All the things the discerning necromancer could want: knucklebones, a noose from the neck of a hanged murderer, a pack of cards made up of aces and eights, and a pouch I hang from my belt full of powdered grave-yard dirt, salt, ground bone, and blood dried under a full moon.

And a 9mm Browning Hi-Power made special for the Wehrmacht after the Nazis got hold of the factories and before the Belgians started sabotaging them. Thing's got Waffen marks aplenty.

I'm not a big believer in evil, but this thing is just ugly. It's a murderer's gun, a sadist's gun. Every kill is burned into it like the Third Reich stamps that cover its frame.

When a guy like me uses it, all that energy gives it a wallop that makes a .44 look like a popgun.

I don't like shooting it. I don't like touching it. Feels like cockroaches scurrying under my fingers.

But sometimes the best tool for the job is a tool that shouldn't exist. It's not as nasty as the watch, but it'll do. I clip the holster on the inside of my waistband, hope I don't blow my balls off.

The sun in West Texas is brutal, baking everything into a blur of burnt caramel. Why the fuck anyone would put a bar out in the middle of this limestone wasteland, I have no idea. Yucca, creosote, a scattering of agave and a wind-blasted Quonset hut are the only things to mar the endless landscape.

Charles Tyrone Washington is a real piece of work. Skipped out on a manslaughter charge in Detroit in the sixties and moved into a double-wide in Florida. Started up this bullshit Voodoo church where he bilked the lo-cals and slept with their daughters.

Sweet deal if you can get it, I suppose. Helped that the guy's the real deal. So, he talks to the dead, curses his enemies, divines the future. The whole shebang. Got some real muscle and he's pissing it away on Evil Eyes and picking horses.

Eventually talking to Voodoo spirits paid off, and he pulled together enough dough in the nineties to pick up a burnt-out husk of an antebellum mansion in the middle of the Everglades. Six months later some of his followers came by and found his rotting corpse in the middle of a circle of salt and candle wax in the foyer.

And that's when he really went to town.

"Hey, Chuck," I say, looking at the carnage. "You're getting creative." I stand in the doorway looking over a grim tableau that would make Hieronymus Bosch blush.

It takes a lot to keep my cool and not throw up all over the place. I've seen death, but this is insane. The lucky ones died in their seats. Five, maybe six guys. Hard to tell in the tangle of body parts. He exploded their heads, leaving open stumps to dump a sea of blood onto the floor.

The others, particularly the Troopers, got the royal treatment. Pinned to the far wall with the blades of a ceiling fan, chests peeled back to show empty cavities, impaled on barstools, shredded by a thousand cuts from broken glass. One poor bastard is just a torso. Christ only knows what Washington did with the rest of him.

The worst one suffered an aborted transformation. Limbs stick out at odd angles, tufts of fur and chitin instead of skin. A dozen small mouths lie open, tongues lolling. The only recognizably human thing about him is his cowboy boots.

There are no ghosts around. This much devastation, you better believe somebody'd leave a ghost. Washington's already eaten them.

He looks like a wiry, seventy-year-old black man in a Hawaiian shirt and khaki cargo pants. Round, thin-rimmed glasses perched on his nose. Typical Florida retiree. Plays some golf, maybe. Hangs out on his porch watching the Cuban chicas go by.

But that's on this side. Over on the Twilight Side, that between world where the dead park their carcasses waiting for whatever comes next, he's a burning, churning mass of faces. The Loa, those same Voodoo spirits who gave him enough keno numbers to keep him in booze and cigarettes, dance under his skin, glowing like hot coals. I'm not sure he's even human anymore.

After Washington died, word started getting through the grapevine that he was doing some really nasty magic down there. It happens. Cheating death for a bit isn't as hard as you'd think. He'd been screwing around with the Loa, feeding on ghosts he'd hunted down in nearby towns.

Nobody tried to stop him, of course. That's not how wizards roll. The only interest anyone took was purely academic. We couldn't give a rat's ass as long as he doesn't rain on our parade or draw too much attention from the normals.

Magic's like Fight Club that way. You don't talk about it. Can't have the regular folk knowing this shit's real. We might have to share.

"You are one tenacious motherfucker, Eric Carter," Washington says. He tips back a Miller, takes a drag on his cigarette.

"It's part of my charm," I say.

On the other side, I see the faces in his skin flare up like gasoline dumped on a bonfire. Seeing the land of the dead overlaid onto our side has its uses, though it's sometimes hard to see what's real and what isn't. But I've had years of practice. Mages are born with a knack. Illusions, transformations, divinations. Some people are just better at some things than others.

I got dead things. Yay me.

"I've been wanting to talk to you. I knew you'd come here," Washington says. "Once I killed enough people I knew you'd sense it. Come straight for me."

I'm good, but I'm not that good. I point a thumb over my shoulder. "Nah. Just lucky. Got a scanner in the car. Heard the cops roll out. I was about to head south. I figured you'd fucked off to Mexico by now."

Washington had been in his swamp palace doing his thing for a while. Not really dead, not really alive. At some point, probably about a year or so ago, he took things a little further off the reservation. Instead of begging the Loa for favors, he started trapping them, experimenting with them, slicing them into snack size pieces. Stitching them together and wearing them on his soul like a psycho killer's skin suit.

This has made some things very not happy. As a general rule of thumb, you don't fuck with things that have big brothers and sisters. They might come after you. Or worse, they might send someone like me.

"You could just leave me be," he says. "Drop this whole farce and let one of your own live his life in peace. One necromancer to another."

I'm not a big fan of that word. Makes me think of towers on the moors and medieval skullcaps. Sure I bleed the occasional black ram under a full moon, but come on. It's the 21st fucking century. Get with the program.

"Two things," I say, ticking off points on my fingers. "One, you don't have a life to live. I'm not sure you're even human anymore, not that I have a problem with that. Different strokes, you know. And two, this is kind of my job. I have a contract. Sorry."

"Don't say I didn't give you a chance, boy," he says.

"Yeah, 'cause that worked out so well for you back in Florida."

I'd hit him down at his mansion in the swamp. He'd been using that as a ritual and research space. Smart move. The place sat on top of a nexus of wild magic that bubbled up through the swamp like methane. Whoever built the place knew what they were doing. Gave his spells a lot more oomph.

I almost didn't make it. Got lucky. While he was pounding the shit out of me and tossing me around the room, I saw a piece of one of the Loa hanging off him like a loose thread. That's all I needed. I tossed a banishing spell at it, tore it loose and sent it home to mommy.

Like an unraveling sweater, it started pulling out the rest of the Loa. Washington's hold on them wasn't as strong as he'd thought. Scared the holy fuck out of him. He tossed me through a window and bugged out, salvaging what he could.

Took me three days to track him to Miami. Holed up

in a four-star resort on Fisher Island. Thought surrounding himself with salt water would hide him. It did for a while. But like a lot of mages, he keeps thinking magic's the only way to do anything.

I found him by grilling the local prostitutes until I found one he'd hired. Man spends a thousand bucks a night trying to hide from me and goes for a cheap hooker with a meth habit. Twenty bucks and a fake badge is all it took.

"Look," I say. "We've been playing hide and seek now for the better part of a month. I know I'm sick of it. I figure you probably are, too."

"You sound like you want to make a deal with me."

"No, I just want to get this over with." I draw the Browning, unload a couple of rounds at him, bolt for an overturned table. Even with damn near perfect shots, the bullets are just a, "Hey, how ya doin'?" If they make a dent in Washington's defenses I'll be surprised.

I hear a loud snap of splitting wood and the building shudders. A tremendous crack tears through the floor, ripping it in half. I jump aside, pop another round. That's three. I don't want to lose count.

Washington calls up a purple fireball and heaves it in my direction. He tried that crap in the swamp. I learned the hard way how to deal with it.

I pull a fistful of powder from the pouch on my belt and throw it between us, making a point of scattering as much as possible on the closest corpses.

The spell in the powder works a treat. It'll do fuck all if he pulls out the good china, but this is just a warm-up. The fireball fizzles the second it passes over the line of scattered powder.

We could do this all day, but I'm really not in the mood. I haven't had lunch yet, and the nearest tacos are twenty miles up the road.

I feint left, pop off a couple more rounds. Five. He levitates a table and throws it at me. I duck and it gets me closer to him. I don't want to make this look too easy.

More gunfire. There's a sense of wounded pride coming from the gun every time I purposely miss. Seven rounds total. It's time to get this over with.

I dive under a thrown chair, smack right into Washington. Before I know it he's got his hand around my throat.

He slams me hard against the wall. I'm beginning to think maybe this was a mistake, hope that the spell that I scattered onto the corpses is doing its job.

"You thought you could kill me with a gun?" Washington says. "You're weak. And I'm gonna enjoy snackin' on your soul."

I make a croaking sound. It's the best I can do under the circumstances.

"You got something to say, son?" I nod and he lets up his grip a little bit.

"Gotcha."

He freezes as he feels the barrel of the Browning press against the side of his skull.

I've been keeping my distance this last month because I couldn't think of another way to take him out. I needed to be close enough to get the drop on him while he was distracted. And I needed help to pull it off. How nice of him to leave me some corpses lying around.

The headless body standing behind him pulls the trigger and bullet number eight—made of silver and gold and engraved with the symbols for all of the families of the Loa: Ghede, Rada, Kongo, Petro, Nago, blessed by Baron Samedi and Maman Brigitte themselves—blows his head off his shoulders.

His body falls to the floor, green flames erupting from the stump of his neck. The fire spreads quickly and I pull his hand from my throat to keep from being consumed with him. He's dying for real this time.

A little shred of his soul stands on the twilight side looking at me, dumbfounded. Then panicked as the Loa tear loose from him, each shadowy figure ripping its way free.

Soon he's nothing but a withered image, glowing dull as wind-blown coals, and then gone.

Chapter 2

There's no point cleaning anything up. I wouldn't even know where to start. More Troopers will be here soon and I'd rather not have to talk my way out.

I leave the truck in the lot. It's stolen and I like Washington's Caddy better. It's a sweet ride. I throw a don't-look-at-me spell on it and head north to New Mexico. About ten miles up I see a line of State Troopers barreling down the highway.

I'd hate to be them right now. They're going to need a shovel to pick up all the pieces. I pull over to let them pass, watch them disappear in the rearview mirror. And that's when the shakes start.

You'd think by now, after a lifetime of dealing with the dead, after years of honing my craft and seeing horrors even worse than what Washington did in that bar down the road, that I'd be used to it. That it wouldn't get to me.

You'd be wrong.

I get out of the car and throw up all over the side of the road. Bodies I can handle. The dead I can handle. But what he did back there, what he could have done to me if I'd fucked it up.

I get back into the car, wipe my mouth on a crumpled up map, pull onto the road. Take all those thoughts and shove them deep in the back of my head where they can't get in my way.

I cross over into New Mexico about an hour later, make good time and roll into Carlsbad before sunset. Hit a motel on the outskirts of town by the college. Twelve-unit deal with cable TV, wireless internet, a cafe and grocery next door. I grab a bottle of Johnnie Walker Red from the store.

I pick up a few wanderers on the way to my room, un-tethered ghosts that aren't tied to a place. Most of them are trauma patients from the nearby hospital. Burn victims, car crashes, gunshots. Yeah, I run with the cool kids.

Ghosts come to me like moths to a flame. I can see them and they can see me. They hover like groupies. I scatter a handful of sunflower seeds outside the door, stick a couple of Post-its with palindromes written on them to the doorjamb. If I really wanted to get rid of the ghosts I'd nail a dead cat to the windows, but that's always struck me as a bit extreme.

They stop at the door, counting the seeds, reading the palindromes backward and forward and doing it all over again like good little obsessive compulsives. I close the door on their empty faces.

I take a shower, wash off the sweat and dust. Adrenaline had me going back at the bar and I didn't notice Washington had smacked me around pretty good until I was ten miles down the road. Bruises, cuts, one of my ribs feels like it's been hit with a sledgehammer. Butterfly bandages take care of the worst of the cuts.

It's hard to see the bruises. I'm tattooed over most of

my body. Neck to wrists to ankles. Wards and sigils. Symbols in dead languages to help ward off threat, divert attention, help me focus my magic. Started collecting them years ago and I keep adding ink.

I've got one that looks like a starburst in an eye that wards off spells that affect the mind, another of an armadillo that's pretty good against gunshots. Does fuck all for baseball bats. Found that out the hard way in an alley in Philadelphia.

Got a murder of crows in flight that covers my chest from shoulder to shoulder. I can't look at it too long in the mirror. It keeps moving. Gives me a headache.

Compared to me, the Illustrated Man's got a tramp stamp he tore off a yoga mom from Orange County. One patch on my left forearm is bare of tattoos, but covered in small scars. A lot of my spells need blood, and there's not always a black ram around when you need one.

I crack open the bottle of Johnnie Walker and pour some into a glass that's been thoughtfully sanitized for my protection. I sit in the one chair in the room, a recliner that only goes partway back. Feels like home.

Which it pretty much is. I don't do well staying in one place for very long. Roots are not something I want to lay down. Been there, done that. Didn't work out so well. My life is a succession of rest stops and cheap hotels. Walmart fashion and estate sale finds. I've got three suits from Goodwill that were in fashion in the sixties. Most of my stuff belonged to dead men. Like my new Cadillac.

I'm getting settled in with my second glass of whisky when there's a pounding on my door. I pull the Browning, look through the peephole. Hotel staff. I thumb back the hammer of the gun, open the door onto two men and a woman I've never seen before.

Then I notice one of the men isn't wearing any pants.

"Oh, it's you. Come on in."

The woman and one of the men step into the room with an almost regal bearing. The pantsless one half-lopes, half-skips in. Thank god he's at least wearing briefs. And for some reason, his socks and shoes. I offer the chair to the lady, let the men figure out where they want to be. I stand next to the door.

As Loa go the Barons Samedi and Kriminel and Samedi's wife, Maman Brigitte, are about as high-ranking as you get. They head up the Ghede family, the Loa that oversee the Dead. Loa aren't the only spirits that do that sort of thing, of course, but they're some of the better known.

The Loa possess their followers, riding their bodies like horses, rather than appear on their own. If they don't have a member of their flock around I suppose some random housekeeper will do in a pinch. Their hosts won't remember any of this. Which is probably good for the guy with no pants.

"Barons," I say. "Madame. I wasn't expecting you until tomorrow night."

"We come when we fucking well want to come," Kriminel says in a thick Haitian accent that sounds weird coming out of a middle-aged white guy in tightie whities. He snarls, spit running down his chin. He's always like this.

"We thought it wise to come sooner, Eric," Maman Brigitte says.

"Is something wrong?"

"Wrong?" Samedi says. Compared to Kriminel, his and Brigitte's accents are almost unnoticeable. "No, nothing's wrong. Our children and brothers and sisters have come home to us."

When they hired me, Samedi told me that he was representing all of the families. Washington had stolen Loa from each one. They weren't afraid of Washington per se, but they were concerned. He had ensnared so many of them that the Royalty didn't want to take any chances and end up in his hands.

"Okay. So . . ."

"We wanted to say thank you and give you your payment," Brigitte says.

"And a warning," Samedi says.

Ah, I knew something was wrong.

"Piss on his payment and his warning," Kriminel says. He's cracked open the bottle of Johnnie Walker and is pouring it into his open mouth. Most of it ends up down his shirt. Glad I didn't buy anything expensive.

Brigitte pulls a small leather purse from her handbag, hands it to me. I open it up. Doubloons.

"This isn't what we agreed on."

Kriminel gets right up my face, spitting as he says, "Who do you think you are, making demands?" The longer they stay in their hosts the more the hosts will begin to resemble them. Already Kriminel's host is starting to smell like grave dirt and decay. I push him away from me.

"I know," Brigitte says, hesitating and looking like she's bit into a lemon, "but we are having trouble. Kriminel agreed too hastily and we were bound by it. We don't understand what a 'bank transfer' is."

And apparently couldn't find someone who did. "Don't you blame this on me, Brigitte," Kriminel says.

"I understand," I say. There's no helping it. "Not a complaint, merely an observation. This is more than adequate." I know a guy in New Jersey who can move the coins, so that's not a problem. "You said something about a warning?"

"Beware what you trust," Samedi says.

"Oh, it's one of *those* warnings." Some things like to be cryptic, some things have to be cryptic. And some are bound by old laws to be cryptic only about certain things, like prophecies and fortunes. Seems this falls into one of those camps.

"I wish we could say more," Brigitte says. "We like you." She glances over at Kriminel, who's finished the scotch and has moved onto the shampoo on the bathroom counter.

He scowls at her. "Fuck him," yells Kriminel. "Fuck him to hell."

"Well, Samedi and I like you," she says.

"We would hate to see anything untoward happen," Samedi says, "and lose one of our most talented friends. So please, take care."

"Can we leave now?" Kriminel says. "I've run out of things to drink." Good thing he hasn't noticed the minibar. His shirt and face are caked with shampoo, scotch and shaving cream. I feel sorry for the guy he's taken over. That is going to be one nasty hangover in the morning.

"Yes," Samedi says. "You have your payment, we have given your warning."

Kriminel is the first out the door, muttering something about black roosters, Samedi right behind him.

Brigitte stops at the threshold, turns to me, puts a hand on my cheek. She searches my eyes for something.

"Truly, beware. Things have already been set in motion, but your part has not yet begun. It starts tonight."

What would be so bad that they would hand deliver a warning? And get Kriminel to go along with them?

I close the door behind them, wondering what Brigitte meant, when the phone rings.

I stare at it like it's a rattlesnake. Coincidences are few and far between with magic. I wait for it to stop and kick over to the hotel's voicemail. It's got to be a wrong number. Nobody knows I'm here.

And I mean nobody. I've got so many redirection spells inked into my skin it's a wonder I can find myself on a map. Sure, I can be tracked, but it's not easy.

Five rings. Ten, twenty. I disconnect it from the wall. It keeps ringing.

That's what I was afraid of. It's *that* kind of call.

We get into a rhythm, the phone and I. It rings. I don't answer. I can do this all night. I let it go and toss back a couple more drinks.

There's a banging on the wall from my neighbor, a muffled shout telling me to answer the goddamn phone. I let it ring some more.

The more it goes on, the more pissed off I get. Somebody's gone to a lot of trouble to track me down. I've got a voicemail number I check every few days for clients and job offers. It's easy to find.

Finally, after the ringing's gone on for almost half an hour, I pick it up, say nothing.

"Hello Eric," says the voice on the other end. Quiet, hesitant. "I know you're there."

Now there's a voice I haven't heard in a long time. No use denying it. "Been a while, Alex. What, ten years?"

"Fifteen."

"Tough to track me down?"

"Yeah. You're not easy to find."

"Good. I'm not supposed to be." I hang up the phone. It starts ringing again before I get the handset into the cradle.

More ringing. More shouting from the neighbor.

I might as well talk to him. It'll just keep going. I pick it up. "I give up already. What?"

A beat of silence, then, "Lucy's dead."

I want to ask "Lucy who?" but I know who he means. I haven't seen my younger sister since I left Los Angeles behind. Is Alex right? Has it been fifteen years? That would make her, what, thirty-two?

"What happened?" I say.

"I'm sorry," he says.

"Alex, the fuck happened?"

There's a pause on the other end of the phone. If he's expecting me to wail and gnash my teeth he's going to be waiting for a long time.

"Murdered," he says. "Something attacked her in her home."

"Some thing? I assume you're not talking about an animal."

"No. Though the cops are saying that. They don't know what else to call it. Eric, she was torn apart. It's bad. And it stinks of magic."

"When did it happen?"

"Couple weeks ago. Been trying to track you down since."

There's no question in my mind that Alex might be wrong. Lucy wasn't powerful at all, but she would have known enough to buy wards for her home, something. Unless she blew through the inheritance and trust fund she got after our parents died, she'd have been able to afford it.

This numb feeling is shock. I've been here before. A wave of grief starts to crack through. I want to scream. Beat something. I slam that feeling down, bury it where it can't get to me, where it can't get in the way. I can control it or it can control me.

"Do you know who did it? Or why?" My voice doesn't even crack.

"No. I tried a divination when I was in the house, but whatever did it covered its tracks really well. But I'm wondering . . ."

"What?"

"Well, I know it's been a long time, but, Boudreau? That is why you left, right?"

"Yeah, that's why I left." That's a name I haven't thought of in years. Haven't let myself. Put it behind me, never looked back.

"Well?"

"Hang on. I'm thinking."

I left L.A. in a hurry. Didn't tell anyone I was leaving, but everybody had to know why I disappeared. I killed a guy named Jean Boudreau. I was as surprised as anyone else when it happened. I was raw then. Angry. I've learned a lot since.

He ran a mob that was fucking around with magical types. Had some powerful mages on his side. Pissed off a lot of people when I killed him.

"No," I say. It can't be him. "I don't think so. You ever hear of a guy named Ben Duncan? Black guy. Probably be in his fifties now. Was working for Boudreau."

"I stayed out of that mess, man. As much as any of us could."

"Smart. He was pretty high up the food chain. Got hold of me after it happened. Gave me a choice. I bail or he'd kill me, Lucy, and pretty much everybody else I know."

The silence on the other end of the line stretches a long time.

"Well, that explains a lot," Alex says, though something in his voice tells me it doesn't excuse anything.

I press the heels of my hands into my eyes. Now's not the time to get into it.

"There's no reason he would have done anything," I say.

I'm trying to treat this like it's a job. But my control's wavering.

"Where are you now?" Alex says.

"New Mexico."

I haven't thought about Lucy in a long time. Our parents are long dead, and I've never heard of any other family.

Fuck. Somebody needs to make arrangements. Set up the funeral.

How do I do that? I don't go to funerals. Hell, I don't go to cemeteries. I hang around real dead people. Nobody dies in a fucking cemetery.

I'm getting dizzy, short of breath.

"Funeral. I need to . . . Fuck. Alex, I need to set up a funeral." The room starts to spin around me.

"It's okay," Alex says. "It's done. She's with your mom and dad. I took care of it."

Suddenly I'm angry at Alex. I was supposed to do that. I'm her brother. I couldn't make her safe when I was there and I couldn't make her safe when I left. The least I could have done, the least Alex could have let me do, is set up her fucking funeral.

Did a lot of people show up? I don't know even who her friends were. Was she dating anybody? Did she get married? Holy fuck, what if she had kids?

I pull myself together. Take a deep breath.

"Right. Thanks. I'll be out there in, fuck, give me a couple of days. Where can I meet you?"

"I run a bar in Koreatown. I'm there every day." He gives me the address, a place on Normandie, and his phone number.

I'm not sure which of us is more surprised. Him about me coming out there or me that he owns a business. Last I saw Alex he was running short cons down in Hollywood using magic to bilk marks out of cash. Jesus, what else has changed?

"There's a bouncer," he says. "Tell him you're there to see me. He'll let you in."

"Sounds like an upscale joint," I say.

"I prefer to keep the riff-raff out."

"I'll see you there."

I hang up the phone, realize too late I didn't ask any of those questions about Lucy. I'd get him back on the phone, but that wasn't the kind of call that leaves a return number. I get my breathing under control, fight the urge to throw the phone across the room. Do it anyway.

They say you can't go home again. Guess I'm about to find out if that's true.

Chapter 3

The early morning sun bleaches the landscape. Scrub brush, dirt. Miles and miles of nothing but miles and miles. Kind of view that'll drive a man crazy. I'm exhausted and look it. Spent the night running scenarios in my head, coming up with a plan. Too many unknowns. Anything beyond, "Get to L.A." is pretty pointless. But I keep trying, anyway.

The desert isn't helping. I've had everyone from the guy at the motel counter to the woman I bought my coffee from tell me it's a dry heat. Yeah. 'Cause that somehow makes it better.

As a guy I know from Texas is fond of saying, "Fuck all y'all."

I'm not a fan of the desert. Not the heat, the dryness, or the magic.

Most of us don't have enough power to light a monkey's fart, much less chuck a fireball, so we tap into the local pool. The way the flavor of soil leaches into wine grapes, so the character of a place leaches into its magic.

The desert tastes dry like dust and wind. Air spells are easy here. Water spells take a bit more effort. Go down to the Everglades and it's a different story.

Down there it's all wild green and wet, loamy earth. The insane growth and deadliness of the swamp is great for plant magic, fertility magic, death magic.

I cut up through to the 82, head west and down to Alamogordo and Holloman Air Force Base. The magic tastes of airplane fuel and oil, hot metal and order. The feeling stays until well after White Sands.

Each city is different. Their character is in their people, their history. New York is heavy like brick and mortar, metallic like hammers. San Francisco is dark and intricate like gold-filigreed chocolate. Vegas tastes like despair.

I don't know what L.A. tastes like, anymore. It changes. Tears itself down, builds itself up again. Recreates itself a thousand times in one day. One block it's the heaviness of Kabbalah, the next it's the dust of Africa. Take two steps and you're steeped in Aztec magic brought up by Mexican immigrants mixed with the not as old, but just as powerful illusions of Hollywood.

Cities turn to counties turn to states. I'm popping Advil and Tylenol for yesterday's fight. Ease my bruises, tear up my stomach. Every mile I get closer to home the urge to turn back grows. But I keep going.

I start to see shrines on the side of the road. Ones I've seen in Juarez, or closer to the border in Texas, dedicated to Santa Muerte, a skeletal version of the Virgin Mary. Patron Saint of drug dealers and killers. I haven't met her myself, but I've heard things. She's got quite a following. Not just among the Narcos, either, but by families living in war zones where two guys can go into a club, gun down twenty people and walk away.

Place like that, you better believe they're praying to Death.

I pass another shrine coming into Arizona on the shoulder of a blind curve, withering flowers at the skeleton's feet. Most of the ones I've seen have been carved from wood, about half life size. But this one's more than five feet tall, skeletal hands peeking from the sleeves of an ornate wedding dress, skull visible beneath a gauzy veil.

I look in the rearview as I pass, and I swear it turns its head to watch me.

———

I stop at the Chiriaco Summit above Indio not long after I cross the California border. Gas up, stretch, toss back a couple Red Bulls. Haven't stopped for more than gas and taking a piss since I left Carlsbad. The sun's starting to set and I'm fighting exhaustion.

I grab an overcooked burger at a diner next to the George Patton museum, a plain building surrounded by World War II-era tanks that were used for training. They sit in a field of gravel and scrub brush, weeds growing up against their tracks.

Not a lot of men died in these tanks, but there were a few. Haunts in tanker gear tied to their machines. Sitting on the turrets, leaning against the tracks, watching me.

I wave, and one of them gives me the finger. I'll take Haunts over Wanderers any day. They're stuck. Tied to a house, a car, a spot on the road. The ones who didn't move on and couldn't move out.

Of course, Haunts tend to be a lot pissier. How'd you like to spend a couple hundred years staring at the same four moldy walls somebody sealed you into to die?

I leave the Haunts behind and head down into Indio.

The Eldorado glides over the 10 Freeway, deep rumbling bass of the V-8 chugging along, and the cities stream by. Magic shifts from place to place. It's like a tasting menu at eighty miles an hour.

Top down, wind in my hair. I can almost forget about my dead sister. Lucy was what the circles my family moved in called "special." Not Jerry's Kids special, though you wouldn't know it the way they talked.

The magic set's a bigoted lot. Race, wealth, family, none of that matters. It's whether you can read next week in a pig's entrails, curse a man with a piece of string, call down the moon.

Lucy could barely manipulate a coin toss. That puts her ahead of most people with talent, but still at the bottom tier.

I wouldn't say she was a disappointment to our parents, but she was the black sheep. Mom and Dad had power to spare. Some of it got to me. Almost none of it went to Lucy. She practiced relentlessly. Kept telling me one of these days she'd get that coin toss down pat and show me. She never did.

I pull over for some dinner in Riverside. From here on in, the freeway's a parking lot. All I can do is wait it out.

Growing up near-normal around magic types is tough. Lucy was the problem child we couldn't talk about. Not because we were embarrassed by her, but because she was too weak to defend herself. We did a good job hiding her. Most people didn't even know I had a sister. Magic and money helps hide a lot of sins.

The traffic clears up to a sea rather than a tsunami and I down more Red Bulls. Should last me until I can find a place to crash in L.A.

Two hours and I can't go any farther. The caffeine and guarana are useless. My eyes are blurring and I'm driving the Caddy by Braille. Should have gotten hold of some cocaine. A couple lines right about now and I could drive this thing to Hawaii.

Instead I pull over onto a side street in Pomona, tell myself it's just a nap. Few more hours and I'll be on my way.

Seven hours later, I wake from a dream of my parents on fire, screaming in our house as they burn, Lucy running in after them.

I stopped her that night, saved her when I couldn't save them. But in the dream I'm too late, and she burns with them.

Chapter 4

The motel is full of ghosts. This is, oddly enough, a good thing.

A lot of the time they can be annoyances. Visual clutter and background noise. But they can also be camouflage. Ever since Alex called me, I've been wondering if my redirection spells are holding up. Magically speaking, a crowd of ghosts is just as good a hiding place as a crowd of live people. The harder it is to see me, the better.

"Forty bucks a night, whether you use the whole night or not."

The woman behind the counter is wearing a pink babydoll three sizes and twenty years too small for her. Bad dye job, painted-on eyebrows. A half-smoked Marlboro hangs from her lip.

I hand her a couple hundreds. "I'll be here a few days."

She snatches the bills from my hand. "Few days, huh?"

"More or less."

She hands me a key. "Number eight. In the back."

The room is pretty much what I expected. A hole. It

could use a good bug bombing, but the sheets are relatively clean. Not like I'm going to spend much time here.

I draw some half-assed charms on the walls to keep the ghosts and gangbangers out. Spend the next hour pacing, wondering what I'm going to do now that I'm here. Don't want to hit Alex's place just yet. Need to get a feel for the city. It's been such a long time, I'm a stranger here.

I take a shower, put new bandages on my cuts. They're scabbing over and the rib isn't giving me as much trouble, but I still feel like I've gone a round with Tyson. I stare into the mirror, try to see how I've changed, try to remember what I used to look like. Hair's shorter, I've lost weight. The rings around my eyes are probably darker.

Let's face it, I look like shit.

I'm not in the desert anymore. Jeans and boots get replaced with a suit and tie. Almost convinced myself I'm out here on business. That if I treat this like any other job I won't let sentimentality get in my way.

I'm here to find out who killed Lucy. And return the favor. That's all. In, out.

Yeah, right.

I blow that idea in the first hour of cruising around. Things are gone that should have stayed, things have stayed that should have been demolished. The Farmer's Market on Fairfax is a giant outdoor shopping mall. Hollywood Boulevard's full of hipsters. Some asshole tore down The Ambassador. Who the fuck thought that was a good idea?

L.A. pisses on its history. Tears it down or spackles it

into something different. Always changing, always trying to be something new. Always failing. An ugly town to grow old in.

I finally bite the bullet. Time to see if things are so far gone I just can't be here. There are some memories it's better to leave buried than to have destroyed when you try to bring them back.

Roscoe's Chicken and Waffles on Gower. Need to know if it's as good as I remember.

It isn't.

———

Alex's bar is in K-Town between Western and Normandie. Brownstones with barred windows and high-rise banks. Shop signs in Hangeul as much as English and it's a good bet a third of the people walking these streets barely speak the latter.

Stuck on a corner next to a place that sells t-shirts and pleather bags, the bar doesn't stick out. Black stucco exterior, awning-covered door. No name, just an address.

My first clue that this is more than a bar is when I step up to the door and feel the warning buzz of magic on my skin. The charms are written in brass designs inlaid in the door and the doorjamb, each a subtle message; don't cause trouble, buy a lot of beer, tip your waitress.

When I left, Alex was doing small cons, using his talents to give him an edge. Never had much power, most people with talent don't, but he had enough to get himself into trouble more often than not.

A guy built like a side of beef is hanging out in the

foyer on a barstool. "Hey," he says with a voice somewhere between a bear and a landslide.

"Looking for Alex Kim."

"You Carter?"

"Eric Carter, yeah."

He pulls the inner curtain aside to let me through. "Ask at the bar. Somebody'll get him."

"Thanks."

"No problem."

Past the curtain the bar's got a mellow vibe. Pretty standard place, but larger, nicer. Less 'bar' and more 'nightclub.' Something about the layout's bugging me, though I can't put my finger on what.

Couple of bars, a few stages and a dance floor. TVs in the corners, neon signs for Sapporo and Kirin on the walls. Floor's clean, chairs are overstuffed leather. Alex has sunk a lot of money into this place.

A cute Korean waitress wanders by with a pitcher of beer for a table of three upscale banker types in slick suits and ties talking money.

She throws a glance my way. "Grab any seat you want," she says.

"Actually, I'm here looking for Alex Kim. He here today?"

"Yeah," she says. "I'll go get him." She deposits the pitcher of beer at the table, exchanges a couple of pleasantries in Korean and heads back toward the bar in the corner where she disappears through a door.

There's no seat in the place where I can watch all the exits so I grab one next to the corner bar where I can see the front door. I've had enough shit happen in bars to know you always pay attention to the exits.

The place has a weird arrangement. There's a bar in the center of the room, five stages laid out equidistant from each other. Half the chairs look bolted to the floor. Who the hell bolts chairs to the floor in a bar?

The waitress comes out from the hallway a minute later and makes a beeline toward my table. "Hey," she says. "Alex'll be out in a bit." She sticks her hand out. "I'm Tabitha."

"Nice to meet you," I say and shake her hand. "Eric." Tabitha's a little shorter than me with a slim build, long, black hair pulled back in a ponytail, a narrow, elfin face. She's wearing jeans, a tight, black t-shirt and a black apron.

"Alex said you'd be coming around. Can I get you something? You look like you could use a drink."

"Been on the road," I say. How much has Alex told his people? "Do I really look that bad?"

She laughs and shows me a smile that's probably turned more men to jelly than I can count. "No, not bad. Not bad at all. Just a little tired, I guess."

"It has been a rough couple of days, actually. What's your story? You been working here long?"

"Couple years. Alex is a cool boss. And this is a good place. You? First time here? Haven't seen you here before."

"Yeah," I say. "Been out of town a while. Things are different."

"How long?"

"Since ninety-five."

"Huh. Yeah, some stuff's changed."

"I'll say. Hollywood and Highland. Jesus, who built that monstrosity?"

"What are you talking about? I like that place."

"Really?

"Of course he doesn't like the place," Alex says, coming out from behind the bar and seeing us talking. "He only likes old stuff."

"I like to think of it as vintage."

"I like vintage," Tabitha says. "I have tables to get back to. See you around?"

Good question. I can't say I won't bolt for the door right now. "Yeah," I say, instead. She winks at me and heads back to the Asian bankers getting hammered on Sapporo.

"Eric," Alex says.

"Alex." The years have been nice to him. Little older, little fatter, few more lines around the face. But he's got that same shaggy black hair and impish smile.

I stand. Do I shake his hand? Wave? It's been a long time. What's the etiquette here? Before I can say anything he grabs me in a bear hug and squeezes. I make a strangled sound as my bruised rib shifts in my chest.

"Whoa," Alex says, letting me go. "Shit, man, you okay?" He takes a good look at me. "Jesus, you look like hell."

"No, I'm good," I say, voice coming out as a croak. I steady myself with one hand on his shoulder, catch my breath.

"Good for a punching bag, maybe. Goddamn. I don't remember your lip being that fat."

"Been a long month."

"I hear ya. Tabitha," he says to her as she's heading

back to the bar, "Dos Equis for me and . . ." he squints, trying to pull a memory. Fails.

"The fuck are you drinking these days?"

"Whatever's cheap. Just like always."

He shakes his head. "I will never understand a man who has no taste. Johnnie Walker Black, splash of water," he says to her. "We'll be in my office."

I follow him into the back past a kitchen and some storage rooms into a simple office that's all function and Ikea style. Laptop, phone, cash counter. Betting he's got a loaded pistol in one of those drawers.

Alex drops himself into a leather wingback chair that looks like it seated executives in the sixties and I settle into its clone across from him. The sun was starting to go down when I got here. I pull out the Sangamo Special, flip it open to check the time. Alex startles.

"What?"

"Sorry. Just forgot about that . . . thing."

I slide the watch back into my pocket. "Sorry. Yeah. Safer with me than with anybody else. And it keeps good time."

"Fuck, I would hope so. That thing creeps me the fuck out."

I start to say something snide when I'm interrupted by a knock on the door. Tabitha comes in with our drinks.

She sets the drink on a small side table next to my chair. "You need anything, have him call me."

"Thanks," I say. "I'll keep that in mind." I can think of a couple of things, but I keep them to myself. She shows me that same dazzling smile I got a glimpse of out in the bar and heads out the door.

"I like the help," I say.

"Tabitha's a treasure," he says. "Say, where are you staying? I can get you a cheap rate at a hotel up on Western. I've got a deal with them to steer out-of-towners their way."

"No, I'm good. Got a motel room on La Brea. Starlite Inn or something."

He makes a face. "Down by the 10? You sure about that? Place looks pretty rank from the outside."

"You should see it on the inside."

"Then why—"

"Because it works for me. Drop it, okay?"

Hands out, placating, mock surrender. Was a time I'd have taken him up on the offer. Lived it up in a four-star. Things change. I like this better.

"No worries," he says. "Whatever floats your boat. But if you change your mind."

"I'll let you know. So, how's business doing?"

"It's a living."

"Pretty good one from the looks of it. Neighborhood's kind of ghetto."

"Oh, come on. It's not that bad."

"Noticed the spells on the door," I say. "Still bilking the normals?"

"Beats three-card monte on the bus. Eight p.m. hits and we're hosting everything from frat boys to Japanese CEOs."

"Come on," I say, "there's more going on here than watered-down beer."

"Well, duh. Here, let me show you. You gotta see this." He opens a desk drawer, pulls out a stoppered vial. The liquid inside glows an iridescent green.

"The hell is that?"

He tosses it to me. The glass and stopper are etched with lead-painted runes.

"Magic in a bottle."

"No shit?"

"The glass is special-made. Rock solid. The cork's spelled for intention. You have to want to open it. I had a guy test them down at a shooting range. Took a Brenneke slug from a 12-gauge just to chip it."

I've seen these before, but never this close. When he said it was magic in a bottle he wasn't kidding. I can feel the power pressing against the glass like a water balloon about to burst.

"Where'd you get it?"

"Made it. I get three or four of those a couple times a week."

"Okay, I can think of half a dozen ways to do this and none of them are good."

"It's not that bad. I've got an ebony cage in a hole under the bar."

"Isn't that one of those wicker baskets you make out of demon bones?"

"Yeah. Cool, huh?"

"Uh—You do know that they're not actually dead, right? The demons? Just really pissed off?"

He gives me a don't-be-stupid look that I can't say I've missed. "You don't say. Of course I know. I've got it warded six ways to Sunday. Been siphoning the energy in this place every weekend for a year and a half."

It clicks. "The layout."

Magic is fueled by a lot of things. Belief, emotions, strong experiences. It flows like water. There are eddies and currents. You can channel it, move it around. That's what was bugging me about the club. Alex has the whole place set up like a funnel. From the placement of the bar, the stages, hell, even the front door and the emergency exits. That's why the chairs are bolted to the floor.

It's Feng Shui on meth.

"That's where the real money comes from," Alex says. "Any idea how much energy a place like this pumps out on a Saturday night? The horny frat boys really crank it out. I get some good DJs, half-off cover for girls. Alcohol and hormones does the rest."

"And you tap that energy and shunt it into the cage."

"Yep. Then I just draw off the power and stopper it up."

"And people drink it?"

"That's the preferred method," he says. "Though I know one guy who likes it in an enema."

I decide not to tell him that he's basically bottling demon piss. Probably already knows. I start to hand the vial back.

"No, keep it. I got lots."

I don't know if I want it, but I don't want to be an asshole and turn him down, either. I slip it into my coat pocket.

"Thanks. I think."

"Anyway, that's me," he says. "What about you?"

"Hanging out with dead folk," I say. I take a drink of my whisky. The silence drags between us.

"That's it?" he says. "Come on, Eric. Fifteen years. There's got to be more than that. What are you doing for a living? Where are you living? At least give me some highlights."

"Highlights. Right. Traveling a lot. Studying. Spent some time in Europe, South America."

"I heard some things," he says.

"Were they good?"

"Not really."

"Then they're probably true. I'm an exterminator. Ghosts, demons, gremlins. I kill shit for a living. That about sums it up."

I down the rest of my whisky. There's that silence again. I'm not asking what needs asking and I don't get the idea that Alex much wants to talk about it either.

"Hey, I wanted to say something," he says after a moment. "Vivian—"

"What happened to Lucy?" I say, cutting him off before he can say anything more. I don't want to talk about my dead sister, but I really don't want to talk about my ex-girlfriend.

He looks past me like he's thinking hard about something, taps his fingers on the desk. He leans heavily back into his chair, puffs out his cheeks and lets out a long breath. Punches a button on the intercom. A minute later Tabitha pokes her head in.

"Could you grab us a bottle of the Balvenie '78 and a couple glasses?" He looks at me. "This might take a while."

———

I'm getting drunk on someone else's booze, reminiscing about things I wasn't around for. I feel like I'm at the wake for a woman I've never met.

Three hours in and I've learned a lot. Lucy never married. Lucy never had kids. Turned out she was gay, but didn't figure it out until a few years ago. Never found that special someone.

Instead she had an inheritance that, as far as anyone was concerned, came from a dead uncle in Denmark, a house on the Venice canals, and an eye for design that the hipsters would shell out wads of cash for.

When I skipped town she already had a bulletproof identity of Lucy Van Pelt. She picked the last name when she was five. She loved Peanuts.

Alex kept an eye on her when he could. Tried to keep her from getting into too much trouble. Bailed her out when she needed it, talked over boys, then girls, then what to do with either one. Watched her graduate, nagged her until she picked a college, helped her move. He was big brother, mom and dad rolled into one.

It's hard to hear as he rattles off the last fifteen years of her life, but I make myself listen. I've missed so much. The scotch helps. I'm on my third glass.

"And she stayed away from the magic?"

He shrugs. "Mostly. I had to get on her case a couple of times. The whole 'scared straight' thing. I mean, I don't have a lot of power, but her, Jesus."

He takes a slug from his glass. His words have been slurring the past half hour. "But she still fucked around with it," he says. "I don't know what it was with her and fixing a coin toss. But the day she got that down, man, I'd never seen her so happy."

"Coin toss."

"Yeah. Every time I saw her she'd make me flip this silver half dollar a couple hundred times. She ever do that with you?"

"Yeah," I say, thinking about the months we spent

trying to get that down. Remember the half dollar, a silver Franklin from the forties I bought her at a pawn
shop. "Couple of times."

"I think it got to her," he says. "You know how it is.
Once you get that one spell down? How you keep trying
for more? She tried to hide it, but I know she was doing
it. I mean, we all do, right?"

"You think she fucked something up?" I say. "Maybe
a botched summoning?" I've seen it happen before.
Hell, I've done it before. You think you're pulling down
an imp to help you pick Lotto numbers and instead you
get some pissed off thing that's all teeth and shadow and
appetite.

"I don't know. Maybe. It would explain how she
was . . . you know." He closes his eyes. Is he—? He is.
He's crying.

He's crying and I can't wrap my mind around it. I
can't begin to imagine what he's feeling, what I would be
feeling if I'd stuck around.

The room suddenly feels claustrophobic. I lurch out
of my chair, unsteady from the alcohol. I have to get out
of here.

Everything spins around in my head like a greased
roulette wheel. Guilt, grief, too much alcohol, not
enough sleep. Finally settles on something I can understand: rage.

"What's her address?"

"I know that look," Alex says. "You're about to do
something stupid. Don't do that, man. I can barely handle this stoic routine you're pulling, but I can't handle
The Angry Young Man thing. It didn't work for you
when you were one."

"What's her fucking address?"

"Jesus, Eric. What do you expect to accomplish? I've had ten guys cast divinations and not a one of them can see a goddamn thing in there. It's like there's a fuzz over what happened."

"Who'd you get?"

"Nobody you know."

"What about the Nazi? He still in town?"

"Neumann? Dude, he's dead. Something ate him like six months ago. And why would I? Guy was an asshole."

"Anybody else do dead?" He was the only other necromancer I knew in town when I was here. Alex is right, though. Guy was an asshole. If something ate him, the fucker deserved it.

"There's a guy up in Fresno, but he never called me back."

Of course there isn't anyone else in town who does dead. Sure, you've got a bunch of hack spiritualists that can channel your passed on grandmother, but real necromancy isn't something people want to fuck around with unless you're born to it. Folks buy into that whole "black magic" bullshit or faint at the sight of blood, or have a problem with the whole death thing. Some of us don't get a goddamn choice.

"Everything you've done so far is as good as a fucking Ouija board," I say. I head to the door, anger and purpose clearing my head.

"Fuck you," Alex says. "I did what I could. Where the fuck were you? I—" He stops, closes his eyes. "I'm sorry. I just—I know she was your sister, but it feels like she was mine, too."

I feel hollowed out, numb. Maybe the alcohol's blunting my feelings. Maybe I just don't have them, anymore. He's got more right to call her his sister than I do. He was here; I wasn't.

"No, you're right," I say. "But I have to do something. And I can do something you can't. If I want to find out what happened to Lucy, I need to ask Lucy."

Chapter 5

The Venice canals crisscross through land that used to be a swamp. Guy named Abbot Kinney built them at the end of the 19th century as part of a beach resort, hoping to get tourists to come out and spend their money. The area's changed but the canals are still there. Thin islands connected by bridges, hidden from the traffic just on the other side of Washington Boulevard. If you don't know they're there, you might not find them.

Lucy's house is a narrow two-story built in the eighties with a palm tree out front. Faces the Howland Canal. Curved façade, wide, high windows tinted almost black. The only sound is the wind whipping the water against the canal walls, the nearby traffic on Washington Boulevard.

There's a handful of Wanderers in the area; their flickering images flit along the canals, glowing in the light from the streetlamps, the low hanging moon. Gangbangers, mostly. In the nineties the Shoreline Crips and Venice 13 were going at it like cats in a bag. The bodies stacked up. The ghosts never left.

The front door is still covered in police tape. I take a

deep breath, steel myself for whatever it is I'm going to find. I touch the doorknob, trace a charm with my thumb, and the lock snaps open. I try a light switch next to the door. The power's been cut off. Simple enough. I call up a torchlight, an indistinct glow that hovers behind me and slightly to my right. It's plenty of light to see by, but not so bright that it should get any of the neighbors' attention.

Inside is a designer's dream. Modern art on the walls, vaulted ceilings, colors that should clash but miraculously don't. Alex was right. She had a good eye for this kind of thing.

The foyer gives way to a hall, which goes to a living room. I can feel her here, faint, but she's here. In what condition I don't know. If I'm lucky she left a Haunt or a Wanderer and I'll get my answers.

Not too much time has gone by. She should still have most of her memories. Ghosts fade at different rates. Some might last a week, some might last a thousand years. With luck she'll be able to tell me what killed her. And then I can go kill it.

I walk around the living room, looking at the photos on the wall. The kind of vacation snapshots professional photographers take. Were these her friends? Models? There's so much I don't know. So much I never will.

I move on through the house, feeling for her. So faint. Through another hallway that opens to a den in the back. I stop at a spray of dried blood soaked into the edge of the carpet.

I crank up my torchlight and bring the whole room in view. The carpet is a brilliant white and the crusted blood soaked into it is so dark it's almost black. The shag has dried into spikes that crunch under my feet as I step on it. The walls are a Pollock painting of blood spatter. Thick streaks run across the floor, slide along the walls.

Shattered glass coffee table, an overturned couch, both scrawled with bloody handprints, thin lines running from fingers as she was dragged across them. The fireplace is spattered with thick drops of spray. One window is broken, and is covered with a board.

Every surface is covered in blood. Except for one wall. Wide arcs have been wiped off of it, as if the killer tried to clean up before finally realizing there was no point.

Just because she's here doesn't mean she wants to come out. Or can come out. I could force the issue, but it feels somehow wrong. Sometimes it's better to be patient.

I find a relatively clean spot on the floor and sit down cross-legged. Take off my coat, roll up my sleeves. Soon there's no sound but my breathing and the ticking of my pocket watch. Half an hour goes by. An hour.

And then I hear it. Sound flitting in and out. Phantom noises. Keys on a table, a purse being set next to it. My heart sinks. I know what those little sounds mean, those tiny audio snapshots of her last day on earth. I stand up and get ready for it.

It's showtime, folks.

Lucy appears at the door to the den, her long, flowing hair dyed black from the mousy brown it was when I saw her last. Workout clothes. Just got home from the gym.

She stutters across the room, like a badly remembered dream. No idea I'm here.

Because she's just an Echo. A recording of her last moments. There's no consciousness there, no construct of memory I can talk to. All I can do is watch.

She's in full color because she's still new. She'll probably fade in a couple more weeks to a muddy gray and then disappear entirely in a few months. Echoes rarely last very long.

I stand and follow as she paces the room. She picks up a shadowy item that I think is a TV remote. It fades into view as she gets near it, incorporating it into her image. She puts it down and it fades away. She's not expecting trouble. Especially not in her own home. She has no idea what's about to hit her.

It's sad and disgusting and I wish I wasn't who I was, couldn't see what I can see, didn't know that this shit was real. Because the last minutes of my sister's life are about to play out tonight. She'll do it tomorrow night, and the next night. And the next, and the next, and the next. One long memento mori.

And all I can do is sit here and watch.

She spins toward the boarded up windows, shielding her face with an arm as something crashes through the window. I see hints of glass as they come near. Sound is the first thing to go with an Echo, and I can barely hear her scream.

Her killer fades in as shadowy as the TV remote had a minute before. It's a man, definitely. Or man-shaped, with a man's build. Lot of things look like that and not all of them are human.

From the entrance through the window the summoning gone bad theory is losing ground. For a second I hope I can catch his face, but I know I won't. This is all her show and all I'm going to see clearly is her and whatever she leaves behind. Like all that blood.

She turns to run, but the killer grabs her from behind. The sounds of her struggle, of her being slammed into the wall, thrown into the glass coffee table are getting louder, more intense. She tries to stand, the wind knocked out of her, her hands badly sliced and dripping blood. Before she can get her feet under her she's being strangled again. The killer slams her hard against the wall. Two, three, four times.

Her attacker's not unusually tall. Can't be more than six feet. But he's incredibly strong. His hands go round her throat, choking her as he beats her to death with her own house. He throws her like a rag doll onto the couch, knocking it over. I know no one else can hear the commotion, but I check the door anyway. To me it sounds like a cage match between rabid wolves.

A wound opens in her gut, though I can barely see the knife. It tears and drags through her flesh while she flails against him.

I get up and cross the room to get a better look, fight my instincts to try to save her. I shut down every emotion I can. I have to pay attention. Now's not the time to give in to grief and anger. I stand where he would be, examine the wounds as they open up. I somehow keep from vomiting. Phantom blood sprays through me leaving cold trails that linger in my chest.

She gives a sudden jerk, bucks against the wall. By

this time she's got no air left and her screams fall silent. She's gasping like a fish on land. Her attacker throws her against the other wall with more power than anyone normal would have. Leaving a dent in the drywall I hadn't noticed before.

Lucy jerks again as he grabs her and reams out one of her eyes with a finger. I force myself to watch. Been doing this my whole life and I've seen worse. But this is different. There's nothing I can do but hope the scene drops some clue, gives me some opening to find this fucker and make him pay.

He continues to brutalize her. Breaks her legs, her arms. She's got no fight left in her, but at this point she was still alive. He tears into her flesh, ripping off chunks of her scalp. Her jaw's got to be broken in at least three places. He's making a point of torturing her. Why do that?

He picks her up again, jerking through the air, a blood-soaked Raggedy Ann with the stuffing pulled out. Still alive, but barely. He shoves her against the wall he cleaned afterward. Grabs one of her broken hands, smears it in her blood, slams it against the wall, scrapes it along like a paintbrush. He starts writing.

Was there writing there when the police came? There couldn't have been. They would never have wiped it off. It would be evidence.

I watch the words appear, watch him punctuate his message by slamming Lucy's head against the wall, leaving a blotchy, red period. My rage at what he's done turns into a spike of ice running through me. The room spins, my knees turn to water. This can't be happening.

It's a message the killer never intended for the police

to find. He wiped it out after writing it, leaving it behind in a way they couldn't have possibly seen it.

He left the message for the only person who would read it. The only one who could.

WELCOME HOME, ERIC.

He left it for me.

Chapter 6

I spend the next half hour throwing up in the kitchen sink. While I was watching, yeah, I needed to stay focused, not let it get to me. But it's over now and I break down.

I sit on the floor in the dark, my stomach flipping cartwheels like a gymnast on meth. I tell myself that the tears are just some side effect of all the puking, but I know they're not. Questions spinning through my head and I can't focus enough to answer any of them.

Why did he kill her in the first place? What the hell does this have to do with me? Why did he torture her? I wash my face, rinse out my mouth. Pull it together.

The first question's easy. She was bait. Bet that if he did this I'd come running. Whoever did this wanted me back in town. Wanted to get my attention.

Well, he's got it. Don't know why he's got a hard-on for me, but when I find out who it is I'll feed him his nutsack and ask him.

I can't answer the second question. Not yet. But if I find out the why it might lead me to the who. File that one for later. And then there's the torture question. What did the killer hope to gain out of that? Maybe he enjoyed doing it but I can't imagine that was simple sadism. There was a reason for it. Had to be.

It comes to me as I'm pulling the Caddy away from the curb outside her house. I drive through an Echo in the street. The hastily scribbled wards I drew on the Caddy in black Sharpie shunt it aside, but not before I see a boy in jeans and a black leather jacket get shot in the back of the head.

Maybe he was in a gang. Maybe he was a bystander. Maybe he was a killer, or a saint, or his mother's pride and joy. Whatever he was he was just like everyone else in one crucial way. He had a soul.

When you die it'll go off to, well, to wherever it's going to go. Heaven, Hell, Elysium, Valhalla. Depends on what you believe, how strongly you believe it, whether you've pissed anything off big enough to take an interest.

Sometimes souls stick around a while. You get Haunts and Wanderers. But ghosts don't just happen. Your Uncle Billy's not leaving a spook behind just because he stroked out during Thanksgiving dinner.

It takes trauma: physical, emotional. The more violent the death the more likely you'll leave something behind. Gunshot wounds, car accidents, burn victims. Suicides, broken hearts.

I have no idea why, and haven't met anyone who's ever had an answer. But the kind of ghost you get is a different matter. That comes down to will. Haunts don't have enough will to leave the place they died. Wanderers have it to spare.

Drag the dying out and all that willpower drains away. The soul goes on, but there's nothing left behind but a big old ball of trauma. All you're getting is an Echo.

That's why he tortured her. Lucy's killer knew what he was doing. He wanted to make sure that's what he left behind, not only so I'd see the message, but so I wouldn't be able to ask her any questions.

But there are a lot of dead people I can ask.

I pull the Caddy into the motel's parking lot, next to a beat up Volkswagen bus and a mid-80's Volvo covered in gang tags. I dig around in the Caddy's trunk for a minute and grab all the things I'll need, then check that the wards I put on it haven't faded.

When I get in the room I lock the door, push all of the furniture in the room as close to the edges as I can. I pour a circle of salt about five feet wide in the center of the room, place red glass grave candles at the cardinal points. Another circle of the last of the powder I used in Texas goes inside. I strip to the waist and touch up some of my tattoos with a black Sharpie. I lay out my straight razor, an antique silver soap dish to catch the blood. I do some stretches. I'll be sitting cross-legged inside the circle. I'm going to be there for a while and I don't need a cramp.

Some of this shit's just pomp and circumstance. Some of it's a focus for me. Some of it's running on ancient laws that were laid down before men knew how to talk. I have no idea which is which, so it pays to follow the rules. Finally everything's ready.

With a single wave and a whispered spell I light the candles, blow away the sunflower seeds and strips of palindrome-inscribed Post-it notes from the room's threshold. The wards I set up on the room blow away like sand.

I can feel the ghosts taking notice. They can smell me. The ones who haven't figured out I'm here yet are going to in a minute.

I hate this part. When Odysseus called forth the shade of Tiresias he bled a ram and fed the dead prophet its blood. You ever try to get hold of a goat after midnight in L.A.? Sure, maybe in Hollywood, but I'm not up for trawling through Craigslist ads.

I flip open the straight razor, press the tip of the blade against the scar-marked patch on my forearm, slice fast and deep, send out a mental invitation. Deep red blood hits the silver cup and the room lights up like Christmas. Standing room only in two seconds flat. Sound like a jet engine that only I can hear.

Wanderers from miles around burst into the room, eyeing the cup, licking their lips. A seething mass of stab wounds, suicides, bullet holes. Forty or fifty of them, it seems like. Hard to tell with them all crammed into the room, flowing in and out of each other in a blur of limbs and faces.

They yammer for a taste of the blood, for a lick of life. Please, please, please. Some tiny reminder of what it's like to be breathing. Pathetic faces stare at me like the orphans in Oliver Twist.

It's easy to forget how dangerous they are. Seeing them is one thing, but this is different. I've thinned out the barrier between worlds. Given half the chance, they'd eat me.

It's not the blood they want, it's the life in it. They'll suck it dry if I let them. The silver dish is a focus to keep their attention. If they noticed it was my blood they'd be on me like a Sunday pack of church folk at a Home-Town Buffet.

The tattoos help divert their attention, and they can't cross the circle of salt and graveyard dirt I've poured onto the carpet unless I let them, but it doesn't mean some of them won't try.

"Here's the deal," I say. "You want a taste, I want answers."

The noise increases. Too many voices, too many sounds. They're all shouting random shit like the audience of a game show, hoping they've got what I'm looking for, answering questions that haven't been asked.

I start by culling the herd. I put my hands together in front of my like I'm praying, focus my will to weed out the dead. First, let's see who's been in Venice in the last month. The crowd parts in front of me like flesh under a scalpel as I separate my hands. Still too many. I split and shuffle, rearranging the dead like packs of cards.

I concentrate on the Canals, the day she died, the week before, the week after. Two weeks, two months. The long-gone, the newly dead. Every shuffle refines it down to the ones with enough awareness of the outside world that they can actually watch it.

I'm one of the few living pretty much all of the dead can see. For good or ill I've made myself known to them enough times that it's stuck. Most of them have no clue there's even another side. I split the group further to match my needs, pulling some back, pushing others away. They don't like it, but fuck 'em.

Each time I ask my questions. What did they see? Who was there? Describe the place, the people. I scatter a few drops of blood into the crowd as payment whether or not I like the answers. I don't.

Five hours into it, the parade of dead an incomprehensible blur, I get a hit. Barely more than a kid. Mid-1920's, maybe. Slicked-back hair, smart suit with cravat, straw boater on his head. Half of one, at least. The rest looks like it went the way of most of his skull. He's missing the left side of his face. Gunshot, sledgehammer, who knows. He probably doesn't remember himself.

"A man," he whispers. "Dressed in rags. He was there that night. I saw him crash through the window. I heard screams."

I've heard a dozen stories so far, most of them vague hints at events that were either too late, too early or never happened. The dead don't lie very often, but their memory's for shit. So far none of them knew anything about the window.

"How tall was he?"

He looks me up and down. "Tall, but not overly so. Thinner than you." He looks around the room. Points at a ghost near the bathroom. "His height." From what I recall of the gray blur I watched kill Lucy, I'd say he's two for two.

"Did you see it happen?"

He shakes his head. "Only the end. He wrote something on the wall. He used her body as a brush. Are you Eric?"

Bingo.

I drag a description out of him that narrows it down to about fifty thousand medium build, black haired, men. Maybe Latino, maybe Hawaiian. Dressing like a homeless guy might or might not help, but I'm not going to bet on it. He didn't have anything with him. No backpack, shopping cart, suitcase. Nothing.

"There was something about him that frightened me," the ghost says. "He glowed with a white fire. He felt dead, but he wasn't. And he had black eyes. I'd never seen that before."

"Black eyes? Like he'd been punched?"

"No. Like he had no eyes. Black pits. Nothing more."

I can think of a dozen different things that look like men and don't have eyes. But most of them aren't urban. And what's with that white fire?

"How long you been around?"

He shrugs. "Long enough."

"You got a name?"

"Herbert, I think, but I'm not sure."

"You're a lot more put together than most," I say.

He laughs with a sound like leaves on the wind, points at his head. "That's one I've never heard before."

The candles are almost burned out, the sun is peeking through the blinds. I could go on another five hours and not get anything else. Time to wrap it up. I've been steadily dripping blood into the cup all night. A drop here, a drop there. It adds up after a while. I'm feeling a little woozy. I'm going to need a steak after this.

I squeeze a few more drops from my forearm into the cup, push it out of the circle with the tip of my straight razor. It breaks the salt line, but that's just a marker for the border. The magic is what's holding the circle together.

I don't let any part of me cross it, though. Herbert looks like a decent sort, but I don't doubt he, or the rest of them, would jump on me the second I crossed that line and drain me dry.

"Thanks for the information, Herbert," I say. "Here you go."

He doesn't look at the blood. He's got a lot of self-control. Damn few ghosts would wait. "What's your surname if you don't mind my asking?"

"Carter."

"You're welcome, Mister Carter. I hope you find what you're looking for." He reaches down to the cup, dips his fingers into it. The cup clatters as he pulls the life out of the fresh blood. He's neater than most, too.

He seems to get more solid for a moment, then fades back to transparency. "Good night, Mister Carter," he says.

"Good night, Herbert. See ya around." I watch Herbert step through the wall and disappear. The rest of the assembled dead look on, envious.

"As for the rest of you freeloaders," I say, "beat it." A few hastily scramble away, but some of the others, more hopeful or more stupid, don't get the message.

"I said fuck off." I clap my hands together and they make a sound that ripples through the room like thunder, breaking the ghosts into shards that fade away like smoke. I know more than I did earlier, but not enough to make a damn bit of difference.

Chapter 7

I manage to pull out a few hours of fitful sleep. My dreams are full of bloody writing and broken bones. Lucy asking me over and over why I left and didn't come back. Blaming me for all of it. Her body shattering like glass.

Before I can say anything I wake up in a clammy sweat, shaking. It doesn't matter. I didn't have an answer, anyway.

I take a tepid shower in a scummy bathtub with no water pressure. It helps some, but not enough. I need to do something. I need to move. I doubt digging through the dead is going to get me any further that it did last night. I should talk to Alex, but I don't want to. He'll ask me what I found out, and for some reason I'm not entirely clear on I don't want to talk to him about this just yet. I need to get my head straight. I'm running on too little sleep and too much punishment. My bruises are throbbing. My legs scream when I get up from bed. Sitting cross-legged for five hours takes a toll. My body's getting tired of paying it.

I decide to take a drive, see if maybe that will jar something loose. I hop onto the 10, take the 110 through

Downtown, cross over to the 5. Breakfast is a drive-thru burger joint on Los Feliz.

I take my grease bomb and fries over to Griffith Park and head over to Travel Town. Built in the fifties, Travel Town is an open-air train museum at the edge of Griffith Park. Locomotives and passenger cars from all across the nation ended up here. Heavy iron and history.

I eat my burger on the edge of an Oahu Railway passenger car from 1910, the wind whipping at the trees. The Santa Ana winds that were only beginning to gust the other day when I was in Koreatown have picked up speed.

I used to come out here a lot as a kid. Lucy and I would climb across the train engines, hang from the pipes and handholds. I can't help but find trains soothing. After a night dealing with the dead I want to surround myself with solidity, sturdiness. Fifty tons of steel and iron fits the bill.

Besides a few Wanderers and a couple of faded Haunts tied to the boxcars I've got the park to myself. No one wants to be out here when the winds blow this hard. Rain threatens on the horizon in banks of crystal-white clouds shot through with streaks of dull gray. Waiting for that moment when the Santa Anas let up long enough that the clouds can swoop in and cause panic in the streets with nothing more than a light drizzle.

From the feel of the air that's not going to happen soon. It's too dry, too crisp. Red flag warnings will be up any day now in hopes that people will actually pay attention and not start a brush fire with a stray cigarette.

It takes me a long time to realize that I'm not really

here for the trains, revisiting my childhood or anything like that. Comforting though it is, this is a rest stop. A place for me to pull up my big boy pants and go somewhere I've been dreading since I got Alex's phone call.

Forest Lawn cemetery is right next door.

I know she's dead. I watched it last night. That's more real than any funeral or viewing or obituary listing can be. But I need to see her grave, anyway.

I don't know why, exactly. It doesn't make sense. She's just ashes in an urn. Chunks of carbon ground down in a cremulator.

There's really no point in putting this off any longer. I ball up the burger wrapper and toss it into a trash can, pass by the ghosts on my way to hang out with corpses.

The clerk at the cemetery office, a large black woman dressed in purple and black, horn-rimmed glasses perched on her nose, sells me a bouquet of chrysanthemums when I stop in to ask for directions.

I don't know why I buy them. It's not like the bodies care. Memories come flooding back as I drive past grave markers, the occasional mourner. I stop across from a funeral in progress, family and friends huddled under a large tent, copper casket waiting to be lowered into the ground.

The last time I was here was for my parents' funeral. We had no casket. There hadn't been enough of them left to bury. Cremation was almost redundant. We stood outside the Court of Remembrance, an open-air columbarium alongside movie stars and the not so famous but plenty loaded.

Nobody teaches kids how to mourn. Everything churns together and you don't know which way is up.

Sadness and anger and regret all ball up together in knots. That night I should have been there for Lucy. I should have taken care of her and protected her and sat with her while she cried for our parents. I should have been her older brother, the grown-up, the strong one.

Instead, I lost my mind.

I hunted down the man who'd killed them. Jean Boudreau. Hadn't a hope in hell that I'd be able to do it, but I did it anyway. It was stupid. Would have been better if I'd failed. Even better if I hadn't tried it in the first place.

I walk along the rows of interred ashes. A slot in the columbarium isn't cheap. I'll have to find out from Alex how much it cost so I can pay him back.

Carl and Diane Carter are in the north wing, third row from the bottom. Lucy is next to them. Even in death she kept the cartoon last name. I don't know why it surprises me, but it does. It was hers, after all. She picked it.

I trace the letters on the plaque with my finger, feeling the weight of reality crashing down on me. Last night I could almost pretend that I was seeing someone else, or that it was distant, like watching it on television. But this is real, solid. A tangible reminder that she's really gone.

I put the chrysanthemums in the holder hanging next to her plaque. They smell wrong. Like roses. And smoke.

"I grieve for you, Eric Carter."

I spin around, call flames to my hand ready to let them fly. If my world were normal I'd think it was a tasteless if elaborate joke. Somebody stuck a skeleton in a wedding dress and plopped it behind me when I wasn't looking.

The bones are bleached white, the eye sockets pitch

black. The wedding dress is clean, if a bit tattered. She holds a scythe in one hand, a small globe in the other. Roses are braided in the veil pulled away from her face and along the sleeves and folds of her dress.

The last time I felt a presence like hers was in Carlsbad. She has the feel of one of the heavy hitters, like Baron Samedi, or Maman Brigitte. Not quite a goddess, but close enough as to not make a difference.

I've never met her in person, but I've heard of her. You don't run in the circles I do and not hear about the Narco Queen herself.

I remember passing her shrines on my way through the desert. Remember thinking one of them had turned to follow me with its gaze as I drove past. Didn't know she knew me. That can't be a good thing.

"Thank you, Señora de las Sombras," I say, bowing my head, letting the flames die around my fist. I have a general rule about showing respect around avatars of death.

She has a lot of names. Señora Blanca, Señora Negra, La Flaca and, it's rumored, Mictecacihuatl, the Aztec goddess who watches over the bones of the dead in Mictlan. Mostly, though, she goes by Santa Muerte, patron saint of drug runners, murderers and thieves. Her cult numbers a couple million at last count.

I'm not talking the typical Día De Los Muertos crowd. These aren't your Hot Topic goths and mariachi bands in white makeup who come out once a year to put out *ofrendas* and *calavera catrinas*. They're not even in the same ballpark.

The Mexican drug cartels routinely lop off the heads of their enemies and burn them as offerings to her. Saint

Death. The only goddess who always keeps her promise. She's very popular on the other side of the border, particularly in places like Juarez where the homicide count is astronomical. Not so much up here, but that's changing fast.

She reaches out her hand and the scythe she's holding turns to dust to blow away on the wind. "Walk with me," she says. Her voice is smoky like Lauren Bacall after three packs of Camels, her accent generically South American. "Take my hand. We have much to discuss."

That's where I draw the line. "I'll walk with you, Señora," I say, "but we both know the power of a touch."

She nods her head. "Agreed," she says, a hint of amusement in her voice. I think. The thing I hate most about skeletons is you can never tell when they're smiling.

I follow her as she glides along the pathway between the walls of interred ashes then out onto the manicured grass and rows of grave markers. Though the wind is whipping at my tie and jacket, it leaves her untouched.

"Do you know what my supplicants ask of me most often?" she says, breaking the silence.

"Can't say as I do."

She's got some angle. All these fuckers do. Gods, goddesses, nature spirits. She wouldn't have appeared to me if she didn't want something. The question is, what?

"That their babies survive to adulthood," she says. "Young mothers with husbands gunned down in the streets of Juarez or the Arizona desert. Rotting in prison cells, hanging in meat lockers."

I mull that over for a second. "Forgive me for saying this," I say, "but that sounds unusually domestic."

She laughs, long and loud. Fucking scary though she might be, she's got a beautiful voice.

"It does, doesn't it?" she says. "That's only half of it, though. The reason they want their children to grow into strong and powerful men and women? So they can avenge their fathers' deaths."

"That sounds a little more like it."

"At one time I watched over the Dead and brought their souls to Mictlan. Bathed them in sacred waters when they passed my tests, judged them, weighed their worth. And then the Spanish came."

"Things went downhill pretty fast, I hear."

"Almost overnight," she says. "Instead of calling me to honor the dead, they called for vengeance. They didn't want to sacrifice these enemies with honor, they wanted to slaughter them."

"This is all fascinating, Señora, and please don't take this the wrong way, but why are you telling me this?"

"I know something of vengeance, Eric Carter. I know what you need to avenge your sister."

"Thanks," I say, "but—"

"I know who killed her."

My heart stops. She glides forward a few steps before realizing that I haven't kept up and turns to me, that perpetual smile on her face.

"You know who murdered Lucy?"

"Yes. Would you like me to tell you?"

There's a catch here. There's always a catch. Everything has a price and things like her don't barter in cash.

"It's something I'd consider," I say carefully.

"You're a rare breed, Eric Carter," she says. "Not many can bend the dead the way you can. How many do you know who can even see them without the aid of powerful rituals?"

"I'm nothing special," I say, not liking where this is going.

"On the contrary, you're very special. You're, how do they call it? A natural. And you've made quite an impression. You're a topic of conversation more than you know. I hear Baron Samedi and Maman Brigitte were very pleased with your work in Texas."

"I pride myself on customer service," I say. "But I'll admit, I haven't really followed up with them the last couple of days," I say. "I've been a little preoccupied."

The last thing I want to be is watercooler talk around the demigod offices.

"Nonetheless," she says, "you've built yourself quite the reputation over the years. I could use your particular expertise."

"You want to hire me."

"No," she says. "I want to own you."

Chapter 8

"Come again?" I've had weird job offers before but this is a bit much, even by my standards.

"Do you know how many of my followers I can communicate with directly? How many I can appear to the way I'm appearing to you now?"

"I wouldn't even hazard a guess."

"None of them. My will comes to them in dreams, flashes of insight, a half-remembered whisper in a cocaine-fueled frenzy. Even my mages must perform rituals to hear me speak."

"Must make it a little hard to get them to do what you want."

"We get by. It's the particulars that are a challenge. Detail and nuance."

"So you're looking for a high priest?" I don't know what the hell she's getting at here.

"No. Let the Catholics have their Pope. That's something I don't need."

I stop at a marble sarcophagus at the edge of the building and lean against it. Try to look nonchalant, but the truth is that I'm scared shitless. I'm getting the sense that this is one of those offers I can't refuse.

"Then what do you need?"

"A courier. Someone to carry out my will."

"An errand boy," I say.

"No. An enforcer. A champion."

"You're looking for a thug?" I say. "Considering most of your followers are murderers and drug runners, don't you already have somebody better qualified for the job?"

"Killers of men," she says. "How many demons have you destroyed?" she asks. "Ghosts you've banished? Vampires, lamiae, ghouls? You've destroyed things almost as powerful as I."

"Yeah, and?"

"I have, as you've pointed out," she says, "an abundance of murderers. But can they survive a Redcap? Face the Jersey Devil and live?"

Things I'd rather forget. Things I've never told anyone. "How do you even know about that?"

"As I said, you're a topic of conversation. I'm truly not asking you to do anything you don't already do."

I make a pretense of thinking about it. I already have my answer.

"Say I sign on with you," I say. "What do I get?"

"You're already a powerful mage. You have control over the dead. You see things that only a handful like you can. Now imagine my power coupled with your own. Imagine that power tenfold."

"I'm listening."

"With me as your patron I can enhance your already

impressive abilities. And give you things you've never dreamed of."

Take what I already know and tack on what she can give me? The things I can learn. It's tempting. Incredibly tempting. Only there's a catch.

"You own my ass," I say. "You tell me where to go, what to do."

"More or less, yes."

"I'm nobody's meat puppet."

"Which is why I want you for the job. I don't need an unthinking drone. That would defeat the purpose. Your will is your own."

"So long as you keep me wrapped around your finger. Steep price." I pull my jacket tight around me. The wind has picked up, chilling the already cold fall air. "No," I say. "I don't care if the job comes with full dental and a weekly blowjob. It was nice meeting you, Señora. Good luck filling that position."

"I can give you your sister's killer," she says. "Is your vengeance not worth it?"

"And lose my freedom? Not by a long shot. I'm not one of your gun-toting narcos. With all due respect, being a gopher for a manifestation of violent death doesn't really do it for me. I'll find the guy on my own."

I turn my back to her, walk away. Ignore her. Which is pretty much the biggest insult I could toss at something like her. Whatever. If she wants to take me out there's not much I can do about it, anyway.

"A favor then," she says behind me, "for a clue."

I slow my steps, come to a stop. Still not facing her I say, "What sort of favor?"

"Something small that fits with your particular expertise. I would like you to kill a man."

"To ask me to do this must mean he's not just any man."

"He isn't. He's a powerful mage. Here in Los Angeles. There is no hurry, though sooner rather than later would be preferable."

"What's he to you?"

"Nothing," she says. "I merely want to see if you can succeed against him."

"No time frame?"

"That wouldn't be much of a challenge," she says, "would it? Let us say, in a week's time?"

Tracking this guy down, figuring out his weak spots. It'll take time, pull me off focus. But a clue from La Flaca herself? That's worth considering.

"I'm not sure I'm up for an assassination," I say.

"Come, now," she says, her voice chiding. "Is this so different from Charles Washington? That was an assassination."

"That was a rescue."

"And yet, Mr. Washington is dead."

"I don't have anything against killing," I say. And I don't, not really. With powers like mine, my relationship with death isn't exactly the same as everybody else's. "But murder's never really at the top of my list."

"Would it help if I told you he was a very bad man? Would that soothe the hypocrisy of your conscience?"

"It might," I say.

"Then he is a very bad man," she says.

I think about it for a minute. If I accept there's not

much wiggle room. Deals with things like her are deals carved into your soul.

"This clue," I say. "It's not something I already have. And I get it now, not in twenty years. And it's useful." One has to be explicit about these things. The simplest contracts are the most easily twisted.

She laughs. "Of course," she says. "Death keeps her promises."

It's a tough call. But what's one more dead mage?

"What's his name?"

"Benjamin Griffin."

"Doesn't ring a bell."

"I wouldn't expect it to."

Kill a stranger, get a clue. It's just another job with a slightly different payment. I turn back to face her and step back startled. She's right behind me.

"Deal," I say. There's a pop in the air that's more feeling than sound and the contract's set. I owe her a dead mage, she owes me a clue.

We're both bound to the pact now. Breaking this sort of contract leads to Bad Things.

"Look for the ghost of Jean Boudreau," she says.

Not what I was expecting. "Boudreau didn't leave a ghost."

I know this for a fact. I know this because when I killed him, I tore up his soul into little pieces and tossed them out like chum. I'd have pissed on them if I could have.

"You're very sure of that," she says.

"I am."

The scent of smoke and roses grows to an overwhelming stink. I start to gag, my eyes water. After a moment, the scent disappears as thoroughly as though it had never been there.

And so has she.

———

"Fuck me." I slam my hands on the Caddy's steering wheel, slam the horn at some old lady walking across Los Feliz just because she's there. She flips me the bird.

My mind is bouncing around like monkeys playing ping-pong. The fuck did she mean look for Boudreau's ghost?

I've been played. Only I couldn't have been. But I have to have been. The information had to be useful. It was in the contract. Which means she couldn't lie to me.

But she could be cryptic. And I thought this was going to be a step forward.

Now I have next to fucking nothing and I have to kill a guy in the next week.

Stupid, stupid, stupid. Goddammit. Here's me being clever. Here's me being a fucking idiot.

This is amateur hour stuff. This is not the kind of mistake I make. I know how to deal with her kind. Lucy's death has me spun so much I don't know which way is up.

I need to get a better read on Santa Muerte. I don't trust her agenda, can't trust her agenda. But I don't know enough about her to see what sort of play she might be making. What I need is some dirt.

Baron Samedi or Maman Brigitte might know, but they won't talk. They're in the same club, or near enough for the difference to not matter, and they don't tend to narc on each other. They're not gods, they're not spirits.

They're somewhere in between. They keep to themselves and though they might gossip with one another, they're not prone to talk to outsiders.

I pull onto the 5 Freeway, merge with traffic. Feels like a game of Frogger. One more thing about this town I didn't miss.

Who to talk to? Who do I still know in L.A.? Who'd even talk to me after all this time? The dead would be useless, though they might help me track down Griffin. The living even less so. My contacts at the higher levels aren't going to talk. I'd just waste my time and burn their goodwill.

Hang on. Maybe I don't need to ask someone who knows her now. Maybe I can ask someone who knew her way back when.

The doors move.

Last time I found one was behind a dumpster on the alley wall of the Roxy on Sunset. Before that was next to the telescope at Griffith Observatory. These doors led to nowhere good.

There are large doors and there are small doors. Sometimes they're traps. Sometimes they're opportunities. They're hard to find but they're always where the people are. No point in having a door if there's no one to go through it.

The particular door I'm looking for now I haven't seen in a very long time. But I know it's around.

The thing it leads to hasn't moved since Cabrillo came over from Spain almost five hundred years ago. If it had, I'd have heard.

People have been looking for it since before he got it off an Arabian trader in Barcelona and lost it somewhere in Southern California in 1542

I park the Caddy in the lot at Union Station on Alameda. It's gotten busier since I saw it last. Thousands of people pass through this place every day. Now I guess they have local trains and a subway? Jesus. When did L.A. get a subway?

The main terminal is a hall of Spanish tile, twenty-foot ceilings, enormous chandeliers. Light slants in through the massive windows. The footsteps of commuters echo through the hall. They wait for buses and trains, talk and text on their cell phones. Oblivious wanderers.

I've spent the last two hours looking for this door. There was one in the Doheny Library on the USC campus once, and I found one at the back of a porta potty in a park in Compton.

Neither of those is there, anymore. I found one here in the eighties and one on the ceiling of a house on Catalina Island. I'm hoping this one is still here. The boat ride to Avalon always made me sick.

I buy a ticket for the Gold Line to get to the trains, duck into the men's room. I wait a few minutes for the handicapped stall, latch the door behind me, pull out a piece of chalk.

I press on the tiled wall of the stall, close my eyes and feel for any magic that might indicate the door is still here. With so many people passing through, Union Station has become thick with it and it's hard to feel past all the background noise.

I taste the smoke and ash in the local pool of magic. Hints of lumber and steel. Oil, blood, stolen water. Subtle notes of so many cultures it's dizzying. This is L.A.'s magic condensed. Thick and cloying.

I think I have it a couple of times but it slips away. It takes me a few minutes but then I catch the taste of a history far deeper than anything Los Angeles has produced. Touches of the Middle East, sex, lots and lots of alcohol.

I hang onto it, make sure I have a good grip, then I draw a rectangle in the wall with a handful of symbols I've memorized but never learned the meaning of. When I draw the spell inside the rectangle I know the cursive's as crude as an epileptic third grader's, but it's the intent that matters.

I finish the last character and the chalk lines blaze into light. There's my door. I knock on it, hope I'm not intruding, not that that's ever stopped me before. Shove it open.

The chalk lines glow brighter beneath my hands. There's a hiss of escaping air and the wall slides in to a space that isn't really there. When it gets in about six inches it stops, slides to one side. I step through.

And I'm immediately assaulted with music.

The room I'm in is a 1940's jazz club. Smoky, dim. A smoking hot Asian woman in a green dress so tight it looks painted on sings "Stormy Weather" to a full house. A large black man in a bow tie and an apron stands behind the bar, cleaning shot glasses, looking at me.

"As I live and breathe," he says as I step up to the bar. His voice is deep, melodic.

"You don't do either one," I say, stepping up to the bar and sliding onto a stool.

"Anybody ever tell you you're too literal?" he says.

"Yeah," I say. "You. It's good to see you, Darius."

"And good to see you, too. I was wondering if you'd ever come back. I heard about your sister."

I notice he doesn't give me condolences, say he's sorry. Darius is never sorry. He has his own agenda. Does things for his own amusement. Can't blame him. He's got to be bored. He's been stuck in here for a very long time. Gods willing, no one will find his bottle and he'll be stuck even longer.

"I like what you've done with the place."

"Yeah, I thought I'd go back a couple years. The punk scene was getting stale."

When I first met him he was trying to recreate CBGB in New York. Somebody told him about it in '74 and he was intrigued, but didn't really know what it looked like and he couldn't go there. I headed out that way for a week and came back with a ton of pictures and recordings. I never asked for anything in return and I've always paid for whatever he's given me. So he still owes me.

He looks me up and down. "You've gotten bigger," he says. "A lot bigger."

"Same size I've always been," I say, not sure what he's talking about.

He laughs. "Okay. Have it your way. What can I get ya?"

I dig out a twenty and lay it on the bar. "The usual, barkeep," I say.

He pours a dozen colored liquids into a shaker. I have no idea what they are. But as long as I have a hold over him I can trust him. More or less.

"I know you didn't just pop in here to say hello," he says.

"You cut me to the quick, sir," I say. "Yeah, I need some information on somebody you might have run into a while back."

"I've run into a lot of people."

"Santa Muerte."

"No shit?"

"No shit."

"Huh. Man, I haven't talked to her in a long time. She's done pretty well for herself, you know. Used to be Aztec."

"Mictecacihuatl," I say.

"Yeah, what you said. Man, I can never pronounce that Aztec shit. Used to just call her Miki. Guardian of the dead, but I guess you already know that."

"That, yeah. But I don't know *her*."

"Short version or long version?"

"What's the price?"

"Short version's on the house."

"Let's start with short and see where we go from there."

"Okay. Short version is she is one batshit crazy bitch."

He pours my drink into a martini glass and hands it to me. I take a couple of sips. One second it tastes like a Tootsie Roll. Another it tastes like an Islay single malt.

"Excellent as usual. So, what's the long version gonna cost me?"

"I got a pest problem." He points over to a table where a man in a rumpled suit is being generally obnoxious to a cigarette girl. He's pretty hammered.

And dead.

"You're kidding me," I say. "You let a ghost in here?"

"He wasn't dead when he showed up."

Darius likes to entertain. I don't know where all his doors are and he's not about to tell me, but about half the people in here are real. Some of them are really here and some of them are just dreaming that they're here.

The rest, like the cigarette girl, probably the singer and the band, too, are all products of his imagination. This is his kingdom, small though it may be, and he's got complete control over it.

He'll randomly open doors and let people in. Some of them stay a long time, some are out in less than an hour. Most of them don't remember they've been here except in dreams. I guess one of them died before Darius could get rid of him.

"I can't get him to go," he says. He sounds almost desperate. "I've tried everything. Banishings, exorcisms. Tossed his body out into an alley. Hell, I tried to pick him up and throw him out."

"Master of your domain, huh? Couldn't even get a grip on him, could you?"

"No, and goddamn it, it's driving me nuts. Get rid of him. That's the price."

"Done and done," I say. "Any of those bottles of hooch real?"

He looks at the rows of booze behind him, selects a half-empty bottle of Stoli, hands it to me.

"Be right back." I grab a couple of whisky glasses from behind the bar, walk over to the drunk's table, pull up a chair.

"Hey, buddy."

"Hey buddy, yourself," he says, his voice slurring. I'm thinking he kicked from alcohol poisoning. I've never known Darius' concoctions to get anyone drunk. Darius' place is about as sealed an environment as you can get. I'm betting that when he died his soul couldn't get out. He's not a Wanderer or a Haunt, or even an Echo. He's just stuck.

"It's last call," I say.

He blows a raspberry, leans on a spectral arm. "Been last call for—Hey," he yells, "how long I been tryin' to get a drink outta you?"

"Eight years, two months and fifteen days," Darius says. I can see why he's so desperate to get rid of this guy. A weekend with him would be enough to drive me nuts.

"Well, one last drink and then I'll take you home."

"Screw you, I like it here."

"Wasn't a request." I pour a measure of the vodka into a glass, put it in front of him.

He reaches for it and his hand passes right through. Tries again. No go.

"Man, that sucks," I say. "Try mine." I pour a measure into the second glass. Same result. I flip out my straight razor under the table, nick my wrist just enough to get a little blood going.

"Maybe you should try the bottle." I set it down in front of him. "Might have to get real close, though."

As he leans in I get a drop of blood on my finger and pass my hand down through him, flicking my blood into the bottle. His eyes widen. He starts to shake. He tries to pull himself away, but it's too late. His face and body stretch and thin out as he gets sucked into the bottle.

A couple seconds later it's done and I screw the cap back on. I etch a rune on the bottle cap. Even if it's opened he won't get out without my say so.

I shake the bottle and peer inside. Hard to see, but he's in there.

I feel a little sorry for him. He doesn't know what's happened. Sure as hell didn't ask for it. Stuck in his own little hell with no idea how he got in there or how to get out.

Just like the rest of us.

Chapter 9

"I'll take him out when I leave," I say, sliding the bottle of Stoli into my jacket pocket.

"You do that," Darius says. He wipes at a non-existent stain on the bar with a towel. "All right. So, the long version."

"If you wouldn't mind." I'm starting to get antsy. I don't know how much time is passing in here. It's really up to him. I don't want to lose any more than I've already lost trying to track him down.

"She's got a sweet gig. Lot of the old gods, they either bailed or turned into tiny things. One guy, old Chumash feast god, I hear he's got himself a drum circle in Santa Monica that keeps him going. Best he can do is get a bunch of New Age wannabes to follow him around as their guru. Nobody believes anymore. In any of them."

His eyes go distant and for a moment I can see the sands of the Sahara reflected in his eyes, the red and gold of the Brass City. I've never known Darius to get maudlin, but after hundreds of years stuck in here, maybe he's getting a little cabin fever.

"Never like the good old days," he says. "Anyway,

Miki. Party girl. Not as big on the whole vengeance, retribution thing like she is now. More a guardian. Took the souls to the underworld and watched over their bones."

"What happened to her?"

"The fucking Spanish happened. That Cortez fuck. Before I came over here. Drove her believers underground, enslaved her people. For a while I heard she was scraping together an existence in Xibalba, chewing on scraps of the dead." He shakes his head. "Couple hundred years of that shit'll twist your head around."

"Can I trust her?"

"Oh, fuck no. Especially not now. Like I said, her head's twisted around. Batshit crazy. From what I hear she's running angles and schemes, short and long cons. You'd think she was fucking Coyote or something."

"Will she try to break the laws?"

"No, she won't lie to you," he says. "She's got that much going for her. She keeps her promises. Death always does. But like the best grifters she knows how to fuck you with the truth."

"So I'm pretty much back at square one," I say. I give him the lowdown on her clue and the job I'm doing for her.

"Yeah, that sounds like her. Wish I could tell you more. She and I, we don't talk. Not since her husband took himself out, what, 1800's?"

"She was married?"

"Yeah. They shared the underworld together. Real badass but he couldn't take the pressure. Some gods do that. They just sort of give up. That on top of everything else and she went off the deep end. Hey, there's a cheery thought."

"What?"

"She said, what, champion? That's what she's looking for? Sure it wasn't 'consort'?" He makes air quotes with his fingers, waggles his eyebrows.

"Oh, dude, don't even go there."

"Just sayin'. Could be she's looking for a replacement." Darius slaps me on the shoulder. "Could be worse. She doesn't have to do the skeleton thing, you know. When I knew her she was smokin'."

Great. Now I've got a crazy death goddess making googly eyes at me.

"I know I probably don't have to tell you this," he says, "but watch your ass. Miki's not somebody to fuck around with."

I tap the side of my head. "Not something I'm likely to forget. Thanks. Appreciate it."

Darius has a wicked sense of humor and who knows what time it will be when I leave, but he's acting weird. The way he spoke about "the good old days" makes me think he could use a little company.

So I stick around for a couple more drinks, listen to some more jazz. He tells me about some new hotshot he's been hanging out with. A girl running a flophouse in Skid Row for wayward supernaturals. Vampires and shit. Weird. I think he's got the hots for her. God help her.

When I finally leave only about an hour has gone by outside. Twenty bucks gets my car out of the parking lot. Rush hour traffic has the freeway backed up and the surface streets are a crawl. I pull the bottle of Stoli out of my coat pocket and look at the drunk ghost inside. Poor bastard. I should let him loose, but I'm not about to do it here in the car. Christ knows what he'd do.

I haven't run into too many stuck ghosts before and they've all been unpredictable. I put it back into my coat pocket. Besides a drunk in a bottle of Stoli and the terrifying idea that a death goddess might be looking at me for a boyfriend I've gotten fuck all from the trip.

One thing, though, at least I know she's telling the truth. Or at least Darius thinks so. Which makes it even harder to wrap my mind around her saying to look for Boudreau's ghost. What if it's not his ghost, not literally? There's a thought. Maybe it's something else. Something he left behind.

Alex might know something. You run a bar you're going to have connections, right? All that business isn't entirely legit. Somebody from Boudreau's old gang must still be around.

When I asked Alex earlier if he knew Ben Duncan, Boudreau's right hand, he said he'd never heard of him. If he's gone I'll have to track someone else down. I drive until I find a payphone on Broadway near the Orpheum Theatre. At least that place hasn't changed. In the land of iPhones and Blackberries a payphone's a rare breed. I tap the side of the phone and get a dial tone. Who needs quarters?

I know I should get a cell phone, but it feels too much like a tether. I don't want to be tied to anything. I dial Alex. He picks up after a few rings.

"It's me," I say.

"Where have you been? I've been trying to get hold of you since this morning. Is this your cell phone?"

"Payphone."

"You're kidding."

"I don't own any credit cards, either." I start to tell

him what happened to Lucy but I can't do it. I'm used to gruesome death scenes, but my brain seizes on this one. The image of Lucy being used as a gruesome paintbrush flashes in my mind and the words die in my throat. Just thinking about it makes me sick all over again. "Killer left a message," I say instead. "For me."

"What? Where?"

"I—Later, all right? I'll tell you later. It's tied in with Boudreau, somehow. Something he left behind, maybe. You said things have changed. Things have calmed down. Did anyone take over when he died?"

"I heard people tried, yeah. But everybody just sort of petered out. Are you all right? Head over to the bar. Let's talk about this."

"Hey, buddy. You gonna be long? I gotta use the phone."

I turn to see a guy in a tailored gray suit behind me, a Mercedes with tinted windows parked in the lot next to the Eldorado.

"Give me a minute," I say. I turn back to the phone and stop. Why would a guy in a tailored suit driving a Mercedes need to use a payphone?

I step back into him and duck just in time to see the taser stab over my head where my neck would have been. I reach up, grab his wrist. Pull forward as I twist myself up and back, throwing him over my shoulder into the payphone. Hand still wrapped around his wrist, I shove my foot on his throat. Anger flares up inside me and I want to kill him, just because I want to kill something and he's a damn good candidate right now, but I rein in the impulse.

I start to pull in the magic around me with a lightning

spell that should knock him out long enough to stick him in my trunk when I hear, "Hey, asshole," behind me.

I let the spell loose in a sphere around me instead of at the guy at my feet, not sure exactly where or how close the second guy is. The guy I have on the ground jerks as the wattage pumps through him and I hear his buddy drop to the ground. The payphone throws off sparks, starts kicking out quarters and dimes.

I turn around to see another suit, this one sporting a Sig-Sauer instead of a taser, twitching on the ground. I kick the gun out of his hand.

"Guns and tasers? Whoever sent you after me gave you some bad intel," I say. Two more suits exit the back seat of the Mercedes, blue flames of magic ringing their hands.

"Or maybe not."

I bolt past them, jumping and sliding over the Eldorado's hood as they let loose with bolts of plasma the size of melons. The fireballs pass by as I get the door open, shielding me from the heat, but cracking the windshield, bubbling the paint on the hood. A tap on the steering column and the engine roars to life. I slam it into reverse, spinning out of the parking space. I miss the guy on my side but clip the Mercedes hard enough to shove it out of its spot.

It blows the mages' next shots. Instead they take out a parking meter and the top of a concrete street lamp from the forties.

Cars swerve to miss my ass end as I throw the Caddy into traffic. In the land of Beemers and Priuses nobody knows how to deal with a boat like the El Dorado. They almost kill themselves getting out of my way.

I cut down Broadway, scream past the 10, cut right on Adams. Almost take out a couple of bikes.

Dammit. I've been so distracted I let a guy with a taser get the drop on me. The two mages I can understand, but a taser? What is this, amateur hour? And who the hell were they?

Guys with guns, spellslingers with money. I was asking Alex if anybody had taken over the reins of Boudreau's old organization. Guess I got my answer.

I figure they've been following me since the cemetery. Otherwise they could have taken me at Travel Town. Probably had the mausoleum camped to see if I'd show. Which means they don't know where my motel is. Yet.

It's time to do what I do best. Take a runner. I'm not skipping town, but I'll be goddamned if I won't stay mobile enough to not get trapped. I pull into the motel lot, scanning for cars. There's a beat up Civic and a Jetta that have been there since I got in. I park in front of my room.

Most of my gear is in the car. Just have a suitcase with some clothes in the closet. I spelled the Do Not Disturb sign to keep people and various supernatural riffraff out of the room. From the feel of it the ward hasn't been disturbed.

In, out and I'll be on my way to the other side of the city before they can track me down. I throw the door open, run in. Turns out it is amateur hour.

The guy sitting on the bed fires two barb-tipped wires from his taser right into my chest before I can react. Everything locks up and I hit the floor. My muscles spasm to the rapid ticking as he pumps me full of voltage.

The thing about a taser is you have to keep it going if

you really want to keep somebody down. I guess it's a good thing he doesn't want to keep his finger on the trigger, too much and my heart might stop.

He lets up on the voltage but I'm not thrilled with his choice of alternatives. He kicks me in the head until I black out.

Chapter 10

As bad men go Jean Boudreau wasn't the worst. He was just more ambitious than most.

From what I hear he started small. Dealt a little weed, diversified. Heroin, meth. Kept it pretty clean all things considered. Toss some magic into the mix and you can throw shit together that makes crank look like Nyquil. Instead he used his magic to keep the customers coming. A little influence got the word out, got some attention, gave him an advantage.

He pulled together a crew. Normals and magic types. Held his own and kept his head down. When the bigger guys came sniffing around wanting a piece he negotiated where he could, threatened when pushed, killed when he had to.

He had magic. Most of his competition didn't.

Drugs led to prostitutes, some legit businesses as cover. But the real money was in his own people. Get enough magical muscle and the rest of the community's got no choice but to pay protection. At least until somebody stands up and says fuck you. Like my parents did. Told him to take his threats and shove them up his ass.

And that's when he summoned a host of fire elementals to burn the house down with them in it.

———

I come to with no idea where I am. When my vision clears and I can take in the scene, I still don't know. It's a plush room, wherever it is. An office with green walls and dark wood wainscoting. Old English hunting prints, shelves lined with leather-bound books, lamps on the walls that wouldn't be out of place in the nineteenth century. A desk with a heavy leather chair and old-style ledger books. I'm sprawled in one of two high backed Victorian chairs.

I've been kidnapped by Charles Dickens.

It's a bad sign when you wake up longing for the days when all you had was a bruised rib. My nose is definitely broken. Every breath through it is like sucking in fire and it feels about the size of a casaba, dried blood crusted all over my face. Lip split and swollen, body screaming in bruises.

I pull myself straighter in my seat, ignore the pain, try to stand up. Before I can get my legs under me a heavy hand clamps down on my shoulder and forces me back down. I feel familiar cold steel against my throat.

"You should stay in your seat, buddy," says the man with my straight razor. "Wouldn't want to do anything premature, ya know?" He takes the blade away from my neck.

That thing is so sharp it barely touched my neck and still drew blood. I hope he slices off a couple fingers folding it back up, but no such luck.

I can see five guys behind me reflected in the glass of

one of the hunting prints. The four from the Mercedes, one of them looking almost as bad as I feel, his nose taped up and his arm in a sling. Didn't think I'd yanked on it that hard. I look up at the fifth guy holding me down.

"You're the fucker who tased me." Guy's built like a gorilla. Nice suit though.

"Yeah, what of it?"

"I think I'll kill you first."

The room erupts into laughter. Thank you everybody. I'm here all week. Don't forget to tip your waitress. I shift in the chair, feel the weight of what's in my pockets. Gorilla boy's got my straight razor, but my watch, the Illinois Sangamo Special, is still in my coat.

They clearly don't want me dead yet, though from the firepower the two mages were packing in the parking lot I don't think they'd mind too much if I was.

I'm not going anywhere for a while. Might as well make the best of it. I start to tap into the local pool. Just a little. Sip at the power. I might need a boost. I can't draw too much too quickly or the two other mages will know.

People don't walk around with badges that say Magic Boy on their shirts. But we can tell when somebody's pulling a bunch of juice out of the local pool. Feels like a tug on the back of your mind. I have to be careful or this won't work.

The door behind me opens and an older guy steps through. Black guy, in pretty good shape, but definitely getting on in years.

"Mister Carter," Ben Duncan says in that same reasonable tone he used when he told me to leave L.A.

fifteen years ago or he'd kill my sister. "Glad you could join us."

"Ben Duncan. Sonofabitch."

"There's a name I haven't heard in a while," he says. "It's Griffin these days."

They have to punch me a couple more times before I stop laughing.

"Not the reaction I was expecting," he says. He crosses to the desk in front of me, slides into the chair behind it.

"Must be punch drunk," I say, my voice thick and nasal. Blood is running down the front of my shirt. One of my molars is loose. My left eye is starting to swell shut. Jesus, one busted nose and I sound like a commercial for cold medicine.

"You're lookin' good," I say. "Well, better than last time."

"Last time I had second degree burns on half my body because of that little stunt you pulled."

There was no way I was going to get close enough to Boudreau to take him out, so I had followed him to a warehouse he had in San Pedro and rigged a car to drive in through the front door. It went in as he came out. Then I remote triggered the fifty feet of detcord I had wrapped around a dozen propane tanks. It had been surprisingly easy.

"You gotta admit, though," I say, "it looked pretty fucking cool."

He shows me how good his right hook is. It's pretty good. I spit out that loose molar.

He wipes my blood off his hand with a handkerchief

one of his men hands him. "Yes, well. From your vantage point I'm sure it did," he says. "I understand you came back to find out what happened to your sister."

"Yeah. Seeing as she's dead and all. I figured our little agreement was, you know, kind of quits."

"I wasn't responsible for your sister's death. You should know that."

"Yeah, actually," I say. "Kinda figured. You know who did it?"

"No."

"Fair enough. So, any particular reason you decided to beat the crap out of me and bring me here?"

"Eric—Can I call you Eric?"

"Only people who don't beat the shit out of me get to call me Eric. So that'd be a no."

A small frown creases his face. "Eric. You were a dangerous boy when you killed Boudreau. You're more dangerous now."

"Nah, your guys are just pussies is all."

He fixes his men with a cold stare. Particularly the guy whose arm I broke.

"Oddly enough I agree with you. Be that as it may, you're still a dangerous man. And I can't have someone like you causing more problems than you've already caused."

"Oh, man, you haven't begun to see the problems I can cause."

"My point. And seeing as you've come back I doubt there's much that will keep you out again. I had been hoping this meeting would have gone better, but things got a little out of hand. I'm sorry about that."

"Yeah, me too." I can see where this is going and when one of the goons behind me puts his gun against my head I'm not surprised.

"Interesting way of showing gratitude," I say.

"I'm sorry?"

"Gratitude. You know, for clearing the way for you. Come on. If it hadn't been for me taking out your boss you'd still be begging for scraps."

"I was never grateful," he says. "Yes, you moved up my timetable, made it a little easier for me to take over, but I already had everything in place. If you'd come in and torched the place before that night it would have all fallen apart. As it was I had a hell of a time picking up the pieces." He pauses, like something's just occurred to him.

"If it helps, this is nothing personal."

"Gee, thanks. Awful magnanimous of you."

I'd figured as much. Going to all this trouble to beat the crap out of me wasn't going to end in him giving me a lollipop and saying sorry.

I know if I make a move the gorilla behind me will pull the trigger. I have an idea, but I don't have enough power, yet. If I can keep him talking, maybe I can stay alive long enough to get out of here. But what will grab his attention enough to want to know more? In a moment I have it.

"You know Boudreau's not dead, right?" It's a long shot and I know it's not going to work, but every second will help.

There's a flash of something on his face and for a split second the mask of hard competence crumbles away before coming back.

It takes me a second before I realize what I'm seeing in that look. Fear. He's scared.

"Why do you say that?" He's trying to not show it, but I've got him hooked. Interesting.

I tell him about Lucy, about how her death brought me home, about the message. I fudge a little and say the dead helped me track him down, confirmed that he's on his way back from the dead.

"He's gunning for me. And when he's done with me, I'm willing to bet that he'll come for you."

Griffin sits for a long moment looking at me. "Thank you," he says finally. "That actually explains a few things."

Wait, what? Explains a few things? What the fuck? He's not really buying this, is he?

"Well, when you run into him I'm sure the two of you will have a lot to talk about," I say. Almost ready to go. Just another few seconds. I shape the spell in my mind. Pull in the different threads of energy I need. "Out of curiosity, how'd your guys find me? I mean, I didn't ex-actly advertise I was in town."

"I have sources," he says. "Interesting thing. Did you know your friend Alex doesn't actually own most of his bar? Bad debts. Almost half a million dollars. Sold me a sixty percent stake in it a few years ago. We're business partners."

Where punches couldn't shut me up, that does. I can't believe that Alex would sell me out. That doesn't make sense. But my brain runs with it, anyway.

I find myself wondering if he used Lucy's death as an excuse to lure me back, then quash that thought as hard as I can. I can't believe he would do that. I won't believe it.

Griffin nods at his lackeys and I know I've run out of time. I've been slowly pulling in energy and tying together my own spell. It was touch and go there for a while when they were beating the crap out of me, but I was able to hold on to that thread of the magic, letting it leech into me. And now I've got plenty.

I give reality a hard shove and toss out a variant of that lightning spell that I used earlier. More shield than blast. Good thing, too. I let it loose a second before the gun goes off.

A wall of blue light pulses out from me in a hemisphere, expanding through the room with lightning speed. Shoves the gorilla to the floor and his hand goes high as the gun fires, sending the bullet meant for me into the ceiling. The shield expands outward with enough force to slam Griffin's desk a foot back, pinning him against the wall and knocking back the other guys behind me.

If you can avoid it, I really have to recommend not having a gun go off next to your head.

My hearing goes to a high-pitched whine. If it weren't for the beating I've already taken I'd probably notice the headache. I lurch out of the chair, hit with a sudden wave of dizziness. I ignore it and weave my way over the stunned bodies of Griffin's men, grabbing my straight razor and the gun from Gorilla Boy. His eyes are crossing and he's trying to catch his breath.

I point the gun at his forehead and he gets the message. Stares at me with cold fear.

I say, "Bang," and leave him shaking on the floor pissing his pants in fear.

Outside there's a hallway and a staircase leading down. Path of least resistance. I head downstairs.

It's a big house. I'm not really sure where the door is. But I've got a lot of motivation to find it fast. I can hear noises upstairs as Griffin and his men pick themselves up off the floor.

A door ahead of me bursts open. Of course Griffin would have more than five guys working for him. Cocksucker. I pop off a couple rounds in their general direction and the men coming out of the room ahead of me duck back in fast.

I double back, head down a side corridor. This place is a fucking maze. Every hallway looks the same. Who lives in a place like this?

I feel the gunshot before I hear it. Shooter behind me. Bullet grazes my right forearm. There's a flash under my shirt. I have a tattoo for protection against gunfire. Without it I'm betting he'd have drilled me in the head.

My arm is a searing lance of pain. I drop the gun. Trip over my own feet. I roll over to get a better look. It's the gorilla who tased me. Stupid me. I let him live. The gun's too far away for me to reach it before he can shoot or get to me.

I reach into my coat pocket with my left hand, pull out the pocket watch, thumb the dial. The watch is a masterwork of engineering and magic. I don't even understand how it works. Beautiful in its complexity. And horrific in its operation.

I focus my will at the guy coming for me. I feel time compress around me. Compress, stretch, turn into a thin lance that bursts out and wraps around the man trying to kill me.

I'm shooting for a day or two. Maybe a week. That

usually slows people down from the shock, but it doesn't kill them. But the watch has other ideas.

Instead of a week the energy bursts in a bubble of eighty years or so. He shudders, stumbles. Screams in unholy terror. Years tack onto him in seconds. He drops the gun. Muscles waste away, hair grows gray, long, brittle. Skin sallow and spotted. His eyes cloud over, his teeth fall out.

I try stopping it, jabbing at the crown with my thumb, but it just keeps going.

He drags himself forward. Keeps coming, anyway. His mummified fingers, nails like claws, reach for my foot. His raisin eyes stare at nothing. By the time he reaches me he's been dead ten years.

This is why my watch freaks Alex out. I pull myself up, grab the gorilla's gun in my left hand, the right almost useless from the pain. I tell myself I hadn't wanted to kill him, but I have to wonder if maybe I had.

The hallway leads into a foyer. I run to the door, jump back as machine-gun fire stitches a line in front of me. I duck back into the hallway, look for the shooter.

The foyer has a larger staircase in it than the one I came down at the back of the house. I'm betting the shooter's up there. I can't get to him from here and I can't get to the door.

My arm's starting to feel a little better, if you count numb as better. Some of my tattoos are helping with the pain. I flex the fingers, the pain burning in my forearm. I doubt I'll be shooting with that hand, but at least I can use it.

Options? Run out there. Try to shoot a guy I can't see with a gun in the wrong hand. Brilliant idea. Think I'll pass. I put the gun on a side table, place my hand on the wall, close my eyes and concentrate. There. I can feel him. Up on the balcony. Crap. I can feel *them*.

Three guys. I can handle three guys. I pull in more power, which just gives away my position to any of the mages in the house, but it's not like they don't already know I'm here.

I think of the wood in the stairs, visualize complex knots. Say a charm of shaping. Last time I used it was to straighten out a bent axle. This time I do the opposite. There's a wrenching sound as the banister tears out of its base on the stairs and whips around like a snake. Screams, thuds as the wood twists around in a spiral clearing the staircase.

I grab the gun, run out, hope I got them all. Find out the hard way that I hadn't.

It's not gunfire this time. An inferno of angry, green flame bursts from a side room, blocking off my path to the door. I jerk back, firing blindly into the room, realizing too late that the bullets will vaporize before they come close to a target.

"You're surrounded, Eric," Griffin says. He steps from the doorway, his hands ringed with flames. I should have known. I was paying so much attention to his lackeys it didn't occur to me that Griffin might have talent.

He's right. I can hear running footsteps behind me closing in fast. I've got Griffin waiting to fry me in the front, half a dozen guys with automatics coming up my ass. No windows, no doors. The trick is, as they say at Disneyland, to find a way out.

I've got one. It's not fun and it might just kill me. But it's an option rapidly rising to the top of the list the closer sudden death gets. If they want to send me to the other side, the least I can do is accommodate them.

I close my eyes, take a deep breath, block out the sounds of running and gunfire, the swell of heat from Griffin's flames searching me out. This is one of those spells I've never been able to do without blood. I know a couple folks who can, but whether it's a psychological block or just the fact that this is more closely connected to my particular knack, I don't know.

Good thing I'm already bleeding. I wipe my hand across the wound where the bullet grazed me, scatter a fine spray of blood into the air. I spin a series of images through my head like a visual mantra. Each one clicking into place like the tumblers on a safe. Scenes of burn victims, murders, suicides. Grief, mourning, the emptiness of death.

I pull myself from the land of the living to the land of the dead and the bullets punch through empty air.

Chapter 11

I haven't gone anywhere. Physically I'm in the same place. I've punched through the barrier between worlds, but they occupy the same location. Same house, same walls, but gray and shadowed. All the color has been sucked out.

Like being able to see the dead on the living side, I'm able to see the living on the dead side. Griffin's men are still coming down the hallway, gray blurs of indistinct light. I don't get out of their way fast enough and they run through me, a cold wash as our bodies intersect, leaving me nauseous and dizzy.

I stumble away from them, fighting the nausea until I get to a side hallway then puke my guts out. Between the broken nose, gunshot, and vertigo-inducing flip between worlds I spend a good couple of minutes emptying my stomach.

I pull myself up, wipe my mouth with the sleeve of my coat. This is a temporary respite at best. If I stay too long here I'll die.

This side of the fence isn't designed for the living. Everything here is dead and drained. The very air sucks at your energy, saps your memories, your will, your life with a creeping inertia. The place itself will kill me in short order. Provided the ghosts don't do it first.

The walls look insubstantial, but they're solid enough. This is an old house. Been around long enough it's become a part of the landscape. The furniture's another matter. It's too recent, too transient. It's barely visible and I can step through it with ease.

The rules are different for me over here than they are for the Dead. They're the predators, I'm the prey. I won't be walking through the walls of this place, but they won't have a problem.

I pick my way past Griffin's searching men. They can't see me, but it doesn't mean one of them might not be sensitive enough to pick up I'm here. I'm one monster of a roving cold spot.

The front door's going to be a challenge. I can move things on the other side from here, but it's not easy. I take a look out the window. It's going to be tougher than I thought.

I'm a beacon for the Dead at the best of times. And that's on the other side. Over here I'm a fucking bonfire barbeque with a blinking neon sign that says GOOD EATS.

They're lining up to get a taste. The yard is filling up fast with Wanderers. Clusters of them are already at the door and piling up at the windows. When they spot me a mob of them start hammering on the glass, howling and screaming.

They're not coming in despite the fact that most of them could slide on through without even knowing there's a building here. I crane my neck over to get a look at the outside of the door, catch a pulsing purple glow. So that's what wards look like on this side. That's good. Means I've got some more time to figure out how to get out of here.

I hear a snarl behind me and realize I've spoken too soon. I turn and there's Gorilla Boy. What's left of him, anyway. He stands there as he died; thin, emaciated, ancient. But that's just a look. He's just as dangerous and vicious as any other ghost.

He leaps at me, mindless with need and hunger. There's really not much left of him in there. There probably wasn't much to start with.

I duck and jump to the side, thankful he hasn't been around long enough to figure out he doesn't have to move like a living man, anymore. He hits the ground, rolls, kicks off for another pass. His bony fingers rake across my back as I dodge past him, a searing cold tears across my skin.

I hit the ground in a flash of agony. The cold spreads like an explosion over my body and just as quickly it fades, leaving me shaken and numb. All that from one touch.

He comes at me. I'm easy pickings now. Feeling's starting to return to my legs and hands, but I won't be able to get out of his way fast enough.

There's not a lot I can do over here. I have to preserve what power I have left. I'm cut off from the pool of power on the other side and I used a lot with that spell in the office and jumping over here. I'm running off my own reserves and those are draining rapidly. Would suck if I didn't have enough left over to get back home. Fortunately I've got a couple wild cards.

I've got so much ensorcelled ink on my skin I've forgotten what some of it is for. I had it written all down once, but I lost the list in a car fire about five years ago.

There's one in particular I picked up on an Indian reservation in Montana; a murder of crows on my chest. They're constantly shifting color and formation, number and size. One day they're in a V pattern on my chest, the next there's only one and the rest have migrated to the spaces in between other tats. They like to move around. And they really like to be let loose.

I give a low whistle, a short tune the artist taught me. There's a tearing sensation on my chest like I'm losing a layer of flesh and I cry out from the pain.

The birds erupt from my body, tearing through my shirt in a shower of screeching black. They circle the ghost, pecking and tearing at him like spectral piranha. I've never used them against the Dead before. Wasn't sure it would work. Didn't know they had a taste for ectoplasm.

Within seconds they've shredded him into wisps of insubstantial smoke. I don't know if he's gone. I doubt it, but with some luck it will be a little while before I have to worry about him again.

The crows circle a bit, then fade to nothing. I open my ruined shirt. On the other side they would have lasted longer. Here they lasted less than a minute. Tells me I don't have a lot of time myself.

They're back where they started, but now they're just ink. The magic I bound into the tattoo is spent. If a touch from one ghost could screw me up so badly, there's no way I can take on the crowd outside. Screwed if I stay here, screwed if I go back. I need something to get their attention off of me.

I get a really nasty thought. I know what to do. I've done it before. I find a window over to the side. I shove on the latch, trying to push it open. It's not just that it feels like it's stuck, it's hard to get any kind of grip on it, like sinking my hands into mud.

I switch to hammering on it with the butt of the gun, and after a few seconds it clicks over. I look to see if any of Griffin's men are coming over. They can't hear anything I do on this side, but they can hear anything I influence on the other.

Some of them have scattered, I assume to look for me in other parts of the house. A few are still hanging out here, whether waiting for me to show back up or not I don't know. No one seems to notice the latch opening. I'm careful not to try to open the window. It'll probably take some force, but I don't want to break any of the wards on the house. Not yet, anyway.

One hand on my open straight razor, the other on the doorknob I wait by the front door until I see one of Griffin's men come my way. On this side they all look the same to me, man-shaped blobs of light. Maybe I'll get lucky and one of them will be Griffin. There are a few teasing moments when one of them comes almost in range, but not quite. The timing on this is going to be tough and I can't afford to fuck it up.

Finally one of them gets close enough and I flip back to the land of the living. There's an explosion of light and sound and life. I can feel the magic flooding back, color bursting into everything. Shouting as I suddenly appear, guns being drawn.

I loop my arm around the guy's neck, kick open the front door, flip back to the twilight side. Take him with me. The amount of power it uses is enough to leave me dizzy and I really don't know if I'm going to have enough to get back now. He's not expecting it. He probably doesn't deserve it. Hell, not a lot of people do. I take advantage of his surprise and disorientation from the transfer.

"Sorry, man. Nothing personal," I say, slicing the straight razor fast across his neck, arterial blood spurting high into the air. I spin him around and throw him out the open door.

The ghosts go batshit. They descend on him in a seething mass of piranha love. Ripping him to shreds, drinking his life. When they get done with him there won't be anything left to move on to whatever afterlife might be waiting for him. They'll eat his soul.

I don't wait to see the process. I've seen it before. After the car went up at Boudreau's warehouse I went in, found him torn and broken inside. I dragged him, barely conscious, already dying, out into the night. Threw him onto the still smoking hood of the car.

I took him over to the other side with me and fed him to the Dead. Listened to him scream. Waited until they tore up every shred of that man's soul.

I don't think I've been the same since.

I run back inside the house to the window I unlocked. I don't have much time. That many ghosts on a guy, he won't last long at all. I take a running jump at the window. It's like hitting concrete. I bounce back, take another jump at it. I'm running out of time.

The third one does it. The window pops open and I hit the ground on the other side. There are a few wanderers still lingering who haven't figured out the main event's by the front door. They fall in behind me, taking swipes as I run past them. The grounds of the house are pretty big. I want to find an exit. I run across the circular driveway past dim outlines of Mercedes and BMWs.

I skid to a stop when I see it. The vague shape of a Cadillac Eldorado. It's glowing the same purple the front door had with wards and protection spells.

I can't think of anybody who would do that to a Caddy but me.

I run to the car, try to pull the door open, but I can't get a grip on the handle. It hasn't been here long enough to make a solid impression on the landscape. The ghosts are getting close. I try a second time, realize I'm an idiot and flip back over to the living side.

The world bursts into color and sound again. I yank the car door open, slide into the driver's seat. One of those assholes shoved a screwdriver into the ignition. I turn it and the engine roars to life.

In the rearview I can see Griffin's men running out the door. I throw the car into reverse and stomp on the gas, scattering most of them and bouncing a couple across my trunk. I swerve into the cars in the driveway, bouncing my already battered bumper into the cars' wheel wells hard enough, I hope, to tweak the steering and make them undrivable.

I kick the car back into drive and peel out onto a small private road that's more of a glorified driveway. A vine-covered gate looms in front of me and I give the car more gas, speeding into it and tearing it off its hinges. The doors bounce into the street.

I hit the street hard. Sparks fly up from the car's undercarriage when it smacks off the asphalt. Griffin's house turns out to be on one of the side streets north of Sunset. Should have known. Ritzy place. I toss out a small misdirection spell, hopefully powerful enough to give me a head start. I head for the freeway.

———

I'm not feeling so good.

I find some Kleenex in the glove compartment, tear off a chunk and stick it up my nose to stanch the bleeding. The second it goes up a nostril, pain flares between my eyes and I almost swerve into a truck.

I hate having a broken nose. Getting it reset is going to suck. After driving around for half an hour and not seeing anyone following me I pull over to the side of the road and take stock. The rib's definitely broken. In the rearview mirror I can see my face is one massive, purple bruise. Dizzy, which is never good. But I'm not seeing double, so that's something.

But my thoughts are like Teflon. I can't get anything to stick for very long. The adrenaline dump I got back at the mansion has left me shaking.

I push past the mental Slip n' Slide. So Ben Duncan, the asshole who kicked me out of L.A., is Ben Griffin. I have to kill him to pay for my cryptic clue from Santa Muerte.

I can work with that.

But did he kill Lucy? Even through the beating my head took I know he didn't. No profit in it. Why go through all that trouble just to bring me back here and then try to kill me?

He wanted to see me first. Find out why I was in town

before he took me out. His surprise when I mentioned Boudreau was genuine. Or he's a really good actor.

I find my mind wandering past that to how he tracked me down. Still think he had somebody camped at the cemetery, but how did he know where my motel was? I look around at the seat. Takes me a minute, but I find it, the wadded up receipt for my motel room. Stuck between the cushions. Okay. So they broke in while I was in having my talk with Santa Muerte and found it?

I'd buy it if the receipt hadn't been so tightly wedged in there. But how else could they have figured it out? And how would they know what room I was in? I hadn't told anyone.

Oh. Wait. Yes, I had. Son of a bitch.

———

I pop two wheels up on the curb down the street from Alex's club and shove down on the parking brake. The day's getting on and already the parking lot is full. Happy hour.

I dig around in the glove compartment. The Browning's still there. I pull it out, make sure it's loaded. I get out of the car and immediately regret standing. I stagger, catch myself on the door as dizziness washes over me. I pull it together and lurch down the street to the club. The effect I'm going for isn't subtlety. It's entirely possible I'm not exactly in my right mind. Being repeatedly beaten can kind of have that effect.

I throw the door open and get a face full of bouncer. He could wipe the floor with me, but I'm ready for him. And I'm in the mood to hurt somebody. I drop him with a blast of electricity without bothering to say anything first. He falls backward through the curtain in the foyer to the bar floor.

None of the customers have seen a mage in action before. Part of me cares enough to keep it that way. All they see is the bouncer land on the floor, skid a couple feet and lie there. He'll probably get up thinking I've got one hell of a right hook.

"Where the fuck is Alex?" People are ducking behind chairs, running toward the fire exit. The bouncer stands, a little unbalanced, and comes stalking toward me, his face contorted with animal rage. I step in and shove the Browning against his head.

"I've killed two people today," I say, "and tore their souls into shredded fucking wheat. You really want to fuck with me?"

He hesitates, unsure of what to do. Whether because I've got a gun in his face or because I'm talking bugfuck crazy I don't know. The fact that he got up from that blast and hasn't backed down says I may have picked a fight with the wrong guy. I don't really want to have to kill him. There's been too much of that today already.

"Back off, Max," Alex says, coming out from the back. The bouncer looks at both of us, glares at me and steps aside. Alex comes up to me, pointedly ignoring the gun. "What's going on, Eric?"

On the drive over I did the math. Alex is the only person who knew where I was staying. And then there was that crack from Griffin about Alex half a million in bad debt, how he'd sold most of his club to get back into the black. The more I thought about it, the more plausible it sounded.

"You sold me out, you sonofabitch." I'm slurring my S's and the dizziness has kicked up a couple notches. That spell took a lot out of me.

Alex frowns. He takes on a tone like he's talking a crazy man off a ledge. "I don't know what you're talking about. Come on, Eric, you look like hell. I've been trying to find you since your call cut out. Let me get you some help."

"Fuck you," I say, loud enough to make him flinch. "You sicced that sonofabitch and his fucking band of thugs on me." Alex blurs a little, the floor tilts enough to make me stumble but I hold on to the gun.

"I'm not doing anything, Eric. You're bleeding. Your nose is broken. Your face is nothing but one big bruise. We need to get you some help."

"You're not fucking touching me. Griffin told me about you. Told me about your deal. Right before he tried to have me killed."

"Griffin? Ben Griffin? The hell does he have to do with anything?"

"See, you know him. You knew he was around. You knew he was looking for me. You gave me to him to clear the half million you owe him, get your club back."

"The fuck are you going on about? No. I mean, yeah, I know him. Everybody knows him. And yeah, I owe him money. But he sure as fuck doesn't own any of this club. We've got a revolving account with him. He's one of my suppliers."

"What?"

"He sells me beer, Eric."

Did I get the name wrong? I don't think so. I can't remember. There's something else to say, but I can't think of it.

"You didn't fuck me over," I say, somewhere between relieved and feeling like an asshole. I blink away the double image of Alex. My thoughts slide off each other. The room takes another tilt and I stumble, suddenly too woozy to stand up straight.

He catches me as I go to my knees, grabs the gun with one smooth motion. "No, man. I didn't do anything like that. I wouldn't do that."

"He was with Boudreau." My voice sounds very far away. "Changed his name from Duncan."

"I don't know what you're talking about, man. Let's get you patched up and you can tell me all about it, okay?"

Alex thinks he's just his beer guy. I laugh. "Boy does he have you fooled," I say, and slip into unconsciousness.

Chapter 12

It's 1994 and Vivian is patching me up again. We've been dating almost three years now. I've been in another fight. I've got another broken nose. Took on three guys in the parking lot behind a shitkicker bar on Pico because I wanted to hurt something.

I didn't lose, but I didn't exactly win, either. Story of my fucking life. I'm not stupid. I know I've got issues. Who doesn't? The world pisses on everybody. I'm not special. That pisses me off even more. Angry young man, that's me.

But Viv doesn't deserve this. Doesn't deserve the anger, the fights. Me showing up on her doorstep with cuts and bruises. Broken bones. More evidence I can't rein in my own fucking temper.

"I'm sorry," I say. For what I'm not sure. There's so much to choose from, after all. Let's settle on me being such a raging asshole. That should cover pretty much everything.

"You should be," she says. "Fifteen years is a long time. You didn't even say goodbye."

My eyes snap open and 1994 slams into 2010.

"Vivian," I say. I try to get up, but dizziness and weakness overwhelm me. She pushes me back down with a fingertip. I don't fight it. It's an awfully nice fingertip.

Short red hair, porcelain skin, a smattering of freckles across the bridge of her nose. Time's barely touched her.

"Eric."

"What are you doing here?"

"Fixing you," she says. "Again. Do you know where here is?"

It looks like a storeroom with shelves and boxes loaded with booze, cans of peanuts, cleaning supplies. I'm on a folding table with a rolled up jacket under my head for a pillow.

"We're at Alex's bar?" I say.

"Hey, you're not as concussed as I thought."

I should say something more, but what? Apologize? How do you apologize for disappearing the way I did?

"Viv, I—"

"Have a broken nose," she says, cutting me off. "A fractured rib, lacerations, contusions, a missing tooth, broken capillaries in your left eye and a couple minor gunshot wounds. You're lucky. Bullets just skimmed the surface. By the way, nice tats."

"Thanks. Kept me alive today. You say a couple gunshots?" I only remember getting shot once.

"Right forearm, and a really nasty one on your back."

"Oh, that. Ghost tagged me."

"Do I want to know how that happened?"

"Probably not." I flex my arm, look at the neat stitching cutting through a tattoo of intertwining snakes in a band. I can't remember what that tattoo does. Just to be on the safe side I'll want to get it touched up.

The wounds are sore, but not what I'd have expected from a gunshot. When I breathe I don't feel that hitch from the broken rib that's been bugging me since Florida. I prod my nose with a finger and it explodes with pain, making my eyes tear up. "Jesus fuck that hurts."

"Quit your whining. It's not like you haven't broken your nose before. Quit poking at it and it'll heal up fine."

The pain subsides slowly. All things considered, including the nose, I'm in pretty good shape. I should be in a lot more pain and a lot more fucked up.

"You've gotten better."

"I should hope so," she says. "Spent enough on the medical degree."

"You're a doctor?"

"You sound surprised."

"Kinda, yeah."

"What, you think I couldn't make it through med school?"

"What? No. God, no. I was just—" I let the sentence trail off. I'm not sure what I was thinking. Things had changed. Alex runs a business, Viv's a doctor. Lucy, well . . . before she died Lucy was a success.

And then there's me.

"Just thinking how much things have changed around here. Feeling a little lost is all."

Her face softens a little. "I'm sorry about Lucy."

"Thanks."

"Let's get you up." She helps me sit upright. I'm still dizzy, but it's nothing compared to earlier. She hands me a juice box. "Drink this." I suck it down in record time.

"You got another?" She's already handing me one before I've finished my sentence.

"So," I say, slurping the last of the juice, "med school, huh?"

"Top of my class."

Not surprising. Viv's scary smart. Smarter than me, that's for damn sure. Like Alex she wasn't big on power, but she was good with memory enhancement spells and things that required control and finesse. Couple that with an already brilliant mind and I could never win a goddamn argument with her.

I flex my back. Even the soreness I felt a little while ago is fading. "Private practice?"

She nods. "Through UCLA. I do some work at County, too. I can't do miracle cures, but I can speed things up."

I point at my taped up nose. "Like fixing busted noses?"

She gives me a smile that's got all the warmth of the North Wind. "I could fix that easy."

"Right." Of course she's still pissed off at me. I would be if I were her.

"Oh, I'll take care of it. I just don't have what I need here. Look, Eric. Yes, I was hurt. And angry. I wanted to wear your balls for earrings. But it's been a long time. I've moved on."

I haven't.

The thought comes so suddenly and so unbidden I know it's true. Everyone's kept moving forward, following their path, changing with the times. They've grown up and I'm still the angry young man playing with dead things. I've just gotten better at it is all.

I think, I know, that I've had this hope in the back of my mind that someday I could come home and everything would be fine. That I could pick up where I left off.

I know it's not possible. I can't bring Lucy back, I can't bring my parents back.

But maybe I can get Vivian back. Stop running, get a second chance. If she can forgive me.

"I'm sorry."

"You said that."

"I was delirious. This one's more heartfelt. And conscious."

"Don't, Eric. I can't accept that apology. Not yet."

"Fair enough. But maybe we could—" I don't get a chance to finish. The door opens with a knock.

"Hey," Alex says, stepping inside with a shopping bag. "How you doin', tiger?"

"I've been worse," I say.

"You were pretty messed up when you came in here."

"Yeah, sorry about that. How's your bouncer?"

"Wants to rip you a new asshole, knows it's a bad idea." Alex shrugs. "Shit happens."

He steps behind Vivian, wraps his arms around her in a hug and gives her a kiss on the cheek that's a lot more intimate than just friends.

If either of them has any clue how I'm feeling about this they're doing a good job covering it up.

So much for second chances.

"I got you some new clothes. Moved your stuff to a different hotel. Hid your car. Have you considered getting something that doesn't steer like the Titanic?"

"How'd you know which room I had?"

He holds up my motel room key. "Found this in your pocket."

Of course. My paranoia ratchets down a notch. "Where's the Caddy?"

"At the new motel. Parked in the back. You always drive it with a screwdriver in the ignition?"

"Present from Griffin," I say.

"Oh. Speaking of which, he's why I moved it. Figured if you weren't just being delirious and he's the badass you say he is, might not be a bad idea to get it out of the way. Turns out you're right."

I tense up, my heart hammering in my chest. "Did he come here? What happened?"

"He and three guys with guns. Side of him I'd never seen before. He made noises. Wanted to know where you were. Don't worry about it. I've got this whole place warded for privacy. He wasn't going to find you."

"Helps you're a good liar," Vivian says.

Yes, it does. I don't know if I'm having doubts because I really think Alex would hand me off to Griffin, or if I just want something to hate him for besides Vivian.

"Thanks," I say.

"I got your back. Know that. Please. Now, what the fuck happened?"

I tell them about being grabbed at the payphone, getting tagged at my motel room. The fight, me getting away. I leave out a few details, like how I got out of Griffin's house.

"Jesus," Vivian says. "You've had a hell of a day."

"I've had worse," I say before I can catch myself.

Her eyes narrow and she does this thing where she bites her lip when she's thinking. I'd forgotten how cute that was.

"I'll look into that," Alex says. "I don't like the idea of doing business with a guy who's picked up where Boudreau left off."

"He seems less crazy than Boudreau," I say.

"Doesn't make him less dangerous. I'll ask around. He's not the only one who's got people, you know."

"What, you're gonna have your waitresses tail him?"

"No, Max."

"The bouncer?"

"Ex-LAPD."

"I should probably apologize to him, huh?"

"Might not be a bad idea," he says. He hands me the shopping bag. "I got you some new clothes. I figure you walking out of here half-naked in bloody pants would just confuse the customers."

"I thought I scared them all off," I say.

"This is the late night crowd. Trust me, these folks, you're not gonna scare off."

I look into the bag, pull out a cell phone.

"No more payphones," Alex says. "Get with the fucking 21st century."

I snort, toss it back in the bag. There are jeans, shoes and socks, a t-shirt and a hoodie with a Lakers logo on the front.

My shirt and tie are little more than ribbons. I ball them up and toss them into a wastebin. I put the t-shirt on. Pulling it over the stitches in my back and my broken nose isn't fun, but it's a good fit.

The Browning is in its holster at the bottom of the bag. I leave it there and toss my shoes in with it. A good polish and they'll be fine.

I swap my torn-up suit pants for the jeans and pull on the tennis shoes. I'm transferring the contents of my suit coat into the pockets of the hoodie when I catch Vivian's expression.

"Jesus," she says as I pull out the pocket watch, her eyes going wide. "You still have that thing?"

"What is it with you people and watches?"

"I had the same reaction," Alex says. "He's got good reasons for keeping it."

Vivian looks from Alex to me and back again. "I'd love to hear them."

"The watch is an entropy trap. Causes aging, withering. Sucks time out of things."

"Like living things," she says, "I remember. Tell me you haven't used it on anyone. That accident with the cat was appalling. You said you were going to get rid of it."

"I lied."

"Viv," Alex says quietly. He puts his hand on her shoulder, but she shrugs it away.

"Would you rather I had just tossed it in a dumpster and let some other poor bastard find it?" I say. "Imagine a normal getting their hands on this thing. Any idea the kind of disaster that would be?"

She closes her eyes. I can almost hear her counting to ten. "Fine," she says. She won't look at me.

"You were asking earlier about any of Boudreau's people taking over," Alex says, steering the conversation back. "Well, looks like you met one. Why'd you want to know?"

"Oh, the getting my ass handed to me portion of my day was preceded by the finding out of why Lucy was killed." I give them a rundown of Lucy's murder, the message the killer left behind and how he left it behind. I spare the details, but not much.

By the time I'm done both Alex and Vivian are crying. Me, I can't access that emotion anymore. I just get angrier.

I tell them about my failed attempts to ask the Dead, about Santa Muerte, her clue about finding Boudreau's ghost. I leave out the part where I have to kill Griffin. I don't think either of them would take it very well.

When I'm done I'm met with a heavy silence from both of them.

"Santa Muerte?" Vivian says. "She's real?"

"Yeah. She's real. Not much different from any of the other things you can call up. Just . . . bigger."

I've spent the last few years dealing with things that are higher on the food chain than most people, normals or mages, ever encounter. It feels weird to hear the question.

"And you think Boudreau is back?" Alex says.

"No. He couldn't be." Could he? I push that thought out of my mind. I made sure of it. I tore every last piece of him into scrap.

"How can you be sure?" Vivian asks.

They know I killed Boudreau. They don't know how. They don't know what I was willing to do to make sure that fucker never took another step in this or any other world. I'm not sure how they would react to the truth.

"I just know, okay? I'm thinking it's maybe something he left behind, instead. Some significant memory or something that symbolized him that's still around."

"That could be anything," Vivian says.

"That's why I'm thinking that whatever it is, Griffin's got it. You said he's the only one of Boudreau's old crew left?"

"Not the only one, no. I was thinking about this a little while ago. There's one other guy I can think of who's still around from the Boudreau days. Guy named Henry Ellis," he says.

"The hobo?" Vivian asks.

"You know him?"

"Yeah. I do an ER shift at Harbor once a week and word's around that I'll help out with the magic set. He comes in a lot. Guy's a mess."

"That's what I've heard," Alex says. "Worked directly for Boudreau. Don't know what he did, but I hear he burned out his circuits. Can't channel power from the pool and his talent wasn't all that great to begin with. He might know something."

Burning out happens to mages who hang onto more power than they can hold. One time is fine. Even a hundred, you space it out right. But you do that for too long and one day you find you're pulling less and less and what started out as a waterfall has slowed to a stream, then a trickle, then nothing at all. Then you're dead in the water.

"Know where I can find him?"

Vivian shakes her head. "I treat him every once in a while down at County. Guy's homeless. Lives wherever he finds room. He's a piece of work. I knew he was a talent, but I didn't know he was a burnout. No wonder he's so messed up."

Alex nods. "He could be anywhere," he says. "I don't even know if he's still alive."

The door opens and I tense. But it's just Tabitha, the waitress. Her apron is off, purse slung over her shoulder. She's jingling a set of keys in her hand.

"Hey," she says, giving me a little wave.

"Hey yourself," I say. I pull the hoodie on. "Where's this motel?"

"Over on Lankershim," Alex says. "Tabitha will drive you over."

"Get sleep," Vivian says. "And something to eat. You don't get rest you'll take longer to heal. Especially that nose."

I give her a Boy Scout sign. "Yes, ma'am." I might not have any choice. I'm exhausted.

"Be safe," Alex says. "And don't do anything stupid."

Right. Like I can do anything but.

———

Tabitha's got a little two-seater Pontiac Solstice. It suits her. Both are sleek, classy designs, compact and damn good looking. She slides into the driver's seat and I lower myself into the passenger side like a decrepit 80-year-old.

"Come on, grandpa, you're not that old."

"No, just beat up a lot."

"I heard. Rough day, huh?"

"Rough couple of days, yeah."

There's a paper bag on the floor of the car. I look inside. There's a bottle of Alex's Balvenie '78.

"You planning a party?" I ask.

"Maybe," she says, giving me a smile that's a little more like a leer. "You never know how things will go."

I think about my day. Started well enough. Burger at Travel Town, hanging off the trains. Then arguing with an avatar of death, fighting off mages and guys with tasers, aging a guy into mummified insanity and throwing another one to the hungry Dead like I was feeding piranhas.

"Yeah," I say. "You never know how things will go."

She takes a corner a little too fast, a little sharp. We should be skidding but we're not. And it's not ingenious engineering that's got the car cornering like it's on rails. She just cast a spell.

"You're a talent," I say.

"Yeah," she says. "Didn't Alex tell you?"

"Doesn't tell me anything," I say, thinking back to Vivian's and Alex's embrace earlier.

"It's not much, but he's showing me some things."

"Good for you," I say. "Don't let it get you killed."

"Oh, please. What could go wrong?"

Lucy's face slamming against the wall, her bloody hands being used as a paintbrush. Her body broken, her mind nothing but the leftover trauma of the night.

"A whole hell of a lot," I say.

She's silent for a couple of blocks, face tight in concentration. Whether from the magic, the driving or trying to figure out what I meant, I can't say.

"You've been doing this for a long time?"

"Getting the shit kicked out of me? Years."

She laughs. "No. I meant the magic."

"Yeah. Since I was a kid. You?"

"Few years ago," she says. "I think I always knew, though. Little things, you know? A little too lucky with some things, shit you can't explain."

"Yeah. That's how it starts. How'd you find out?"

"Car accident. Was taking a turn in a Mini way too fast on the 110. Blew a tire. Car spun out. I hit the railing and went right through."

"Sounds nasty."

"Would have been if the car hadn't stopped mid-air. I

mean hanging over the street. Fifty feet to the ground and the car's just floating down."

"Impressive. Been able to do it since?"

"Are you crazy? I'm not about to try. I freaked out and the car dropped ten feet. Had a hell of a bruise on my ass and it cracked the axle."

I laugh. "If you don't try, you won't know."

She glances over at me. Grins a little. "Yeah, Alex said you'd say something like that. He's been telling me not to try until I know how to control other spells."

"Did he now?"

"Yeah, he's kind of a dad. I mean, that's great and all. Helped me out. I was working at the bar when it happened. I come in the next day and he takes me back into his office and he just knows. It was freaky. How does he do that? Know shit like that?"

"He's good at reading people," I say. "That's his knack. He tell you he used to do short cons to make money?"

"No shit?"

"No shit. He was good at it, too. Don't know why he stopped."

"Wanted to settle down?" she says.

Yeah. Settle down. Vivian wouldn't want somebody who's just living day to day, bouncing around. Somebody like me. I shake the thought away.

"I guess," I say.

"You ever think of doing that? Settling down?"

"I'm not really wired for it."

"Me either."

"Home's an illusion," I say, more to myself than her, but she nods her head.

"Yeah. Working with Alex is the longest job I've ever had. I've never even had an apartment longer than a year." She takes a right off of Lankershim and into a parking lot. "Speaking of which, welcome to your new illusion."

"Sweet place," Tabitha says behind me as I flick on the light. It's called The Goodnight Inn, down in the Valley. Alex didn't think having me stay so close to his bar was a good idea. Extended stay suites. Two rooms a pop. Nice furniture. Kitchen and complimentary morning newspaper. Everything's all coordinated the way real people live. Even the hotel art is tasteful.

I hate it.

Tabitha sits on the king size bed, bounces up and down a little. Flops down onto her back, snuggles into the blue comforter covering it. "Come here," she says. I do and she grabs my hand, pulling me down onto the bed. I wince, but lie down next to her, anyway. Goddamn, I feel old.

She props herself on an elbow. "Jesus, you weren't kidding, were you?"

"About getting beat up? Figured the taped up nose and bruises were kind of a giveaway."

"Well, yeah, but I figured it'd stopped there." She hesitates, considering. "I heard you were pretty messed up when you came in. Heard you laid out Max. I've never seen anybody budge him."

"I was motivated." And an asshole. When I left the club I tried to say sorry, but he just glared at me. "Do you know why I'm out here?"

"Alex told me some," she says. "Heard about your sister, about how you, Alex and Vivian used to hang out. And that your magic's all about dead people. I figure you're looking for the guy who killed your sister?"

"That about sums it up." I close my eyes for a moment and relax a little. Having Tabitha lying next to me is nice. She puts her head on my chest. I don't stop her. That's even nicer.

I feel her run a finger along the tattoos on my forearm. "This stuff go all the way up?" she says, voice quiet.

"And down." I tug up the t-shirt and show her the tattoos on my side and belly.

"Wicked. Can I see them?"

I cock an eye at her. "When I say they go down, I mean they go all the way down."

"Now I really want to see them."

"How about you?" I say.

"A couple." She sits up, peels off her top, undoes her bra and drops it on my chest.

I'm expecting butterflies and unicorns, but it's an elaborate series of cherry blossom branches from one shoulder, down her side, across her hips, cupping her right breast. The work is excellent. The branches knot back into each other in elaborate patterns and disappear down her jeans.

"Nice," I say for both the tattoos and the woman wearing them.

She rolls over, straddles my hips, slides her hands up under my shirt, fingernails running lightly across my abdomen. Now that's something I haven't felt in a while.

"I want to see the rest," she says.

"Not that I'm implying anything, but are you going to try to eat me and suck out my soul?"

"Does that happen a lot?"

"Enough for it to be a question."

"Only if you ask *very* nicely," she says.

"Well, then," I say, running my hands along her hips and up her back. "How could I possibly say no?"

———

Tabitha's asleep, sprawled out in the king size bed next to me. I can't stop thinking about Boudreau. The idea that he or his ghost or whatever could possibly still be around is absurd. I go over that night in my head a thousand times, play his death over and over again in my head.

He's dead. Dead as he could possibly be. But what if he's not?

That thought keeps nagging at me and I push it aside once more. No, either he left something behind or—and here's something I hadn't considered—someone's trying to make me think Boudreau is back. But why? Griffin sure as hell isn't going to offer any clues. And Santa Muerte, well, she'd be happy to tell me if I gave myself over to her lock, stock and screaming soul.

Alex mentioned some homeless burnout. Henry Ellis. Only lead I've got. And the sooner I find him the better.

Tabitha stirs beside me, cracks a sleepy eye open. "Hey," she says.

"Hey yourself."

She presses herself into my side. "Thanks for that. That was nice."

It was. I'm not sure how I feel about it now, but it was. I don't know what to say. Thanks? Glad you enjoyed it?

"It's been a long time." Jesus. Did I just say that out loud?

She rolls onto her stomach and props her head up on her hands. "Yeah? How long?"

"Honestly? I don't remember. I, uh, move around a lot."

"You said. Home's an illusion, right? How come?"

"It's complicated."

She doesn't say anything for a minute and then, "Because of the dead people?"

"Partly, yeah. I mean, they're always around." She looks around her, a frown of worry creasing her face.

"What, right now?"

"No. We're good here." I tossed some half-assed wards on the room before things really got heavy between us. "But I can feel them in other rooms of the motel, down on the street. I can't get away from them."

"Jesus. I'd go crazy."

"I do from time to time," I say. "It changes your point of view. I don't really know how it is for other people, but for me death is, maybe a little less complicated? More complicated? I'm not sure."

"Different?"

I laugh. "Yeah. Different. It's like, well, dead's not always dead, you know?"

"It's not a big unknown for you," she says. "Like it is for most people."

"It is. I mean, I don't know where everybody eventually winds up, but I think I have a better idea than most. It's more I know there's a waiting room for some people. Just because somebody's dead doesn't mean they're gone, if that makes sense."

"Sure," she says. "I'll be honest, though, it's kinda creepy."

"Oh, hell yeah," I say. "Took me years to get used to it. Before I left—"

"You don't have to talk about it if you don't want to," she says.

I think about that for a second. "Actually, yeah, I do. Is that okay?"

She nods. "Sure."

"Before I left I wasn't very good with it. Weirded me out more than anything else. I was born with this. I was a freak in a world full of freaks. You've got talent, so you know there's more going on. But the thing is nobody, mages, normals, doesn't matter, nobody wants to deal with the dead. They want to not think about it. They want it sterilized and live with their dreams of people being in a better place."

"And they're not?"

"Fuck no," I say. "It's cold and empty. And the dead are always hungry. They want their lives back. And if they can't get theirs they'll be happy to take yours."

Tabitha shudders a little. "You really know how to turn a girl on," she says. "I always love following up a roll in the hay with an existential crisis. Thanks."

"Sorry," I say.

"Joking. If I didn't want to know I wouldn't have asked. I mean, I can't do much of anything and I don't think I even have a knack, but to be a kid with that kind of power? It couldn't have been easy growing up with that."

"It wasn't," I said. "And it wasn't until after I left that I really learned some real control over it."

"Has it helped? Being able to do that? I mean, it can't be a curse all the time. It's got to have its uses."

I think back to the night I murdered Boudreau, to the life I've been living for the last fifteen years. "Ups and downs," I say, "But yeah, it's useful." I let my thoughts wander.

After a moment Tabitha says, "You kinda drifted off there."

"Sorry. Thinking. Would it be terribly rude of me to—"

"Kick me out?" she says finishing my thought, a small smile on her lips. "No. I mean, I'd love to stay, but I think you've got too much on your mind for another go."

"Thanks. Yeah, things are going to get a little . . . weird in here pretty soon."

"Weird like you regretting we slept together and not talking to me later weird?"

"Weird like a parade of the Dead tromping through my hotel room drinking drops of my blood so I can get them to answer my questions weird."

"Oh. Yeah, I don't think I'm ready for that," she says.

"Kinda figured," I say.

"Okay. No problem. Can I take a shower first?"

"Sure. I've got some prep to do in the other room."

"Fifteen minutes and I'll be out of your hair." She flounces out of bed, heads to the bathroom, stops. She turns around jumps up to put her arms around me and kisses me.

"Be careful," she says and disappears into the bathroom.

I stare at the closed door for a couple of minutes, listening to the shower run. Interesting woman. I find myself wondering where she came from, who she is.

Why she jumped me. I shake myself out of it. I can think about that later.

I put some pants on, move the furniture in the other room around to clear a space. Set up my candles, pour out my circles in salt. It all feels like I'm going through the motions. I've got too much on my mind.

I pull the Browning and a cleaning kit out, feel the gun radiate menace. I take it apart, laying out all the pieces on a towel on the coffee table. Scrub each piece, oil the action.

The Browning isn't like the Sangamo Special. It's got energy I can tap into, but it's not magic the way the watch is. Sometimes I think the watch might even have a mind of its own.

Cleaning the gun is a meditation. I get lost in the meticulous nature of the task. Tabitha comes out while I'm in the middle of it. She watches a few minutes, but says nothing to disturb me. She leaves without making a sound.

Yes, a very interesting woman.

I put the Browning back together, take it apart, put it back together again. Empty the clip, reload it. Check the action, weigh it in my hand.

I put it back in its holster. I step into the circle with the straight razor and the cup, light the candles and get to work.

I have better results this time around. I know who I'm looking for. I know who to ask. I call the men and women who died homeless, forgotten, unclaimed. Separate them into the recent dead and dismiss the rest. Bludgeoned, stabbed, raped, shot. A few run over by cars, some set alight. Their lives were hard, their deaths harder.

Henry Ellis is a burnt out mage who's gone hobo and the dead tell me he hangs out in Long Beach a lot, alternating between three or four encampments near the freeway, behind a warehouse, at the edge of the river.

"Yeah," one of them says, an overweight woman with stumpy, sore-ridden legs. "He was there when I got stabbed." She points to a gaping wound in her belly, loops of intestine hanging like garland off a Christmas tree.

"How long ago was that?"

She cocks her head to the side, thinking. "Half an hour? Little more?"

Jackpot. I get the location, a strip of land where the 405 and 710 Freeways converge. I get dressed in my own clothes, leaving the outfit Alex gave me over a chair. He'll be crushed.

I see the bottle of Balvenie on the counter as I head to the door, a note stuck beneath it. "LET'S HAVE THAT PARTY SOMETIME SOON," it reads, with a phone number. I pocket the note. It makes me happier than I expected.

———

At this hour on the South 405 there's little traffic, though it's slow going past Sunset. I know I've got the right place when I see the flashing blue and red lights of the police and paramedics.

I park nearby, reach into the glove compartment for the Browning and a roll of stickers that read "HI! MY NAME IS:". I write DETECTIVE CARTER on one of them in Sharpie. I blow on it, whisper a charm over it, think of a badge, Hawaii 5-0, Adam-12 episodes, stern looking policemen. Serpico.

I slap the sticker on, clip the Browning to my belt and get out of the car. The cops let me through the police line when they see my nametag. As far as they're concerned I'm a Long Beach detective, or maybe it's LAPD. I don't know who's got jurisdiction, but it doesn't matter. They'll fill in the gaps themselves.

I ask one of the officers for an update. I stay away from the other detectives. I might have a badge but chances are they know all the other detectives who should be out here. Don't need questions.

He points out the body of the woman I spoke with a little while ago underneath a white sheet on a gurney. She's come to this place when I released her and recognizes me. She waves halfheartedly, staring down at herself with resignation.

"Any suspects?" I say.

"Seriously?" He points to a spot where the camp residents are sitting, each one being called up to talk to a detective. "We got about fifty of them."

"They're all there?" I say.

"Every last one of them."

"What about him?" I cock my head toward one bum sitting on the edge of the camp watching the scene with interest.

"Who?" the officer says, looking right at him.

"Never mind," I say. "Trick of the light." I think I've found Mister Ellis.

I turn and head toward him. His eyes go wide when he sees me. Wider still when I wave at him. He's an older guy, unshaven, wearing a torn-up parka, mud-crusted jeans, a Dodgers hat. He stands up, looks for an exit. He's got two choices. Run over a small hill of ice plant and jump into eighty-mile-an-hour traffic, or come through me.

I don't say anything because that might draw attention to him and it might break his camouflage spell. Having him in police custody will make it even harder to talk to him. I smile at him, hands out to show I don't mean to hurt him.

He jumps for the freeway.

"Oh, come on," I say. Am I really that scary looking?

I tramp after him, my shoes slipping in the slick bed of plants. Ellis hits bottom, starts climbing over a retaining wall. My feet slide underneath me and I go the rest of the way on my ass. I get hold of his ankle before he tops the wall and yank. Heavier than he looks. He scrabbles, lets out a holler and falls back into the ice plant.

"The fuck, man," he says. "The fuck."

Jesus. With that stink he doesn't need defensive spells. This close and I'm gagging.

"Henry Ellis?" I say.

"Fuck you, man. Cops always hassling me. I know my rights." He looks at the nametag on my coat, blinks, sees it for what it is. "Goddammit," he says.

I stand, reach out to help him up. He stares at my hand, takes it like he's holding onto a snake.

"You're Henry Ellis, right?" I say, trying to only breathe through my mouth. "You worked for Jean Boudreau."

He freezes. Then yanks down on my hand hard, throwing me off balance. My face hits his waiting knee. Pain explodes in my nose with a sound like a bag of broken glass. I hit the ground, half blind.

He heads back up the wall. I pull the Browning, shove

it against his ass hard enough for him to notice. He freezes.

"Keep going and I'll give you a push."

"I didn't mean nothin'. Just, you know, got scared." He slides back down the wall. "Please, don't kill me."

I manage to get to my knees, wipe the tears from my eyes. "I'm not going to kill you," I say. "I don't even fucking know you, Henry."

"But I know you," he says. "Eric Carter. I know you killed him. Now you're gonna kill me, too, aren't you? Oh, god."

I don't remember him there that night, but then things were pretty chaotic. "Henry—"

"Not my fault. I didn't know. Not my fault."

"Henry!" He stops the second I shout at him. "I'm not going to kill you. I need to talk to you. I need to know some things about Boudreau. I'll even pay you. Get you some food." My eyes are watering being this close to him and it's not just the pain in my nose. "And a shower."

"Don't want no shower," he says. "Water. Water's bad. It drowns you. Swallows you up. Fish fuck in it. But I'll do bourbon. Since you're buying." Great. The Caddy's going to smell terrific for a month after this.

I find a nameless Mexican bar over on a stretch of Pacific Coast Highway that cuts through the docks of the Los Angeles harbor. The outside is a garish fuchsia, the word *CERVECERIA* hand-painted on the side. The parking lot is full of beat-up pickup trucks, sedans held together with baling wire. This is where the immigrant workers who get brought in to haul cargo against union rules come to drink.

I go inside leaving Ellis sitting on the curb. I don't think he'll run, not if the way his eyes lit up when I told him I'd buy him that drink was any indication. I buy a bottle and a couple of glasses. I get some looks but nobody messes with me. I take it outside, slide down to the curb next to Ellis and top off his glass.

"Before you start asking your questions," he says, "I got some of my own. How'd you see me?"

"Your camouflage spell's too weak. Fooled the normals, sure, but come on, man. Anybody with talent could see through that."

He sighs, mutters something under his breath. Takes a pull on his beer. "I put everything I had into that," he says. "I'll barely be able to light one of my own farts with what I have left."

"I heard something happened to you. You can cast, but you can't tap into the pool? Something like that?"

"Yeah, something like that. Goddamn Boudreau. Fucking cocksucker. You want to know about Boudreau, sure. Fat lot of good it'll do you."

"Hey, man. Anything will help."

"Why you want to know? And after all this time?"

"Somebody killed my sister and I think Boudreau left something behind that maybe has something to do with it."

"Then you want to talk to Ben Duncan. He got everything. If Boudreau left something behind, he's got it."

I point at my bandaged nose. "I did. He's changed his name. Goes by Griffin, now."

"Just a broken nose? He was in a good mood then." He tosses back his bourbon, holds out his glass for a refill. I pour him another. "So ask. What do you want to know?"

What do I want to know? Now that I've got him I don't know what to do with him. I knew he wouldn't just pull something out of his ass and say, "Here ya go, sonny." But I honestly don't know what to ask him.

"Uh—You worked for Boudreau. Directly?"

He nods. "Yep. Chance of a lifetime. I'd been teaching in Prague. Visiting scholar sort of thing." He gives me a look that I think is supposed to be piercing, but just looks drunk.

"You know anything about," he pauses letting the tension build, "necromancy?"

It hurts to laugh but I can't help myself.

Chapter 13

"What?" he says, indignant. "I know what I'm talking about. Necromancy's very serious business." I'm trying not to laugh, really I am. But having this stinky hobo intone about dead shit like a cartoon villain is too ridiculous.

"I know," I say. "Believe me, I know. How the hell do you think I found you? That dead fat woman told me where you were."

He looks at me considering. "You know the other side," he says.

"Kind of my thing. Yours?"

He shakes his head. "No. I know a few things, but I prefer research. That's what Boudreau hired me for. Knew he was going to die some day. Wanted to find a way to capture his spirit and preserve it in the hopes that he could come back to life."

I chew on that for a second and already I can see holes in it. "Ghosts fade. Can't stop it. Might last a while, but he'd head off eventually."

"I know, but he wouldn't listen. Over time they degrade. Lose their memories, their identities, right? Do you know why?"

I open my mouth and realize I don't. Not really. I've never been much on theory. Everything I've learned I've picked up from other mages or learned on my own. Now he's got my interest. "Always figured it was just them heading over to wherever they go. Heaven, Hell, Elysium, Valhalla. Places like that."

"Sort of. But they don't do it all at once. They're draining away like water. Every day they lose a little more of their substance. But their identities are shot through the entire thing. A person loses a thumb, he loses a thumb. A ghost loses a thumb and there goes its memories of kindergarten."

I've watched ghosts degrade over time. I know what he's talking about. They grow less substantial. Their memories less clear. "Interesting theory."

"That between place is just as toxic to them as it is to us. It strips away layers the way it saps life from us."

The land of the dead is one big waiting room. You can call it Purgatory or Gehenna, if you like, though I hear those are places in their own right. The theories I'd heard all centered on the idea that ghosts were strong enough to resist the pull that would take them to their final destination, not that they were all slowly circling the drain. It's an idea I hadn't run into before.

"And Boudreau wanted you to figure out a way to stop it? How would you even do that?"

"The environment is the key. At best it's an irritant that wears away the ghost. When a piece of grit gets into an oyster it wraps it in layers of material that eventually makes a pearl," he says.

I think I'm beginning to understand. "So, you'd wrap

the ghost in something that the environment—" I search for the idea, "eats instead?"

Then it hits me. "Other ghosts."

"Exactly." Ellis throws up his hands and his eyes sparkle.

I feel like I'm in school again. The first real teacher I had was the ghost of a dead Brazilian guy I met in a jail cell in Vegas after I left L.A. Spent a month picking his brain, so to speak. Then he started breaking down. He was useless after that.

Ellis reminds me of him. Makes me wonder where he ended up.

"That's exactly right," Ellis says. "I created a series of spells that would, when he died, attract more ghosts to him. When they got close enough, they'd stick like flypaper."

I'm not sure, but I think I see a hole in that. "You wrap the ghost to protect it, but what happens before it gets protected? It'd still have lost some of itself, right?"

"That's the beautiful part," he says. "The enwrapped ghost feeds off the others, using them to rebuild itself. Everything is already there, it just needs more substance to grow back the original personality."

I'm remembering back to Washington, what he did with the Loa, how he had fed himself on ghosts. I had thought he merely ingested them somehow, used their energies to sustain him. Maybe it was more. Maybe it was this.

I get this cold, sinking feeling in my stomach. "How big a piece of the ghost would you need in order to rebuild it? What if you just had a scrap. Would it take a long time?"

He shrugs. "I don't know. Tiny, I suppose. And depending on the size and how well it works I imagine it could take years."

Years. Like maybe fifteen of them?

"But I don't know if it took," he says. "I performed the ritual months before he died. He said he didn't feel different and he insisted he should even though I told him he probably wouldn't." His hands start to shake. "That bastard. That bastard."

"What happened?" I say. "What did he do?"

"Forced me to do it again. Locked me up in his warehouse, fed me bread and water and nothing else. I was chained to the floor like an animal." He throws the glass back, winces at the burn. I top him off again.

"And every night he'd make me do it again. He was convinced I wasn't using enough energy. That I needed more. At the end he was so desperate he brought in people and killed them right in front of me. Insisted I use the power their deaths left behind. Prostitutes and the homeless first, then whoever he could get his hands on. One night he brought in a truck of children. Children."

"Jesus." An intense experience can bolster magic. Like the way Alex uses the energy in his club to fuel his Ebony Cage. Getting killed is about as intense an experience as you're going to get. A person dies and they let out a flare of energy that a mage can pick up and use.

I realize now the real horror for Ellis. It's not the children, or the murders. He's a mage. Only one thing he could lose that would really matter to him.

"It was too much and you were doing it too often, weren't you?" I say. "That's what burned you out?"

He nods. "Months of that kind of torture. And for

what? Nothing happened. I heard you'd killed him and nobody found the body."

"I pulled him over to the other side and fed him to the ghosts."

"Oh," he says. A little gleam comes into his eye and his mouth curls up into something I can only call a smile because of its shape. It belongs on the face of a hacksaw-wielding circus clown. "That must have hurt a lot."

"Looked like it. I stuck around to listen to him scream."

Ellis' brow furrows and his hands shake like Parkinson's. "Did they eat all of the pieces? Did they get every one?"

I don't know for certain, but in the words of the Magic 8-Ball, outlook not so good. I give Ellis the story about why I'm here. Lucy's death. The message. It was obviously meant for me.

"I'm still not buying that it's him," I say. "I know what I saw. I know I killed him. Somebody's impersonating him. It has to be."

"But who would do that? Who could do that? Griffin?"

"Griffin, maybe. You."

Now it's his turn to laugh, but there's no humor in it. His bloodshot eyes are just this side of madness. "You don't get it, do you? Most days it takes everything I've got to make sure my piss doesn't hit my shoes. Other days I've got enough to throw a car, but I don't dare use it. What if I burn out more and then I can't cast at all?

"I've got a yawning pit inside me that I hollowed out pumping more and more power through and no way to fill it. It's like being blind, deaf and starving all at the same time. So if you think I could pull off something like this. Consistently. Regularly. On fucking time. Then go ahead. I did it. It's my fault. Either kill me now and end it or go fuck yourself."

"No, I don't think you did it," I say. "But this changes things." I thought Boudreau had left something behind. Some object, maybe. Now I'm not so sure.

"Where did Boudreau spend his time? Where was this place he kept you?"

"Why do you want to know that?" he asks, confused.

"Because the only way to be sure he's gone is to try to summon him. Know for sure one way or another. And it'll be a whole hell of a lot easier to rule out in a place he's likely to be than the middle of my hotel room."

"So you think it might actually be him?"

"No," I say. I hope. "But this way I'll be sure."

"You killed him at the warehouse," he says. "I saw you there."

"Caught him as he was leaving."

"That's where he kept me locked up," Ellis says. He mulls the thought over in his head. "There's a secret room under the floor near the back. Ritual space, smuggler's bolthole, prison. He spent a lot of time there. It was pretty important to him. The fact that he died there would just make it more so. If you're going to find him that's the best place to start."

"So we hit the place tomorrow. Dig around."

"What?" Ellis says. "You're fucking crazy you think I'm going back there."

"I need your help. I don't know where this room is. If he used it as a ritual space then out of the whole building I can summon him there."

"No. No, no and fuck no." Ellis lurches to his feet, knocking the bottle over into the gutter. "Don't drag me into this. This isn't my problem. So he comes back, so what? So what if your sister died? How does that affect me? No. I'm barely hanging onto my own fucking sanity and going back there is just going to hammer my fingers until I let go and fall into full-on crazy."

"Ellis, I—"

"No. And leave me alone. I don't want to see you. I don't want to talk to you. Go ahead. Get yourself killed when Boudreau comes back and turns you into fucking kibble. I won't be there to see it. He'll come for me next." He lurches away, stumbles down the street. I think about going after him, but I don't have the right to make him. He's suffered enough. If I can't get his help then I'll do it myself.

———

Back at the motel I let the shower water get as hot as it can and stand there under the tap scalding the day away. I get out, towel myself dry. It's late, but I still don't know if I can sleep.

Suddenly I'm ravenous. I think to the last time I ate. A burger in Travel Town that morning. I check the refrigerator. It's bare, except for a flyer full of coupons for local fast food restaurants. All this time and Alex still knows me.

I'm pulling on my jacket to leave and get a burger when the cell phone chirps at me. I pick it up. Try to figure it out. Finally press a button that looks promising.

"Hello?"

"Eric, it's Vivian."

My heart starts to beat a little faster, but I force it down. "Hey, Viv. What's up?"

"Did I wake you up? I know it's late."

"No, I was just heading out the door to get some food."

"Oh, okay. I'm back home. I've got the stuff I need to work on your nose. How's it feeling?"

"Broken, but I can breathe through it. You want me to come over tomorrow some time?"

"Actually, was wondering if you'd like to come over now." I look at the clock on the wall. It's after one in the morning.

"Sure," I say. "Not going to sleep, anyway. Give me half an hour?"

"Great." She gives me her address, it's a place in the Wilshire Corridor where the rich people live and I find that my phone has grabbed her number from the call and stored it. After a couple of minutes of fumbling I figure out how to do it myself and enter Alex's number. After a moment of considering it I enter Tabitha's.

I head over the hill down to the West Side. Her condo is in a high-rise on Wilshire near Westwood and UCLA. Doormen and taxicabs, the rich playing at wishing they were in New York, but L.A. will never compare.

I park on the street around the corner. Valets will cost an arm and a leg, and if today's little escapades at Griffin's have taught me anything, having to wait for my car is a bad idea.

The doorman looks at me funny. Can't blame him. Busted nose, bruises on my face. I'm not sure he's going to let me in. But he does, anyway. Must be the tie I'm wearing.

Vivian's condo is easy to find. There are only four on her floor. She opens before I even get a knock in.

"Hey," she says.

"Howdy."

She's gorgeous. Here, at home, she's more relaxed. She's on her turf. Her red bobbed hair, shapely legs. Not quite as tall as me, but almost in a pair of white yoga pants and a tank top. She's wearing glasses that hide the fringe of freckles along the bridge of her nose. I really want to see them.

She says nothing, just looks at me with an expression I can't quite place.

"Were you going to let me in or did you want to fix my nose out here in the hallway?"

"Oh. Yes, come in," she says. "Sorry, I got a little distracted."

"Well, when confronted by such manly magnificence such as myself it's easy to get overcome."

I step inside. The place is huge. Vivian has done ridiculously well for herself. But then I knew she would. She started with money and with magic you're rarely without.

"Oh, yeah," she says, rolling her eyes. "Fistfights get me so wet."

I set myself down on the sofa. The room is clean and white and well designed. I'm suddenly reminded of Lucy's house, flash to all that blood, her head being used as a ghastly brush.

"You okay?" Vivian asks.

"Yeah. Did Lucy decorate your place?"

"She did. Did a fantastic job, too. You should see her place, she—" Her hand goes up to her mouth. "I'm sorry."

"Don't worry about it. I've seen worse."

"Really?"

"Not really, no."

She crosses over to a bar on the other side of the living room. "Can I get you a drink? Water? Juice?"

"Got any Johnnie Walker?"

"God, do you still drink that stuff?" She digs a bit and finds a bottle, dusts it off. "Neat or ice?"

"Neat, thanks."

She pours me my whisky and gets herself carrot juice. She sits on the other sofa opposite me. We have a glass-topped coffee table between us. And a decade and a half.

"I'm sorry about what happened earlier," she says.

"For what? Not letting me bleed out?"

"For Alex. When he came into the room and—He forgot. I hadn't wanted you to find out like that."

I hadn't wanted to find out like that either. I hadn't wanted to find out at all. I drink my whisky, a bigger gulp than I'd planned. There's a way to make an impression, Eric. Toss it back like you're a cowboy on the range.

"You said something about my nose earlier," I say, changing the subject.

She has a small case by the sofa. She pulls it to her lap, opens it up. Finds a syringe and sticks it into a bottle of something. "Xylocaine," she says. "It's a local."

She pulls out a couple of faceted stones and a ball of silly putty.

"I'm pretty sure I can do this without having to break your nose again."

"What if I deserve it?"

"Oh, stop. I am a professional over here, you know.

The Xylocaine's just to numb the area. Most of the work's going to be on the putty. Then I transfer the shape to your nose. Without the anesthetic it hurts like a mother."

"You do remember what my nose is supposed to look like?"

"Big, bulbous. Like Jimmy Durante, right?"

"Ha. You're funny."

"Relax, I remember how to set your nose. God knows I've done it enough times. This way's better. Lie down on the floor."

"The floor?" There must be something lewd in my tone because she gives me The Look.

"I don't keep an examination table in my apartment. Do you want me to break your nose again?"

I put up my hands. "S'all good."

I push the coffee table aside, lie down on the floor. She slides a pillow under my head. I'm suddenly very tired. She gets down on the floor, straddles my hips. I have an image of Tabitha earlier that night in a similar position, know that this isn't going to go that way. Push it out of my mind.

Her weight is comfortable, familiar. I don't mean to, don't want to, but I can't help comparing her to Tabitha. Tabitha's all compact muscle, dense strength. Vivian's lighter, with thin bones. She settles on me like a feather.

It feels right, like going home should feel. Her hands are cool on my face, touching softly. She's whispering something soothing in my ear that I'm too far away to hear. I know that it's a spell, something to help me relax, help dull the pain a little. I can feel my muscles relax. I start to drift off.

And scream when white fire bursts into my sinuses.

"I told you to hold still, goddamn it," Vivian says. She stabs me in the face a second time with the Xylocaine and I can feel the drug swell under my skin, light an inferno in my nose. I'm clawing the floor, tears are streaming from my eyes. I'm gritting my teeth so hard I'm afraid they might break.

The pain subsides a minute later and all I feel is a pinching coldness. My nose feels three sizes too big and oddly, like it's missing. She taps at the skin with the tip of the syringe.

"You feel that?" she says.

"No, but I can see it and that's bad enough. Get that thing away from my eyeball."

She discards the syringe into a plastic container she pulls from the case and pushes the whole thing aside.

"Okay," she says. "This part's going to feel a little weird. So just relax and breathe through your mouth."

"Like I could breathe out of my nose at this point. Jesus Christ that hurt."

"Oh, quit your whining. You big baby."

She slides up to my chest, looks down at me. She's so light. We used to sleep with her on my chest, curled up like a cat. I'd barely notice.

"Close your eyes." I do and I feel her cool hands resting lightly on my cheekbones. Through my eyelids I can see a glow and her hands become warm. I hear her hands molding the putty, feel a gentle tugging on my nose that doesn't hurt and then another. And then a monster wrench and my whole face feels like it's being twisted the same way the putty is.

"Keep breathing," she says. "Told you this would feel a little weird."

"Didn't think you were going to go yanking my nose around like it's Stretch Armstrong."

"I'm almost done." The wrenching and tugging have subsided and her hands have cooled.

"Try breathing through your nose." I do and it's great. Easy. Better than before.

I touch it. Still can't feel my face. "That's great," I say. "I think I'm breathing better, actually."

"You are. I fixed your deviated septum and shaved some space into the nasal cavity. Should help your snoring, too."

"I don't snore."

"You sure as hell did when we were together." I think about it, concede the point.

"Thanks," I say.

"You're welcome." I open my eyes and Vivian is right there. Inches from my face, still straddling my chest, fingers still on my face. She moves a finger up and brushes a stray hair away from my eye.

I lean my face in a little, she does, too. Our eyes are locked. Another inch and I can kiss her. It'll be just like before. Just like home.

She jerks back upright, slides off my chest and stands up. "Hey, you need to get something in you besides whisky. I'll get you some juice and cookies. Like giving blood that way. When's the last time you had a real meal?"

Like that the moment's gone. And with it the feeling that home was just around the corner.

Chapter 14

Vivian orders delivery Persian food from a 24-hour place down on Westwood. I'm wolfing down my second kabob before I realize how hungry I was.

"Good stuff," I say. "Thanks."

She grunts something like "You're welcome" through a mouthful of koobideh. We've moved back to our respective corners, the gulf between us bigger than the coffee table could ever fit. I'm sipping grape juice. The tape is off my nose and the anesthetic is starting to wear off, but besides it being a little tender my nose feels fine.

"Tabitha came back to the club after she dropped you off," Vivian says. "About three hours after. She seemed happy. Bubbly even." Vivian raises an eyebrow.

"She's a positive gal."

"I just wonder what she did in the time it took between dropping you off and her coming back. What do you think she did?"

She's trying to pass it off as cute and it's just irritating. It's none of her fucking business.

"Couldn't tell ya," I say.

"Really? And what were you doing?"

"Called up some dead folk. We had a party. I was looking for Ellis."

She perks up. "Did you find him?"

"Oh, yeah. And then some." I tell her about the spell that Ellis had cast that ultimately led to his burnout. And what it means if it works and I didn't do a thorough enough job.

"What exactly did you do to him? Boudreau? I know he died. How?"

"In a very unpleasant way. Do you really want to know?"

"Yes."

I tell her. I tell her about taking him to the other side, about bleeding him and feeding his body to the ghosts. About his screams and the way I watched him shrivel and shrink in on himself. How he died. How I laughed. How it wasn't nearly enough.

Her eyes go inward and she doesn't say anything for a long time. Then, more to herself it seems than to me, she says, "Okay." She looks at me, as though seeing me for the first time. I know I've lost something.

"I wish you hadn't asked me that," I say.

"Me, too. You're sure you got all of him?"

"I did. There wasn't a scrap left when they were through with him. No body, no ghost, no Boudreau. But I have to be sure."

"How are you going to do that?"

"Try to summon him at the place he died. His old warehouse down in the harbor. Nothing's going to come of it, I know. But I have to try. Otherwise I'll have this nagging at me."

"You can't do it somewhere safer?"

"I could try, but if Ellis is right and Boudreau's still around it means he's different. Doing it from my hotel room might be safer, but it might not work. I want to be sure."

"What will you do if he shows up?"

"I'm more likely to get a blowjob from the President."

"Eric, seriously. If Boudreau is really out there and he was able to kill Lucy like that, he's not someone to fuck around with."

"If he killed Lucy he had to have possessed someone. Whoever was there was alive. If he shows up he's still dead. He can't do fuck all as long as I'm on my side and he's on his."

"I'm coming with you," she says.

"Viv, you don't need to do that. I'll be fine." I wiggle my nose a little with my finger. "See, new nose and everything."

"I'm serious. You know as well as I do that shit happens, and you might need a hand. I know I'm not as powerful as you, but you're not the only one who's learned a thing or two over the years."

"Okay." I stand up, it's after two in the morning and I'm too tired to fight her about it. "Tomorrow, eight sharp. I'll pick you up."

She walks me to the door. "Eight a.m.?" she says. "You still don't sleep much, do you?"

I keep waiting to say she'll call Alex and have him come along, but she doesn't. I hope she'll ask me to stay, but know she won't.

"Sleep is for the weak. Earlier I get this handled the better."

"I'll be ready," she says. She stops at the threshold. "It's good to see you, Eric. I've missed you."

"Missed you, too, Viv. Get some sleep. I'll see you in a few hours."

———

Vivian balks when she sees the Eldorado. She's wearing Doc Martens, loose jeans, a t-shirt with a denim button-down shirt left open over it, sunglasses, a red and blue Angels cap.

"Is it safe?"

"Hey. This is Detroit ingenuity. We're talking tons of good, old American steel in this thing. Get your ass in there."

She slides into the passenger seat looking over-whelmed. The only thing keeping her from sliding across the seat to my side is the small, fold-down armrest. She taps it, pushes it a little.

"You got life preservers? I feel like I'm on a boat."

"Everybody's a fucking critic. Here." I hand her a cup of coffee I stood in line twenty minutes for. "I don't know if you're still into lattes. Two sugars, right? With cinnamon?" Everything else has changed, why not that?

She takes a sip. I can see her trying not to make a face. "This is great, thanks."

"Sure." Probably drinking soy milk now.

I pull the car out onto the parking lot that is Wilshire Boulevard. Drum my fingers on the steering wheel. I should say something. About last night. About my leav-ing. About her and Alex. I don't.

"You like doing the doctor thing?" I say.

"Yeah," she says. "Makes me feel like I'm doing something. Making things better. How many of us do that?"

"By us do you mean people in general or people like you and me?"

"You and me. Alex. Magic doesn't make it better. It makes us lazy and selfish."

"We're not that bad," I say, for some reason feeling defensive. "Not all of us."

She looks at the Caddy's empty ignition slot. I pulled the screwdriver out the night before. "When's the last time you saw the key for this monster?"

"Never. Stole it from a guy I killed in Texas last week." I sit there slack-jawed for a second. Did I just say that out loud? Vivian stares at me in horror, pulls back in on herself.

"It's not like that," I say. "He was a really bad man. Really. He was kidnapping children and doing really nasty things to them. Honest." I leave out the fact that they weren't human. Or strictly alive.

"Children?"

"It's a long story," I say.

"I don't want to hear it." She's shaken, but she doesn't push.

I try to get the conversation back on track. "I just made your point for you, didn't I? About magic."

"A little more extremely than I'd meant, but kind of, yeah."

"Okay, what about Alex? Does it make him lazy and selfish, too?"

She looks away out the window. "That's different."

"Different? He runs a bar and sells bottled demon

piss. You honestly think he's selling that stuff to philan-
thropists?"

"Okay. Yes, he makes my point, too. But he's a good
guy. He takes care of his employees. He took care of
Lucy."

My fingers tighten on the steering wheel. "Yeah. I
heard." We drive in silence for a few minutes.

"Before I left," I say, "Alex was running short cons at
gas stations and doing street magic to gather a crowd so
he could lift people's wallets. What happened?"

"Your parents happened."

"Excuse me?"

"Come on, Eric, we don't have a community. We're a
bunch of selfish, narcissistic assholes. We get a little
power and we want more. Fuck the other guy. Your parents weren't like that. They tried to pull people together,
not tear them apart. You were too busy being a self-
centered prick to notice. Maybe you didn't pick up on
that lesson, but Alex did."

"They weren't saints, Viv," I say, but my words don't
have much conviction.

"None of us are. But they knew they had power to
make a difference. Why do you think Boudreau went
after them the way he did? They were a threat to his
power base. God, you can be so dense, sometimes."

"That why you became a doctor?" I say, hoping we
can get off this line of discussion. I've got enough on my
plate without thinking about it.

She snorts a laugh. "Like it's that simple. No," she
says, "not quite."

"Okay," I say after a moment. "I'll bite. Why then?"

"I was already pretty good at patching you up," she

says. "And I'd been thinking about it a while. But what really cinched it was my mom got brain cancer a couple years after you took off. I couldn't do anything about it. She was gone in a few months."

"I'm sorry," I say. I had no idea and it hadn't even occurred to me to ask. Vivian's father had died when she was a kid before I met her. I never got to know her mom very well. But I know they were close.

She waves it off. "That was a long time ago," she says. I don't have anything to say to that. We drive the rest of the way in silence.

Chapter 15

The Port of Los Angeles sits on the edge of an industrial pit called Wilmington that stinks of diesel, burnt oil and dead dreams. Everything's covered in a layer of soot from fuel depots, docking ships and refineries. The roads are pocked with holes like war-torn Europe.

We pull off the 110 at Anaheim and head south to the docks. Outside the gates I pull off a few nametags from the roll in the glovebox and write GRAY HONDA CIVIC TOTALLY NOT A CADILLAC on one, slap it on the outside of the windshield.

Then THE GUY WHO'S SUPPOSED TO BE HERE on another for me and one for Viv that reads HOT, VAGUE LOOKING CHICK WHOSE CHEST YOU KEEP LOOKING AT. She glares at me but puts it on anyway. I say charms over all three and feel the disguises settle over them.

"What are you doing?" she says.

I let my eyes stay firmly fixed to her chest. "Just following instructions."

She laughs and hits me. "Jackass."

"Never claimed to be anything but."

The bored looking security guards wave us through, giving Vivian an appreciative glance that turns into confusion as they can't quite recall what she looks like. We drive between rows of red and blue shipping containers stacked stories high like city blocks made of Lego bricks, even taller cranes standing above them. We pass trucks, longshoremen loading or unloading them.

The last time I saw the warehouse the front was on fire and I had a car stuck through the doorway. I never got a good look at the inside. Just enough to grab Boudreau and drag his ass outside.

It looks pretty much the same. Long, free-standing building. A few stories high with massive air conditioning machinery on the roof. Stacks of boxcars sit lined up like cordwood along the sides. Waiting to be loaded, unloaded, used all over again.

I pull up behind a stack of shipping containers far enough away to hopefully not grab much attention and close enough to bug out fast if we have to. Then I realize where I've parked.

I reach over Vivian, open the glove box. I pull the Browning, try to ignore her stare.

"What the hell is that?" she says.

"It's a gun."

"Noticed that," she says. "Why do you have it?"

"I told you this might be dangerous."

"I know," she says. "I just want to get a feel for how dangerous." She unzips her knapsack, pulls out a holstered SIG Sauer P220 Compact. Racks the slide, thumbs the safety off. It's a small gun with a lot of punch.

"Alex buy that for you?"

"I bought it myself. Alex hates guns." She glares at

me, throws her door open and gets out. "And fuck you for thinking that." She slams the door as punctuation.

I follow her out of the car. Was a time she hated guns, too. I suppress the urge to ask her if she knows how to shoot it. She might decide to show me. I turn my attention to the warehouse.

"What?" Vivian says.

"Sorry?"

"You've got this look on your face like a dog trying to figure out physics."

"Just thinking. Looks different in the daytime." And when it's not on fire with a burning Toyota jammed through the front.

"Who owns it now?"

"No idea," I say. "Griffin, maybe. If he took over the organization he might have gotten hold of the assets." I'm less worried about who owns it and more about who's here.

"Do you see anybody?" I say.

"No," she says. "Shouldn't there be workers? Cars in the parking lot?" There might not be people, but there are cameras. Lots of them. Spaced at ten foot intervals. Okay, that's going to be a problem.

"Front door's not really an option, is it?" Vivian says.

"I'm thinking not." A sound grabs my attention. A shoe scuffing on pavement? Vivian hears it, too. Freezes.

"I know you're over there, goddammit," Ellis says on the other side of the shipping container. "You're making more noise than a cat in a bag."

I catch Vivian looking at me. I'd drawn the Browning without realizing it. I slide it back into its holster.

"Over here," I say. Ellis pops his head around the corner of the shipping container. Stops when he sees Vivian.

"Doc?" he says.

"Hi Henry," Vivian says, not missing a beat. "How are you doing?"

"Okay, I guess. What are you doing here?" His eyes are playing ping-pong between Vivian and I. "Didn't know you knew this guy."

"You know how it is. Small world. Especially for us. I heard you had some trouble the other night," she says. "Eric here mentioned you might show up. Was hoping I'd run into you."

Some magic isn't magic. When she wants Vivian's got a voice that could calm a rampaging bull. I can see on his face that he knows it's a lie. How much does he trust her?

A lot, apparently. He nods. Turns to me. "You're looking to get in," he says.

"Yeah," I say. "You know a way that won't walk us in front of the cameras?"

My paranoia tells me not to trust him. Why have such a change of heart? He was pretty scared last night. But if he has a way in, I don't want to poke him too hard and spook him.

"Maybe. Boudreau built a contraband tunnel under the warehouse. I don't know who else knew about it."

"How do you know about it?"

"That's how he'd bring the—" he falters, a shadow passing over his eyes. "Sacrifices. One branch of the tunnel goes up into the warehouse and another goes to the ritual room I was held in."

"It's still around?" Vivian says.

"Don't know. Don't care."

"Henry, why are you here?" Vivian asks.

"I —" he looks lost for a moment.

"I think I know," Vivian says. "I think you're here because you've got a chance to put some things behind you. I think that's a good thing."

"I don't want to go back in there."

"I know. And I'm not saying you have to. But if you could show us where it is, that would help Eric and it might help you, too."

He looks between us with furtive eyes, chews on his lip. Eventually he nods. "I don't know if it's still there, but we can look. It's not far."

"Thank you, Henry." Vivian looks at me expectantly.

"Yeah, thanks," I say. "Appreciate it."

"Uh huh," he says and heads back the way he came. We follow as he zigzags between shipping containers, checking labels, looking at doors. Raps on the side of a couple of them. Eventually he stops at one stack that's eight stories tall about a hundred yards from the warehouse and simply stares at it.

"Problem?"

"Don't know. Things have changed a little," he says. "Looks different in the daytime."

"What do you mean?" I say.

"I only saw this side of it the night Boudreau died. With everything going on I was able to get loose and find my way through the tunnel. Glad I took the right fork and not the left." He lifts a well-worn padlock on the shipping container's door. "Can you do anything with this?"

It's a pretty standard padlock. Master. A simple spell

spins the tumblers and it pops open. I grab the handles, stop when Ellis grabs my arm.

"Hang on," he says. "Look. The edge of the doors." I would have missed it if he hadn't pointed it out. And that would have sucked for all of us. Wards drawn in very thin paint strokes, and so subtle I have to stretch my senses to pick up the magic.

"What is it?" Vivian says.

"Fire wards," I say. "A lot of them." Tiny spells, not much more than a flash of heat and light. But they all interlock with each other.

"Didn't trigger them when I came out," Ellis says. He squints. "They're not new." He traces a finger above them, careful not to touch.

"They only go off if you open the door from this side," he says. If I'd opened the door we would have had a few hundred thousand tiny bursts of flame that would have made one big kaboom.

You have to admire the work that went into creating them. Whoever did it was very good. Thousands of miniscule explosives all knit together like an afghan made out of detcord.

"I've seen similar, but never one this complex," I say. "This could take a while." With spell weaves like this there's usually a stray thread in the pattern. Some loose piece of a spell that isn't tied tightly enough to the others. It's like counting out tiny rosary beads. I go down a path, lose count a couple of times, have to start over.

"This is going to take all day," I say.

"No, it won't," Vivian says, studying the wards.

"You got an idea?"

"Yeah. Figured this trick out in school. It's a lot easier to futz around with organic chemistry when you can actually pick apart compounds." She mutters a spell. The edges of the doors flash a deep red. The whole thing unravels like a sweater thread caught on a nail.

"Nice," I say.

"Thanks. Easier to do in New York when I was in school. L.A.'s magic isn't good for complex."

"Oh, come on. L.A.'s plenty complicated."

"There's a difference. Like I'm complex, you're complicated."

"Point."

"So, it's safe?" Ellis says.

"Yes," Vivian says. "Don't know what's on the other side of this door, though."

"Let's find out," I say, pull the latch and yank. The door opens with a groan of metal gone to rust in the salt air. The air inside is stale, floor covered in dust. No one's opened this door in years. Guardrails flank a wide hole cut into the floor, leading through the bottom of the crate and down into a tunnel dug into the pavement. Heavy bolts line the floor, securing the container in place. Fluorescent tubes hang from the ceiling.

Ellis finds a switch on the wall, flips it up and down a couple of times before one of the old tubes sparks to life with a loud hum. "It goes down at an angle for a while before leveling out," he says. "There are two branches. One leads to the chamber. The other to a freight elevator that goes up to the warehouse."

He turns to leave. Vivian puts her hand on his shoulder, stopping him.

"I know you don't want to do this," Vivian says. "But it might not be bad to see it again."

"No," he says. "I got you this far. I'm not going in there again."

"You have nightmares about this place," she says.

"Often enough."

"Then come with us. See it and see that it's just a place."

He looks from her to me. "You think it's safe?"

"With wards like that on the door? No. But do I think Boudreau's on the other side waiting for me? No. But I have to be honest with you, if I was certain I wouldn't be here."

"We could use your help," Vivian says. "Can't we?"

I think about it for a second. I understand what Vivian's doing, helping the old man exorcize some demons. I can empathize.

"I don't know," I say, "but we wouldn't have found that door without you. Or those wards. What I said last night still holds. You know this place."

Ellis takes a deep breath. "All right. But anything goes pear shaped and I'm out of here."

"We'll be right behind you."

We close the doors, throw an internal latch to secure them. About half the fluorescent tubes in the tunnel are out, but there's enough light to see by. Our footfalls echo loudly on the dusty concrete.

"Which way?" I ask when we hit the fork.

"Left," he says. "That'll get us into the ritual chamber."

We head down the left tunnel, stopping to cast a light spell when we hit a patch of dead fluorescents. The rest of the tunnel is pitch black. A minute later we see why.

"This is new," Ellis says, running his fingers along the mortar lines of the brick wall blocking our path.

"Obviously," I say.

"No," he says, glaring at me. "I mean it's new. Like recent." He digs his finger into the mortar and comes out with small chunks. "Two or three days at most."

"Is there another way in?" I say.

"From the warehouse, yeah. There's a trap door that leads to it."

"I'll go that way, then," I say. "You two go back up the tunnel and wait for me in the car."

"What?" Vivian says. "Why?"

"Somebody bricked this up for a reason," I say. "Maybe I got Griffin spooked that Boudreau really is back. Maybe there's something else in there. If it were ten years old that'd be one thing. But the last couple of days?"

"Don't have to tell me twice," Ellis says. "If the elevator's out there should be a ladder. It ends in a shed at the top."

"And the trap door?"

"About ten, fifteen feet away from the elevator. Look for a metal plate. It looks like it's there to hide electrical work. It's on hinges. Least it used to be."

"I'm not letting you go on your own," Vivian says.

"Look, something's going on. You could help me a lot more by being in the car and keeping the engine running."

"He's got a point, Doc," Ellis says.

She closes her eyes. I can almost hear her counting backward. She'd do that every time I'd done or said something stupid and aggravating.

"How much time do you need?"

"An hour tops."

"You have an hour. If you're not out by then I'll drive that fucking boat through a wall and come get you."

"Deal."

We split at the fork in the tunnel. "One hour," Vivian says before heading back the way we came.

The freight elevator isn't far. Even though it's just a simple platform it's obvious a lot of money went into it. Safety flooring, handrails. Hell, it might even be OSHA compliant.

But it hasn't seen much use. Old grease and dust is caked on it, except the control lever. Skidmarks in the dust expose the metal floor. So they came down this way, bricked up the passage and went back up. I don't know if there's still power to the elevator.

If I go up in this thing it's going to make one hell of a racket. I opt for the ladder instead. It's not a long climb and I get to the loading platform in the shed a couple minutes later, doing my best to be as quiet as possible.

I crack open the double doors. See no one. Sun through the windows and skylights casts a gloomy light. It looks like a normal warehouse. Crates, boxes, forklifts. A small office in the back.

I listen for workers, hear nothing but the hum of the air conditioning units on the roof. The trapdoor down to the ritual space is right where Ellis said it would be. A large metal panel with a DANGER: HIGH VOLTAGE sticker on it. Next to it is a cement mixer, bags of concrete. Looks like they were going to seal this side of the room, too.

I check for wards like the ones on the shipping container, but don't see anything. Must figure that anyone inside is supposed to be inside. That or they just don't want people exploding inside the building.

I grab the latch, pull it open, revealing a narrow staircase. Wide enough for two people to walk abreast. More handrails. That Boudreau, always thinking of the safety of his employees. I look for a light switch when I reach the bottom. Nothing on the walls, but I do bump into a cast-iron candelabrum, almost knocking it over.

I murmur a spell and the candles flare to life, smoke guttering from years-old dust. No one's been down here for a long time. The room's maybe twenty by twenty, with plain black walls, ceiling and dust covered floor. A lectern stands against one wall. More candelabra.

On one wall is the tunnel door. The wards on it are more obvious, less subtle. Just as well we didn't go through it. It's got the same spells the shipping container had. Only we wouldn't have been able to see these. I walk across the floor to get a better look and my foot snags on something, sending my sprawling to the floor. I pick myself up.

A series of metal links are bolted to the floor. I brush some of the dust away and see part of a circle in the floor inlaid with silver and gold and inscribed with runes. Deep, rust-red stains are soaked into the concrete.

This must be where Boudreau kept Ellis chained. Where he chained the people he murdered to create enough power for the spell. But if that's the case, why aren't there any Dead down here? I had noticed some dockworkers outside who had fallen from cranes nearby but nothing down here. I close my eyes and put out more feelers. Extend my senses out of the room, out onto the docks. I get nothing, like I've hit a wall. Like the place has been cleared of everything dead.

An exorcism would do that. Would make sense. For what he was having Ellis do he'd probably want to keep the area clear as much as he could. Having ghosts wander in when you don't want them to can muck things up.

Still, I should at least get a feeling of the collected trauma, a sense of dread, something. I hope there's nothing actively blocking the Dead. Some ward I'm not seeing keeping them out. If that's the case then I wouldn't be able to summon Boudreau's ghost even if it was still around.

I clear a space in the dust, pull out my gear. Get half way done setting up when the floor starts to shake.

A couple of candelabra fall over. Half the flames on the candles still standing sputter, go out. I'm here to call the Dead. Looks like the Dead are calling me.

There's an implosion of light on the other side of the room. A ghost, hazy but solidifying fast. The feel of magic buzzes along my skin like static. And all those missing dead? Found 'em.

They swarm into the room, a seething tornado spinning around this one ghost. The strength of their collected personalities hits me a like a sledgehammer, a screeching whine in my head. And through all that noise, one ghost punches through loud and clear.

Any doubts that Boudreau has come back are gone.

I bolt for the exit. The room shudders and I trip over one of the rings fastened to the floor. Barrel ass over teakettle into one of the candelabra. One sleeve has snagged in a decorative loop of metal. I try to pull myself up, shake the damn thing loose. The sleeve finally tears free. I struggle to stand and hear a footstep inches from me.

"Hello," Boudreau says.

Chapter 16

All things considered, he looks pretty good for someone who had his soul turned into shredded wheat. The ghosts swarming his body have receded, become part of him until they're barely visible. I can see them seething just below the surface. Embedded in his skin, his clothes. He's wearing the same suit I killed him in. Double-breasted, navy blue. Torn, burnt from the exploding propane tanks. Great purple bruises on his face where I took a crowbar to it. He's more solid than he should be. More opaque than transparent.

I search for something to say. Settle on, "Hey, Jean," because what the hell else am I supposed to say?

"Eric Carter. Now this is a surprise."

"Same for me, lemme tell ya."

"Come back to finish the job, did you?"

"I—"

"Shut up!" His screaming echoes loud in the chamber. It shouldn't do that. I should be able to hear him in my head, but he shouldn't be making actual sound. To do that he'd—

"Shit."

"Damn fucking right you're in the shit." He swings a foot and connects right under my solar plexus. I double over, try not to vomit.

Boudreau didn't appear with the veil between us. We're not on different sides of the fence, anymore. This is almost as bad as me being over there. On top of that he's fucking solid. Solid enough to hurt at least. My brain tells me this isn't possible. But his boot in my chest tells me something else entirely. I don't know what the hell's going on. The rulebook's been tossed out on this one.

"I'm not the one you want," I say, teeth gritted, my eyes tearing.

"Oh, I don't know," he says, leaning in to give me a good long look. "You're maybe not at the top of my list but believe me, kid, you're definitely on it."

This close and I can feel the power radiating off him like heat from a bonfire. Most of that is coming from his collection of ghosts. Absorbing them, feeding off of them. I see a few small ones under his skin thin out, disappear as he consumes them. Others leave tiny shreds outside his form like loose threads.

Panic wells up inside me. Think fast. It's a stupid idea, but I can't think of anything else. "You want Griffin," I say. "Duncan, I mean. He changed his name."

"You don't say. Yeah, I want him. But I've got you here."

"You've got him, too. He's in the tunnel. Waiting to see what will happen. You can't take him out on your own. He's gotten a lot more powerful since you went."

"Horseshit."

"No lie, man. He's down the tunnel at the fork, waiting. Hoping you'll take me out for him and then wander

down after him alone and get your ass handed to you."
I'm trying to sell this as much as I can without going
over the top. Avert the eyes, nervous hand wringing, ear-
nest face. Got the hem of my shirt bunched up in my fists
like a freaked out twelve year old. I worry a thread of
the stitching out of its track, pick at it to make it longer.

Boudreau thinks for a minute. I can't tell if he's going
to buy it or not. I'm screwed either way, but this might
buy me some more time. "I don't feel him out there."

"What, you think he'd be stupid enough to not be
shielding himself? Of course you can't sense him."

"And he wouldn't be stupid enough to let you in here
on the chance you'd tell me all this, either."

I can feel the power collecting in the room. He's
drawing in a lot from the ghosts and from the local pool.
I've never known a ghost who could do that.

"Yeah, which is why he shoved me in here. He figures
you for a hotheaded idiot. Thought you'd take one look
at me and smear me across the walls. Said something
about you never being able to see the long game."

"Oh, that is so like him," Boudreau says. "That arrogant motherfucker. He knows fuck all about me."

"Seems to think he knows a lot." I go out on a limb.
"He's been working with Henry Ellis."

That stops Boudreau cold.

"He's still alive?" he says. "What did he tell him?"

"Don't know. But I think he said something about a
way to get rid of you permanently."

Boudreau looks at me with the intensity of a light-
house. "You're telling the truth," he says.

Wow. The dead really are stupid.

"All right," he says, "but I want you in front of me.

You so much as sneeze and I'll rip you to pieces. Understand?"

"You're the boss."

I stand up, the pain in my stomach a throbbing ache. It was a good hit. That's got me worried. Even when a ghost goes poltergeist, pulled to this side and stuck here, they can't do much more than shake some furniture. He's no ordinary ghost, that's for sure. But how much of a ghost is he?

I stop at the door. Tap the runes. "These going to blow if I open the door?"

"Try it and see," he says, a wicked grin on his face. A grin like that tells me that when he does try to kill me I won't see it coming. I pull the door open and step through. It's pitch black. I'm still doing my worried kid routine. Pulling on that thread and winding it around my finger.

"He's not far," I say. The corridor is dusty and there's trash on the floor. Bottles and cans. Somebody knew about it well enough over the years to come down and throw back a few. We're probably ten, fifteen feet from the brick wall blocking the rest of the tunnel. I've got the thread loosely wrapped around my finger, now for the annoying bit.

I trip. It's almost a pratfall. Bring my hand down onto the edge of a broken bottle. It slices the skin of my palm deep enough to start bleeding.

"What is this?" Boudreau says. "You said you could help me against Griffin. And you're just some whiny fuck who can't walk straight. I don't know why—Oh, you sonofabitch. You're bait, aren't you?"

I tighten my hand into a fist, soaking the thread round

my finger and focus my will into a spell of binding. Not too powerful. Doesn't need to be.

"Not quite," I say. I yank on the string, unraveling it from my finger as I reach out to Boudreau's swarm of ghosts. I feel the magic grab hold of one of the ghosts spinning around and through Boudreau like a fish on a hook. Like the thread being pulled from my finger, the ghost is being pulled away from Boudreau. It happens so fast all he can do is squawk, and grab ineffectually against the unraveling ghost.

This ghost is attached to another and another and another. They're all linked, tied together. And they're all being spun off him.

It's almost comical. Like unwrapping a cartoon mummy.

I focus on a banishing spell, pull power in while he's distracted. It's simple and brutal and only works on less powerful ghosts. It tears open a hole to the other side and shoves the hooked ghost through. And whatever happens to be attached to it.

Boudreau unravels before my eyes, becoming thinner, weaker, clawing at the ground with hazy hands. A tremendous wind blows out from the hole, a hurricane gale that's pulling in every ghost in the tunnel.

"You fucker," Boudreau says, his voice barely a whisper over the howling wind. "You think you're so fucking smart, don't you?"

"Yeah, as a matter of fact. Kicked your ass, didn't I? Twice now, I'm thinking." I'd stomp on those grasping fingers dragging across the concrete if I could.

"Yeah? Let's see how you deal with this." He slaps his hand hard onto the ground, a flash of light appearing underneath it. And with that final act he's sucked away, an emaciated, wasted shell. Leaving behind this curious little flame on the ground.

It looks a little like a burning egg. So much so that I'm not surprised when it starts to wobble like it's about to break open. I'm more surprised that it's here in the first place. Boudreau really did throw out the rulebook. Ghosts don't cast spells, either.

The egg pulses, and with each pulse it grows a little. Vaguely egg shaped, licks of flame coming off of it. Cracks form on the side as if a baby bird were hatching from it. I've seen one of these. It took me a second but I know it now. Stomping out the fire won't do any good. It's already too late.

I watched one of these hatch in my parent's living room fifteen years ago.

I head down the tunnel, slam the door behind me, rush up the steps. I get halfway up the stairs, take a moment to weave together a shield across the steps. It won't last long and it won't stop much. But maybe it will buy me enough time to get to the car and the fuck out of here. Screw the cameras seeing me. I'm heading out the front door.

I back the rest of the way up the stairs. Make sure it isn't right behind me. I clear the trapdoor feeling like maybe I'll get out of this mess.

And then I hear, "We should have bricked over the entrance while you were in there."

"This day just won't fucking quit, will it?" I glance over my shoulder. Griffin, half a dozen of his guys. Nasty looking machine guns pointed at my back. "Hey, you got new guys. You trade 'em in? The old ones were looking a little rough around the edges."

I keep walking backward, a little more slowly. I don't want them to shoot me, but I don't want to be near that trapdoor, either.

"Who else is down there?" Griffin asks. His face is pretty banged up and one of his fingers is in a splint.

"Just me."

"Bullshit. Heard you talking to someone down there."

A loud groan of wrenching metal below us shows me up as the liar I am. "Okay, maybe not just me." Sounds like Boudreau's parting gift got through the tunnel door.

Griffin points to one of his men. "Get him out of the way and cover him. The rest of you cover the trapdoor. Last chance. Tell us who your friend is or my men unload as soon as he pops his head out of that hole."

"Would you believe me if I told you it was a really nasty fire elemental?"

Griffin nods at the man covering me, who gives me a glancing blow across the forehead with the butt of his gun. More surprise than pain, it still knocks me on my ass.

A deep shudder rolls through the floor, then another. I can feel the concrete beneath my hands grow warm. Panic threatens to consume me, but I force it down. I inch back a little. The noise gets louder. Worry creases the men's faces. I get ready to move.

A blast of heat and smoke pours out of the trapdoor and a glow like hell's own furnace. My guard turns away to see what's going on and I make my move.

I bowl into him, fouling his aim. He stitches a line of gunfire into the ceiling. This is a stupid move, rushing headlong into a mob of armed men. But the thing behind me is worse.

A blast of furnace heat bursts from the trap door followed by a deafening roar like sequoia falling in a forest fire. A wave of flame shoots out, spreading into a form of two thick forelegs, a long sinuous body and a head that's impossibly huge. It looks like a giant, pissed off weasel made of fire.

More importantly everyone's shooting at it and not me. Which is a plus any way you look at it.

Chapter 17

Elementals are a pain in the ass. Each one is brought into the world with a single purpose, a simple command. Drown this guy, bury that one, fly me to the next county over. Burn a house down with the people still inside.

They're not smart, but what they lack in brains they more than make up for in tenacity. They'll keep going until they accomplish their task, get destroyed, or are ordered to stop by their summoner. Boudreau's not around to stop it and I don't know how to destroy it. That leaves option three, me dying, which I'm really not all that keen on.

I duck between a row of crates, zag toward a door at the far side of the warehouse. I hear the chatter of automatic weapons fire behind me. Screaming. A monstrous roar like a bonfire made out of Molotovs.

I make a run for another set of crates. Bullets follow me, punching holes through wood, ricocheting off metal. I hazard a glance at the fight. It's one hell of a fray. Two of Griffin's men are charred husks on the floor. Everyone else has scattered in a loose circle around the elemental, unloading bullets into it that vaporize before they reach it.

The elemental's tail arches and flows, leaving scorch marks on the cracking cement floor. It paws the ground like a bull, whips its head out at one of the gunmen who doesn't get out of the way in time. It snatches him in flaming jaws. His screams turn into a hiss as he bursts into flame and his bones explode.

The elemental rears up to take a leap, letting loose a roar that shakes the walls, the cement beneath its feet cracked and bubbling. And then Griffin waves a hand and with a blast of magic throws a shipping container at it. The heavy metal box kicks up sparks as it grinds across the cement like a race car, slams into the elemental, keeps going until it crashes into the wall.

Stunned silence. No sound but the ringing in my ears and the heavy crackle of licking flames. That was easier than I expected. Which means I have a problem.

I duck behind another shipping container as Griffin and the last few of his cadre open up on me. Bullets ping against the metal. I hear the whooshing sound of fire extinguishers. I've made one hell of a tactical error. They're going to flank me. I can't cover both sides of the container.

The door on the far side cracks open, Vivian pops her head in, sees me. Waves at me to run. I take a deep breath, wish I did more cardio on a regular basis.

The warehouse fills with a wrenching, bubbling sound. Metal tearing, melting, turning into slag. The sound of more gunfire. I risk a quick look around the edge of the container. Expect bullets for my trouble. But the shooters are a little preoccupied.

The shipping container that just flattened the elemental is glowing white hot. The metal is bubbling and dripping into pools of molten steel. Flame claws spread around the edge. They don't push it out of the way so much as melt it. What's left of the container shreds, flinging superheated chunks of shrapnel that gouge pits in the cement floor. I duck back in time to avoid being sliced and cauterized.

When the rain of shrapnel subsides I pop out from behind my cover to get a look. Useless gunfire popping from cover, shelves of crates bursting into flame. The elemental rears on its hind legs, lets out a bellow like a volcano cracking open. And sees me.

I duck back but it's too late. The elemental launches itself into the air. Leaps across stacked shelves and containers, leaving melting metal in its footsteps. It lands in the wide aisle spanning the warehouse. Spins its body to face me, tail snapping like a whip through a stack of crates that light up like kerosene-soaked flares. Flames crack off the end of the tail, showering more shelves, more crates. The building's going to be a raging inferno in minutes. If this thing doesn't kill me the smoke and heat probably will.

I consider popping over to the other side. Might work, but I'll have a hell of a time getting through the doors. And if I understand them correctly elementals can go anywhere. If it figures out what I've done I won't be in any better shape. But it might give me a couple minutes I won't have here.

Thirty feet away and I can feel my skin blistering from the heat. The flames behind me are cooler than the elemental's inferno. I shield my face with my arm, squint through tearing eyes. I'm constructing the spell as fast as I can, but I don't think I'll be in time. It rolls back on its haunches, ready to spring.

I hear squealing tires and a sound of shredding metal, bursting glass. A heavy shelf of burning crates and stacked pipes creaks and shudders as the Eldorado, crazed Vivian at the wheel, fishtails into it. The elemental sees it in enough time to jump out of the way, but seems taking it down wasn't the point.

Ellis pops open the passenger side door, screams for me to get in. I don't have to be told twice. Vivian floors it before I'm all the way in and Ellis has to pull me the rest of the way inside. Behind us I can see the elemental clambering over toppled shelves, its feet melting through the steel beams, igniting the crates. It lets loose another bellow that shakes the building's frame.

Vivian drives the Caddy to the hole she made in the sliding door of the loading ramp. Bullets punch into the car, ping off the wall as we pass through.

"The fuck is that thing?" Vivian says.

"Fire elemental," Ellis says. "It after you?"

"Yeah. Boudreau was there. I got away from him but he summoned that thing at the last minute."

"And the guys with guns?" Vivian says.

"Griffin showed, too. Guess it's his warehouse."

Ellis pinches his eyes together. "Shit. Shit shit shit. A goddamn fire elemental?"

"It's not a party without one," I say.

Vivian gives a giggle bordering on hysteria. "Yeah, a real barn burner." Behind us the warehouse has turned into a five-alarm inferno. The building burns faster than it has any right to. Support beams start to come down, bringing chunks of the ceiling down with them.

"I don't suppose it'll die from a building falling on it?"

"Not hardly," I say.

As if to make that point I can see the flames leaping from the building coalesce into the elemental behind us. Vivian plows back the way we came, passing rows of shipping containers. A thought occurs to me.

"We can't leave," I say.

"What?" Vivian says. "Why the hell not?"

"Because if that thing gets onto the open road, or god forbid the freeway it's not just us in danger. Imagine how many other people are going to die. Imagine what the news'll do with shots of that thing."

"Fuck." She knows I'm right. "What about the dock-workers?"

"They'll probably see it, but we might be able to run it ragged through these rows of containers."

"And then what?" she says. "It's not gonna just run out of gas."

"I'm still working on that one. Just keep the car moving."

She spins the car around a corner, takes another path. We lose the elemental for a moment, but it reappears behind us. It runs and flows something like a snake and something like a cougar.

"The pocket watch," Vivian says. "Do you still have it?" I pull it out and show it to her. "How close do you have to be to use it?"

"Closer than this," I say.

"Get ready then." She taps the brakes.

The distance closes more than I'm comfortable with. I focus on the elemental's reflection in the rearview, spin the watch's dial. Nothing happens.

"Any time now."

"Fuck you, it's not working."

"Yeah, I got that," she says.

"That's because you used too much, already," Ellis says from the backseat.

"The fuck are you talking about?"

"You have any idea how much magic was being tossed around in there?"

"Shit. Of course."

"Okay, I'm still lost," Vivian says.

"Used up all the juice," Ellis says.

"Between me, Boudreau, Griffin and that monster on our ass, we've drained the local pool," I say. I hang on as Vivian yanks the steering wheel hard to the right, peels around a tight corner. Fucking fire's keeping up.

"Then what the hell do we do?" Vivian says.

"Try harder," Ellis says.

"Real useful. Thanks." I fix the elemental's reflection in the mirror again. Force-feed my own reserves into the watch, spin the dial again. I can feel the power trickle up through me and drain into the watch.

The fires dim, flicker. I keep ratcheting the dial and the elemental stumbles, trips, scatters gouts of flame. Hits the ground and skids into a roll, the fires draining away to a flicker. The elemental goes out.

Vivian hits the brakes. The Caddy fishtails to a stop.

"I think I just peed myself," Ellis says.

What's left of the elemental is a burnt out husk, blackened and smoking like charred wood. Without the fires it looks like a bald dog.

I slump in my seat, spent. I could pass out right here. Vivian doesn't give me the chance. She stomps on the gas again.

"Whoa, what's going on?"

The look of dread on her face is enough to tell me before she says it. "It's not dead."

The husk breaks, flickers of fire sputtering through the cracks. The flames flow out, start to reform. Vivian puts as much distance between it and us as she can.

Why didn't that work? Think, goddammit.

It hits me in a flash. "We need to cut off its source," I say.

"What do you mean?"

"The pool isn't used up, that thing's sucking it all up. That's what was causing the, shit, brownout, I guess. It's not running on its own fuel supply. The pool's just fine."

"Can't we just get it wet, or something?" she says.

"I know you're not stupid."

"No, but I am hopeful. If that won't work, what do we do?"

My stomach sinks as the answer comes to me. "As long as it can feed off the magic in the area it won't stop. We either block its access by doing something bigger or we take it someplace it can't get to the source."

"You can't be serious," Ellis says, catching on. "Boudreau's over there."

"That thing's going to follow us anywhere we go," I say. "Anywhere."

"What are you two talking about?" Vivian asks.

I pop open my junk drawer of a glove compartment. Receipts, pens, a rat's skeleton in a Ziploc bag, a talisman of Chinese coins and crow feathers, packets of powders I can't even identify.

Where the hell is it?

"I can jump us over to the dead side," I say. "It's using so much juice it'll drain itself dry in a minute."

"Aren't we kind of out of juice ourselves?"

"I think I got that covered," I say. "Give me a second."

"Have you moved a whole car before?" Ellis asks. "You can't just move us. We'll still have momentum."

"First time for everything," I say.

"It's a moot point," Ellis says. "There isn't enough power to light a fart around here."

I find the glowing vial Alex gave me back at the club. "There is now." I take a deep breath, pop the cork and upend the contents down my throat.

"Wait," Vivian screams. "That's not how you use it."

Wish I'd known that sooner.

Chapter 18

My brain is melting.

The rows of shipping containers shoot out in front of me into a multicolored blur. The chugging of the Caddy's engine stretches into a solid, heavy buzz. The power pours into me like molten metal. My mind feels like a balloon animal. Expanding, twisting, threatening to pop. I wonder distantly if this is what Ellis felt when he burned himself out. I wonder if I'm about to do the same. I focus on the Dead, the cold darkness of the other side, the emptiness and dread. I grab reality by the balls and give 'em a yank.

The car shudders, snapping me back to reality. The sky flickers. Bright blue sky to dank, empty gray and back again. The steering wheel bucks in Vivian's hands. The world tears. And we're over.

"Fuck me," Vivian says, staring at the shadowy forms of shipping containers speeding by. The air feels empty and oppressively heavy at the same time. Sound barely carries. Ellis throws up in the back seat.

Vivian' puts her hand on my shoulder. "Are you okay?"

"I don't know," I say. "Dizzy. You?"

"Yeah. I think. I've never been here. Why didn't you ever bring me here?"

"Not exactly the kind of place you bring a date."

"It's incredible."

"Not the word I'd use," I say. Faces appear out of the gloom ahead of us, fade in alongside.

"They're all dead?"

"And hungry," Ellis says.

"You doing all right back there?" I ask.

"The fuck do you think?"

"Can they get inside the car?" Vivian says.

"No. I've got it warded."

There's a flash behind us and a dull thud. Flames burst in behind us like a rip in a blast furnace.

Vivian hits the gas, increasing the distance. He's on my turf now, the cocksucker. Let's see how long he lasts over here.

It's hard enough to see where I'm going when I'm walking over here. Driving is a whole other experience. Vivian narrowly misses a wall of spectral shipping containers. The last thing we need is to crash the car.

Is the elemental dimmer? The flames lower? It's hard to tell at first, but the farther we go the more obvious it becomes. It's fading fast.

So am I. I can feel my energy being sucked out of me. And Vivian's breath is coming in more strained. We don't have much time left. The Dead are coming in faster. Drawn in by our scent, or whatever it is they use to find us.

"Let it get closer," I say.

Vivian eases up on the gas. The elemental gains

ground fast. She lets it get close, let the ghosts gather thick in front of us.

"Punch it," I say as it's almost on top of us. Vivian slams her foot hard on the pedal, plowing the car through the Dead. They bounce off the wards like bowling pins. I've only known the Dead to go after the living, but would the elemental attract them the same way?

Turns out that's a big yes. They latch onto it like lions taking down a gazelle. It falters, shakes to throw them off, falls to the ground. And with a sudden, loud whump collapses into nothing.

"Can we please get out of here, now?" Ellis says. "I'm not doing too well over here."

I'm about to say yes, but now I'm not so sure.

"I'm not hearing anything positive," Vivian says.

"Took a lot to haul the car over. I think I can get all of us, but I don't know if I have enough to take the car back."

"The car's kind of secondary, don't you think?"

"It's my car."

"It's our lives."

Dammit. "Fine, stop the car. Everybody out."

"I'm not going out there," Ellis says.

"Then I guess you're not going back." That shuts him up and he pushes the door open. That simple action takes it out of him and I have to help haul him out. I throw Ellis over my shoulder in a fireman's carry. He's really going fast. Vivian's not far behind him. Me, I've got a while left, but I wouldn't last much longer than they will.

Vivian wraps herself around us. The Dead have finished with the elemental and they've turned their attention to us. I focus on sunlight, warm air, blue skies. Tap my heels together three times because, you know, every little bit helps.

There's a wrenching feeling that thins out to the sounds of sirens, the smell of smoke and diesel, the light of the mid-day sun. I collapse and darkness falls around me.

———

I hate hospital waiting rooms. Stink of antiseptic and disease, buzzing fluorescent lights that leech all the vitamin D out of your body. I'm reading a five-year-old copy of *Highlights*, wondering who writes this crap. No wonder kids are screwed up today.

I've been here for four hours. Back at the docks, with the adrenaline pumping through me, I didn't notice the bruises and scrapes, the second degree burns. But now I feel like a grilled steak. My left hand is wrapped in a bandage and antiseptic gel, the cuts on my face are big enough to need butterfly bandages. My left eye is swollen. No broken bones, thank god. Well, no new ones.

"Hey," Vivian says, appearing at the doorway. She's wearing scrubs, looks a mess.

She threw together some bullshit story about us being at the docks to check on hospital equipment coming in on a boat when the warehouse went up. Told the cops she found Ellis passed out behind a truck. They bought it with a little help. The force has power over weak minds and all that.

I lost track of her once we got to Harbor-UCLA. She was holding an IV bag over Ellis, barking orders at interns. She disappeared down the hall while a nurse ushered me behind a curtain.

"How you doin'?"

"Okay. Been better." She yawns.

"Ellis?"

She shakes her head, falls heavily into the seat opposite me. "Where do I start? Malnourished, dehydrated. Had a heart attack."

"The fuck? When did that happen?"

"After we got him here. He's old. And a train wreck. Diabetic. Kidney problems. A staph infection. Other things."

"Is he going to be all right?"

"I don't know. He's still unconscious. I pulled some strings. Got him a room. How are you doing?"

I show her my hand, point at my swollen eye, my bandaged face. "Pretty much what you see," I say. "Hurts, but I've had worse."

"You have, haven't you?"

"Kind of comes with the territory."

She frowns. Like she's not sure exactly what sort of territory that is. Whether she wants to be a part of it. I don't blame her. I'm wondering the same thing myself.

"What happened back there?" she says.

Excellent question. Boudreau showing up is one thing. I always knew there was a possibility. But Griffin? Beverly Hills to San Pedro? On the 405? He showed up awful fast.

If we'd tripped an alarm he shouldn't have been able to respond that fast unless he was close by. And what are the odds that he would just happen to be down near the docks with a cadre of thugs?

"Did you tell Alex where we were going?"

"Yeah, I—" She cocks her head, narrows her eyes. "I don't think I like what you're thinking."

"How would Griffin know we were down there if someone hadn't told him?"

"I thought we'd settled this." There's a tone in her voice I remember that screams at me to back off, but I can't. I'm tired of people trying to kill me.

"Maybe you did. I didn't. Somebody told Griffin I was in town, somebody told him I was at the warehouse. If not him, who?"

Vivian's in my face faster than I can react and gives me a slap. "You sonofabitch," she says, fire in her eyes. "You have no fucking idea who that man is or what he's done. How dare you judge him?"

"How the fuck am I supposed to know?" I say. I rub my jaw. Jesus, she's got a hard hand. "I haven't been here."

"Exactly. You just up and bailed the second things got rough. You left us. You left me."

"You know why I left."

"Yeah, because you're a fucking coward." That stings worse than the slap and it must be showing on my face.

"Oh, I'm sorry," she says. "Did I hit a nerve? What, you can do dead people but god forbid you deal with live ones?"

"I left because it was safer for everyone."

"No, you left because it was safer for you."

"Lucy—"

"Tried to kill herself," Vivian says. "Did Alex tell you that?"

"What?" Kill herself? "No. He didn't say anything."

"About five years ago. Took a bunch of Xanax, washed it down with a bottle of vodka. Alex found her.

And it wasn't a 'cry for help', either. He wasn't supposed to be there. Went over on a whim."

"Why?" I can't process this. The thought just keeps sliding off my brain.

"Why? Jesus, are you really that stupid? Because her parents died. Because her only brother couldn't handle the stress and up and bolted. Because she was afraid what was going to happen to her if anyone found out who she was. You made a choice. She had hers dumped on her. So, don't you dare blame Alex for anything. He took on your responsibilities for you."

I press the heels of my hands against my eyes. I take a deep breath, let it out slowly. "Don't tell me he's a saint," I say. "We both know what he was like when I was around."

"You're really going to try to use that against him? The petty thieving? The short cons? Yeah, I remember them. And I remember how much it cost him. He turned things around. He takes care of people. His employees have a health plan for fuck sake. They get paid holidays. What have you done for anybody?"

"Oh, fuck you," I say. "You have no idea the shit I deal with. It's a wonder I'm still alive. You know fuck all about me."

"I know enough. Alex might have flaws, but he's not a killer."

"Well, ya got me there. You know what? You're right. I shouldn't have left. Because then I'd be dead and I wouldn't be having this conversation."

"God, you are such an asshole."

"Yeah, not like saintly fucking Alex. Too bad you

didn't figure that out then, huh? Could have hooked up with him before I left."

"What makes you think I didn't?"

That stops me. She's staring at me with a defiance I'd forgotten about. I can feel myself deflate and suddenly I don't have the stomach for this, anymore. I remember the fights we had, the screaming matches. Funny, I can't remember any of the good times.

She's right. I am a coward. This is all my fault. And I'm tired of fighting. Maybe that's another reason I left. I push past her into the hallway. She yells at my back but I don't pay attention to her. I've got nothing to say.

Chapter 19

The more I think about it the more I realize she's right. I am an asshole. What of it? I did what I had to do. Sure as shit not what I wanted to do. She works with the living, I work with the dead. We're on opposite ends of the spectrum. No wonder we had so many fights.

I take the elevator downstairs, go out through the ER entrance. The cold outside makes me realize how stuffy and claustrophobic it had been in the hospital. I take a deep breath. It's car exhaust and Southland smog but it's cold and familiar. I walk in between a couple of ambulances where it's a little darker. Close my eyes, let the cold air clear my mind.

"Hey, buddy," someone says behind me. "Got a light?"

I catch a whiff of smoke, something burnt. I turn to see a soot-smudged face, a shirt with blackened cuffs and a type of gun I've been seeing a little too much of the last couple days.

The taser goes off but I'm ready this time. The darts shoot forward but I'm able to throw out a quick burst of energy myself that shorts them out and stops them in their tracks.

"I'm gonna shove that thing so far up your ass you're gonna sneeze lightning bolts," I say. Too bad I don't figure out he's just the diversion until somebody else pistol-whips me from behind and I go down.

———

"This is getting to be a habit," Griffin says. "I hope there's been no permanent damage. Concussions can be nasty."

"I got a hard head," I say. But not, apparently a hard nose. I must have smacked it when I hit the pavement. At this rate I'm going to run out of cartilage.

Griffin's blurry, it's too goddamn bright in here and I can't move. When my vision clears I figure out they've got me in one of the ambulances strapped to a gurney. Two other guys besides Griffin with guns trained at my head. The driver hits a pothole and my head snaps back. Pain starbursts through my skull.

"Please be careful, Alonso," Griffin says. "Apologies. He's not a very good driver."

"Got that." I close my eyes. My head's in agony. "Hey, if you're gonna kill me, can you just get it over with? I'm getting tired of this shit."

"Not yet. I've got some questions."

"Dude, I can barely remember my own name."

"That elemental in the warehouse. It wasn't yours. It was trying to kill you."

"And they said you were stupid." I'm really not in the mood for this. I wish he'd just get it over with and put a bullet in my head or something.

"Who summoned it?"

"Take a wild guess."

"Boudreau's back, then, is he?"

"More or less. I went there to see if I could dig him up. Got a little more than I expected."

"So, Henry's little spell actually worked," he says. "I'm impressed. How'd you get rid of him?"

My visions blurs again. I forget where I am for a second. I think maybe I've gotten a few too many hits to the noggin lately. "Banishing spell. Wasn't easy." I close my eyes again, start to drift. Jerk awake from a sharp slap. Goddammit.

"So, he's not gone permanently?"

"Fuck no." Alonso hits another pothole. Takes me a second to clear my head. "He'll be back." A thought occurs to me and I get lost in being impressed with myself for a second. I really wasn't sure that was ever going to happen again.

"He's come after you, hasn't he?" I say.

"I think so. Something has. I've been having random curses thrown my way. Weak. Annoyances, really. But they've been getting stronger."

"Might want to watch out for the next one."

Griffin doesn't say anything. Looks like he's thinking pretty hard so I leave him to it and try to go back to sleep.

"No," he says. His voice jerks me awake. "I think you're going to need to watch out for the next one. He knows you're here now. I can't imagine he's going to do much else for a while but figure out how to kill you. He was a little obsessive that way."

"You don't kill me, you let him kill me," I say. "Nice plan."

"As long as you're alive his attention's going to be focused on you. You're the best distraction I could hope for." He taps on the wall behind him. "Alonso, pull over when it's convenient."

He turns his attention back to me. "Of course, you could always kill him, instead."

"On my to-do list."

"Thought as much." The car slows, pulls over to the curb. One of Griffin's men undoes the straps, the other keeps his gun on me.

"Out you go," Griffin says.

"Where the hell am I?"

"I have no idea. I'm sure you'll find your way back to that nice little hotel on Lankershim you're staying at just fine." Great. He knows about the hotel. Now I'll have to move again.

One of his men hauls me up, throws me out the back of the ambulance. I hit the curb and roll. Try to stand up, fall on my ass.

"Good night, Mister Carter," Griffin says. "And stay alive a little bit longer, if you don't mind."

———

I find an all night convenience store with a payphone, call a cab. Somewhere in today's mess I've lost the cell-phone Alex gave me. This is why I can't have nice things.

I buy a bottle of cheap tequila and a bag of frozen peas. I've got a lump on the back of my skull the size and consistency of a hard-boiled egg. I sit on the curb and wait for my ride with the peas shoved against my scalp. The cold is helping a little. Every passing light isn't a blinding stab in the eyes. My thoughts are clearing up.

There's something about what Griffin said that's not

fitting right. Now that Boudreau knows I'm in town I'm going to be his favorite target.

That's not making sense, but I can't place why. My thoughts are still a mess. I shake my head, hoping that will help, but all it does is make me nauseous and dizzy. I don't think my nose is broken, but it hurts like hell. My left hand is throbbing under the bandages and every cut, scrape and bruise is screaming like third-graders at a birthday party.

I'm going to have to get a new room. Somewhere Alex doesn't know about. To be safe I don't think I should tell Vivian or Tabitha about it, either. Just pack my stuff and go. Which should take all of five minutes. I've got one bag in the room with a change of clothes in it and a toothbrush. Everything else was in the Eldorado.

That's another problem I don't know how to begin to tackle. How the hell am I going to get my car back? I'm not sure I could even find the spot where we abandoned it.

I think about what I said to Vivian back at the hospital and wonder if maybe I was right. I should have stayed. I'd be dead now, sure, but what good am I now? The fuck kind of wasted life have I led, anyway?

My cab pulls up. Guy sticks his head out of the window. Yells at me asking if I called the cab. I don't say anything, just slide into the backseat. Cabbie's license says his name's Sam Something-I-Can't-Pronounce. Guy needs some more vowels.

"Where to?"

I start to tell him to take me back to my hotel, but I catch something out of the corner of my eye. I'm so out of it I'm not paying near enough attention. There's someone in the car with me, and he's not alive.

"Where to?" the driver repeats, clearly annoyed.

"Studio City. I'll tell you when we're closer."

"You got cash? Not taking you that far you don't got cash." I slip him a fifty, not paying much attention. He looks at it, glares at me in the rearview mirror. Sniffs the bill. Who the hell smells money?

The ghost was young when he died, maybe twenty years old. Thin to the point of emaciated. Leather jacket with a couple too many holes. Tight, tight jeans, close cropped hair. You see guys like him up around Gower at two in the morning selling their asses for cash, drugs, a place to sleep.

He'd look perfectly normal if it weren't for the long, ragged gash that starts from under his right jaw and zips down to his left hip. Deep, too. Intestines are poking out. Hands are covered in blood, presumably his own, and it spatters up into his face.

"What's your name?" I ask.

"Sam," says the cabbie. "It's on the license."

"Not talking to you." I can see him roll his eyes in the rearview, mutter something about picking up crazies.

The boy looks at me, surprised. "You can see me?" His voice is like leaves on the wind. When I nod his eyes grow bigger. "I'm . . . I don't remember."

"It'll come to you," I say. "Take your time." The back seat is pretty clean. New upholstery. The rest of the car looks like shit, though.

"Nice cab," I say to the driver.

"You talking to me now?"

"I am this time. You get the back reupholstered recently?"

"Uh, yeah," he says, brow furrowing. "Few months ago. No, a year. Two years." I go with his first answer. Too nice for even a year with all the pukers and smokers this guy must see on a daily basis. Probably ripped out the seats, reported them stolen.

"Nice. Private cab, right? Nobody else drives it?"

"Yeah. Why?"

"Just wondering. Take pretty good care of your stuff."

"Thanks. I guess." He's not sure what the hell I'm babbling about. And I'm okay with that. He will soon enough. I turn back to the boy. He's got his face screwed up trying to remember his name. When he was killed he could have probably told me his social security number, address and shoe size.

"Brett," he says finally.

"Nice to meet you," I say. I ignore the cabbie's grunt. "How long's it been?"

"I'm not sure. Not long. I think." He looks over at the cabbie, his eyes like slits. "He did this. When I got into his cab. Picked me up. Blew him and the fucker didn't pay." He puts a hand to the gash slicing down his body. "Killed me instead."

He's got a lost look in his eyes. They were blue, I think. Hard to tell now that he's faded so much and I can see the car door through him. Just another Haunt. And before that just another runaway, hustler, addict, fuck-toy for whoever could pay him.

Never leaves the cab. Locked away from anyone who can see him. Sat on day in and day out. And has to endure this greasy fuck every day of the week.

I check my wallet. I've got a handful of twenties. I rub them quickly between thumb and forefinger and now they're hundreds. At least until dawn.

I hand the cabbie a couple of the fake hundreds.

"Changed my mind. Malibu. Head up PCH and up Kanan. I'll give you better directions when we get there."

His eyes light up as he takes the bills. Does his sniffing routine again. "Malibu. Can do Malibu."

That's step one. I concentrate, pull together my will, pull a little energy from the city's pool, mix it with a little of my own, press my finger hard into the car seat. The radio up front sparks with a pop. So does the cabbie's cell phone and the embedded GPS telling the dispatchers where the car is. He curses, waves away a small puff of acrid smoke.

"Problem?" I say.

"No, no problem."

Don't worry, buddy. There will be.

———

Traffic's light up the coast. We make good time. I have him head up Kanan, cut over to Mulholland. Deeper into the hills that they call the Santa Monica Mountains. These people so need to see the Rockies.

The cabbie spends the drive yakking away about his big screen TV, all the women he's slept with, how he's a stud and a ladies' man and god's gold-plated jizz let loose upon the world.

I spend the drive wondering how I'm going to kill him. Because that's what this fucker deserves. On the drive up I started to see tattered wisps of other ghosts in the back. A woman, a couple other boys. Younger than Brett. So far gone I didn't notice them until we were up past Topanga.

The cabbie starts looking at me funny as we head deeper into the middle of nowhere. Really gets nervous when he starts hitting potholes. "You live out here? No-body lives out here."

He's right. Not even the rich folk who can afford to rebuild their houses every fire season. With the wind and dry air a stray spark torches this whole area yearly. Kind of surprised it hasn't happened, yet.

"Sure I do." I hand him another five hundred bucks and he shuts up and keeps going. I look out the window at the stars. Still a lot of light pollution, but not enough that I can't make out the constellations and a thin arm of the Milky Way. My eyes light on Orion. The Hunter. I like that one. That works for me.

"Stop here," I say.

"What? There's nothing here."

"Sure there is. Cabin right over there. Can't see it in the dark, though."

He pulls over to the shoulder, dust kicking up in his headlights. "Get out," he says. "Get out of my cab."

I draw the Browning and tap it against the glass be-tween us. "You first." He can punch the gas, betting that I won't shoot him since he's driving. But there's nothing but dirt and brush on either side. Not even a cliff he can threaten to drive over.

"Fuck you," he says. Reaches for the glove box. I give the dead boy a wink and snap my fingers. The lock on the box fuses. He tugs, panicking. Finally gives up when I tap the glass again. He gets out. I follow him, leave the door open. To his credit he doesn't run. Doesn't cry, scream or beg. Probably thinks this is him taking it like a man. Probably thinks this is just another robbery.

I don't do it this way very often. It's dangerous without a circle and I don't have the trappings that help me focus. But I don't really need them. The magic works because you want it to work. And right now I really want it to work.

I have him face the car, get behind him. Probably thinks I'm going to shoot him in the head. Man, he should be so lucky. I flip out the straight razor. With one quick, practiced move, I slice a gash into his arm. He screams when I cut him, clutches his arm, spins around to look at me. His eyes are wide with terror.

"If you're going to kill me, just kill me. Stop playing bullshit games."

"Don't worry," I say. "I'm not going to kill you." The thing about using another person's blood to call the Dead is that I can use it to bring him into the spell with me. Sam gets a rare, ringside seat to my world.

The ghosts swarm in. Not many this far out in the boonies, but enough. Sam stares in horror at the assembling Dead. They're all paying attention to him, to his bleeding arm. Leaving me alone. Licking their lips, vibrating with want.

I kick him forward into the backseat of the car. He lands on his knees, partway inside the car. Gets a good look at Brett. Lets out a high, thin shriek when he recognizes who it is.

I think back to the years I've spent preferring the company of the Dead over the living, of staying on the road and always moving. Vivian's wrong. My life isn't wasted. Let her handle the living, heal their wounds, mend their broken bones.

But when they're dead and there's no one to speak for them, no one to collect on the debt their killers owe:

that's where I come in. The Dead have already paid for their sins. The living, not so much.

When I cut myself and use the silver cup, it's just to act as a focus. Makes it clear to the dead that it's *that* blood that's okay to eat. And if you're sacrificing something it doesn't matter how it feels about it. It's not like Odysseus asked the ram for permission.

"He's all yours," I say.

His screams echo in the empty air for a long time.

Chapter 20

I find a flashlight in the trunk and use it to pick my way through the trees and scrub brush with Sam's desiccated body. Toss him down a ravine. He'll be picked clean by coyotes inside of a week.

I drive the cab down into the Valley, snag the plates and wipe the seats and steering wheel down. Dump it in a parking lot. Stealing another car is stupid easy, but my options are a Corolla with missing hubcaps and a Hyundai with a cracked windshield. Though I can at least see the road in the Corolla, the clutch grinds when I switch gears. Nobody takes care of anything anymore. I want my fucking Caddy back.

I park the Corolla a couple blocks away and stagger to the hotel, dropping the cab's plates into a dumpster. I want to take some aspirin, drink my tequila and go to bed. Waking up tomorrow is optional.

"About time," Alex says when I open the door.

"You know," I say, "if I'd been more on the ball I'd have shot you."

"Good thing for me that you weren't then, huh?"

He puts the book he's been reading down and stands

from the chair near the window. "Jesus, you took a pounding today," he says. "Vivian let you leave the hospital like that?"

"Not really, no." I sit heavily on the bed, pull the bottle of tequila out of its paper bag. Pop the top. Take a deep swig. "What are you doing here?"

"Well, I had come over to kick your ass, seeing as you almost got my girlfriend killed today. But seeing as somebody beat me to it, I figure I'll give it a pass."

"How fucking magnanimous of you. Last time I checked I wasn't twisting her arm to come with me."

"You could have asked me, you know. I've got people who are a little better equipped to deal."

"I don't think having a bouncer on our side today would have been all that useful. Unless he's a particular strain that's fireproof."

He nods. "Point. But that's not why you didn't call me, is it?"

"You talk to Vivian tonight?"

"Yeah."

"Then you already know the answer to that question."

Alex sits next to me on the bed, takes the bottle of tequila, tosses some back.

"You're an asshole," he says. "You know that, right?"

"So I've heard."

"You honestly think that I'd put Vivian in harm's way because of you? I'm not sure if you're a narcissist or just fucking stupid."

"Can I be both?"

"Sure, why not?" he says. He sucks down more tequila. "You have no idea how much you fucked things up by leaving, do you?"

"I'm getting an idea," I say. I haven't thought about Lucy's suicide attempt since I left the hospital. Haven't let myself.

"The fuck happened?" he says. "I don't mean with your parents, or the shit with Boudreau, I'm talking about you. The fuck happened to you?"

"I left because—"

"I know why you left. I want to know why you stayed away."

"Because it was easier than coming back," I say. "Boudreau was the first person I killed. You know how many I've killed since then?"

"No," he says.

"Me neither. I lost count. Most of them weren't human. Some of them were just this side of dead already."

I take the bottle from him, take another drink. Try not to wince, but this stuff is like drinking paint thinner.

"Vivian called me a coward tonight. She's right. I stayed away because I was afraid of what I'd come back to. I was afraid of talking to Lucy, telling her the things I've done."

"The things you've done, or the things you've done to her?"

"That, too." Who knew I could fuck so much up by *not* being around.

"We all know this shit's dangerous," Alex says. "At least those of us who are paying attention. The monster under the bed's real. She knew that. She would have understood."

"There's a difference between knowing about the life and living it. Lucy wasn't wired for it and you know it."

"What about the rest of us? You think we wouldn't

have understood? You're a killer. Big fucking deal. So's an exterminator."

"Your girlfriend doesn't quite see it that way."

"Vivian's tough, but yeah, she can be a little Pollyanna-ish sometimes. But come on. I get it."

"This is different. You wouldn't understand."

"I think I've earned the right to say fuck you, so fuck you. That's so much horseshit and you know it. Like you've got a monopoly on nasty shit."

He stands, staggers a little to the table, grabs his keys. "Leave," he says. "Take your fucking emo pity party somewhere else. Get back on the road and run. It's what you're best at."

He leaves me alone with my thoughts and most of the tequila. I drink one to drown out the other.

———

"Wakey-wakey," Tabitha says and pulls the sheets off the bed. I flail upright, blinking. I have no idea what time it is. Everything hurts so much I don't know where the hangover ends and the concussion begins.

"Jesus fucking Christ, does everybody have a key to my room?"

"I said I was your girlfriend and they gave me one at the desk," she says.

"Glad to hear security's such a high priority here."

"I flashed some tit, too. I think that helped."

"What are you doing here?"

"Dragging your ass out of your pity party."

"I'm not having a pity party."

She picks up the empty bottle of tequila from the

floor. "Señor Sauza here says otherwise. Come on, let's get you cleaned up before you throw up on the bed."

"But that's so sexy," I say and let her lead me to the shower.

The hot water helps, but not much. A hot shower doesn't do much for the kind of beating I've taken. It's almost noon. I pull on a clean change of clothes. Last set in my bag. Everything else is in the Caddy. I'm going to have to go shopping. I fucking hate shopping.

"All right, I'm up, I'm dressed." The coffee's gone cold enough for me to chug some down without burning myself. "And now I'm caffeinated. So spill. Why did you drag my ass out of bed instead of jumping into it with me?"

"You mean besides the fact that you smell like a three-day Tijuana bender? Alex has been trying to get hold of you. Asked me to bring you over to the club."

Guess he didn't chew a big enough hole in my ass last night, he wants another go at it. Telling me to get out of Dodge and I'm taking him up on it. Soon as I get another car I am the fuck out of this town. I'll square things with Santa Muerte later. She'll probably kill me for not taking out Griffin, or worse. But fuck it. I don't care anymore. I struggled with that for a long time last night. I came here to find out what happened to Lucy. Who killed her. Now I know and I can't do a fucking thing about it.

I can't bring her back and I don't know how to take out Boudreau. For whatever reason he's got a big enough hard-on for me to bait me here. That reason alone is enough to get me to leave.

"And he thought I'd show up?"

She shrugs. "I think he wasn't sure so thought I'd be able to convince you. What happened? You two have a fight? Those look like fresh bruises," she says, ignoring me. She traces a finger along the edge of a particularly nasty one on my cheek.

"Something like that." I tell her about yesterday's fun at the warehouse. Her eyes go wide as I tell the story.

"Jesus. Is Vivian all right?"

"Yeah, just pissed off at me. The old guy's in the hospital." I show her the goose egg on the back of my head. "That's where I got this. Got nailed last night with a sap."

She winces. "Who — uh, who did it?"

"That Griffin guy who owns the warehouse. Guy's an asshole. Should have killed him years ago."

"You knew him?"

"Met him once. Wasn't fun." I tell her about Griffin, about Boudreau. And I can't seem to stop. It all comes pouring out of me. About Lucy, the night fifteen years ago, Santa Muerte. I tell her everything short of the cabbie last night. That might be a bit much this early.

She doesn't say anything until I finally peter out. "No wonder you tried to kill yourself with cheap booze." I almost flinch from that, remembering what Vivian told me about Lucy's suicide attempt. Was it so bad that she couldn't take it anymore?

"That's why I'm maybe not looking my best right now."

"It's, uh, a lot to take in," she says.

"Look, I'm sorry. I'm not the best guy. Ask anybody. You really don't want to hang around me. Sooner or later I piss everybody off. Or get them killed."

"That's not fair," she says, her eyes going hard.

"Sorry?"

"You don't get to make that decision," she says.

"I—"

"No, you don't. I get what you're saying. And maybe I even believe it. I know there's a lot I don't know about. But there's a lot you don't know, either. You made bad choices. We all make bad choices, sometimes. But you don't get to make mine for me."

That was unexpected. "Fair enough," I say.

"Look, you can't change what happened, but you can maybe move forward. So come with me and see Alex. I think you have some things to fix." She gives me a funny look that I can't quite read. "I think I do, too."

"All right," I say. "Let me get my stuff. I don't think I'll be coming back to this room again." I pack up the one suitcase that wasn't lost when I left the Caddy. Not much in there. Couple shirts, some slacks, socks and underwear.

I pick up the bottle of Stoli from Darius' bar.

"Isn't that what got you in this state?" Tabitha says.

"Huh?"

"Vodka? Hangover? Hello?"

"Oh, no. Just an impromptu spirit bottle. Believe me, you wouldn't want to drink it. There's a ghost inside."

"What, really?" she says. "What happens if you drink it?"

"It tastes nasty," I say, tossing it into the suitcase.

"I'll take your word for it." She rummages around in her purse. Starts scanning the floor. "You see my cell phone anywhere?"

"No. You drop it?"

"Must have just left it in the car. Wanted to call Alex, tell him we're heading back."

I'm not sure why I'm doing this, going to see Alex when I should be finding a car and skipping town. I toss my bag into the trunk and get into the car with Tabitha, anyway. We spend the ride in silence. Maybe she's right. Maybe I do have some things to fix. Or maybe I'd like a do-over. I look at her. She's thinking hard about something, though what I can't tell. Me, maybe? Or is that just too much to hope for?

When we get to the club I'm ready to get out of the car. My headache has gotten worse. I want to get this over with. Find out what Alex wants and, I don't know, take off? Stay?

The bar is almost empty. A far cry from the loud mash of people from the night before, with even fewer people than the day I first showed up. Max, the bouncer, glares at me as I walk in, but waves me to the back. Tabitha starts to follow me, but he stands in front of her and transfers his glare to her. She looks at me, surprised and, I don't know, a little scared?

I shrug, try my best to look unconcerned, but I'm not sure what Alex is up to. "Don't worry about it," I say. "I'll be out in a minute."

I knock on Alex's door, turn the handle to a muffled "Come in." He's sitting at his desk like last time, but there's a tension in him that he didn't even have last night.

"I don't know why I'm here," I say, and slide into the chair in front of his desk. "But I'm here. What do you want?"

"You look a little hungover."

"Only a little? That's an improvement."

"How was Tabitha when she picked you up? She seem off at all?"

"I don't really know what off looks like with her. Why?"

Instead of answering me he slides a cell phone in front of me. It's small and pink with rhinestones lining the back. It's flipped open and a phone number ready to be called is displayed on the screen.

"The hell is this?"

"Call the number. I think it might be enlightening."

I pick up the phone. I don't know whose phone this is, but I can guess and I don't like it. "The fuck is going on?"

"Just make the call."

The phone rings a few times, somebody picks up. "Tabitha?" says a voice.

"No shit," I say.

"Who is this?"

"Mornin' Benny. I can call you Benny now, right? Or do we have to stick with Mr. Griffin?"

"Carter? How'd you get this number? How'd you get this phone?"

"Don't worry," I say. "I'll get it back to you later. Along with your girlfriend." I close the phone to distant protests from the speaker.

"I got suspicious," Alex says. "Had Max snag her phone and did some checking."

I don't say anything for a long time. Keep thinking back to my conversation with her in the hotel. We all make bad choices.

"Hey," Alex says. "You with me?"

"Huh? Yeah. Max stole her phone? I can't imagine he'd be all that sneaky."

"You'd be surprised. Anyway, I think you know where this is going."

"Yeah," I say.

Alex punches the buzzer on the intercom. "Send her in," he says when Max answers.

A minute later the door opens and Tabitha pokes her head in. "Hey," she says. "What's going on?"

"Found your phone," I say. "And I just talked to Griffin on it."

Her eyes go wide, bouncing between Alex and I. "Oh," she says.

"You want to tell us what the hell is going on?" Alex says.

"I didn't know all this was going to happen," she says. "I didn't even know the guy before a couple days ago."

"Before I showed up here?" I ask.

"Yeah. Day before. He told me you'd be coming here. He offered me five thousand dollars if I could tell him when you showed up. Where you'd be staying. That sort of thing. I didn't know he was the one that did that to you. Or that anything would happen at the warehouse. I didn't know any of that until this morning."

"You told him we were there?"

"Vivian called yesterday morning when you guys were leaving. I told Alex and then I called him."

"You almost got him killed," Alex says, anger in his voice. "You almost got Vivian killed."

"I didn't know that would happen," she says. Her eyes are pleading.

"Can you give us a minute?" I ask Alex.

He looks dubious. "Okay," he says. Tabitha shrinks back from his glare. He slams the door behind him.

She stands against the door, not looking at me, not saying anything. I don't know what to say myself. We stay that way a good minute.

"Are you going to kill me?" she asks, her voice quiet.

"What?" The question throws me. A second later I realize it shouldn't surprise me. "No," I say. "God, no. I'm not going to kill you."

"What are you going to do?"

That's a good question. I've been thinking about that since Alex handed me the phone. Her words from this morning come back to me. "We all make bad choices, sometimes." We sure do. But it doesn't mean we have to keep making them.

Finally, I find my voice. "It's been a long week," I say. "And you've been a bright spot in it. Thank you for that."

"You're not mad?"

"I'm furious. But not at you. You didn't know who the hell I was. Guy shows up with five K cash to tell him about somebody you've never met? No. I'm not mad at you. I'm pissed off at myself. For a lot of things."

"I'm sorry. I had no idea this would happen."

"I know." A thought has been nagging at me this whole conversation and I don't want to ask the question, but I have to know, even if the answer is one I don't want to hear.

"The other night, when you drove me back to the hotel—"

"I wanted to do that," she says. A hint of a smile plays across her face. "I think you're cute."

I laugh. "You really need to raise your standards, then." My face looks like it's been used as a punching bag, I'm missing a tooth, my hand's been barbequed and I reek of tequila. Yeah, I'm a hottie, all right.

"When I said I had some things to fix this morning, this was what I was talking about," she says. "I was going to call Griffin and tell him it was off. Or, I don't know. Lie to him, maybe. Tell him you'd left town."

"I am leaving town," I say.

"Oh."

"It's not a good idea for me to be here."

"The fuck?" Alex says, opening the door and looking in. "What? It's my goddamn bar, I can listen at the door if I want. What do you mean you're leaving?"

"Look, I'm sorry I've been such an asshole," I say. "My being here isn't doing anybody any favors. Things have been going to shit ever since I got here."

"What, that's it? You're just packing it in?"

"Boudreau killed Lucy to get to me. Came pretty fucking close, too. I can't bring her back, I can't change a goddamn thing. So what the hell am I getting out of this? The fuck am I supposed to do?"

"Kill Boudreau. For real this time. Jesus, Eric. Pull your head out of your ass. You think he's gonna stop just because you left town this time?" He looks at Tabitha for support. She shrugs.

"Got any brilliant insights on how?" I show him my bandaged hand. Point to the bruises on my face. "I've been getting my ass handed to me since I got back in town. I'm pretty fucking tired of it."

"Can't win if you don't play," Alex says.

"Can't lose, either. You know what happens if I leave? Griffin's screwed. He's hiding behind my ass hoping Boudreau'll come after me instead of him. Well, fuck him. Best thing I can do is leave."

"No," Tabitha says. "You can't keep running. Not forever. I mean, I get it. If you have to go, go. But Alex is right. This isn't going to stop just because you're not here."

Alex's phone interrupts him before he can say anything else. He looks at it, glares at me, flips it open.

"Hey," he says, listens for a bit. "Okay. Yeah, he's right here. You want to talk— Oh. Okay." Listens some more. "I'll see if he wants to. Yeah, he's being kind of an asshole. See you in a bit." He hangs up.

"I'll take a wild guess and say that's Vivian and Ellis has woken up."

"Yes on one. No on two. He's still out. She's been there all night. Wants me to pick her up. Asked if you'd come along."

He sees my hesitation. Rolls his eyes. "Fine, at least say good-bye to her this time. Then, hell, I'll drop you at the fucking airport, or something."

Say good-bye. I owe her that much. Kind of missed that the last time. Another thing I owe Griffin. I hope when Boudreau eats him he makes it hurt.

"Okay."

"Are you coming back?" Tabitha says.

Half an hour ago I'd have said no, but now. "I don't know."

"Fair enough," she says. She steps over from the door, kisses me on the cheek. "I hope I see you again some time."

"Me too," I say. "Thanks. I mean for the other night, not, you know."

"Selling you out?"

"Yeah, that. You might want to make yourself scarce for a bit. I doubt Griffin's going to try anything with you. There's no profit in it, but still."

"I have his money and I gave him what he wanted. I think I'll be fine."

I nod. She gets it better than most people would. I turn to Alex. "You're gonna have to drive. My car's stuck in the afterlife."

Chapter 21

"You gonna fire her?" I ask.

Alex shakes his head. "No. She didn't know who you were. She didn't know anything about this. How about you?"

"I'm not her boss."

"You know what I mean. What are you going to do about her?"

I don't know. No, I know and I just don't want to say it. I need to leave. They can call me a coward but I'm a target and anyone standing around me is in the blast radius. If Boudreau doesn't kill me, Griffin's sure as hell going to try.

"Nothing," I say. "She didn't do anything wrong. This is all Griffin."

Griffin. There's something about him that's been bugging me since last night, but I can't put my finger on it. What was it that he said in the ambulance? Something isn't clicking. He'd said, "Now that Boudreau knows you're in town." There's something there, but my mind slides off it as we hit a pothole and my head throbs some more.

I manage to pull myself more or less together by the

time we get to Harbor-UCLA. The headache's dulled to a low throb. A couple pieces of gum and my mouth doesn't taste like a possum took a shit in it.

I'm still hungover, but not so hungover to not notice that shit is really, really wrong when we step into the hospital.

"What?" Alex says, as I freeze at the doorway. I put up a hand to shut him up, close my eyes. Extend my senses.

"There's nobody dead," I say.

"They're having a good day?"

"My kind of dead, smartass. There aren't any anywhere in or around the hospital. This place should be crawling with them."

"The fuck would scare ghosts away?"

I can think of a couple things, but only one of them makes any sense. "Boudreau. He's got to be somewhere in the building, but I can't sense him." A thought hits me. "Where's Vivian?"

"Fourth floor. ICU."

We run to the elevators, almost knocking over a security guard as we pass. Get there as the lights go off. Emergency lighting kicks in, flickers, dies.

"Stairs?" Alex sees them first, grabs my sleeve, yanks me down a short hallway. Get to the fourth floor and my chest is in agony. I don't recommend running up stairs with fucked up ribs. Hit the door, step into chaos.

The ICU looks like it's been hit with a tornado. Equipment is toppled, gurneys on their sides. Through the glass walls of the rooms I can see doctors and nurses doing CPR on flatlining patients.

An orderly runs by with a defibrillator that suddenly

starts emitting an electronic shriek. I yank Alex back into the stairwell and slam the door just as the defibrillator explodes. It goes off like a flash-bang, a loud pop. Then screaming.

The orderly's thrashing around with pieces of plastic embedded in his face and chest, blood running into his scrubs. I push past him looking for Vivian.

"Did she say what room?"

Alex is leaning by the orderly looking like he doesn't know what to do. Pull out chunks of glass and plastic? Apply pressure? Where? I grab Alex, haul him up. "What room?"

"But the guy—"

"Screw the guy. What room?"

"Uh, 412. Around the corner."

I head down the hall, dodging gurneys, nurses, exploding fluorescent tubes raining glass from the ceiling. Turn the corner.

Room 412 is worse than the rest of the floor. The entire glass wall facing the hallway is gone. Pieces of tempered glass cover the floor like gravel. Somebody threw a nurse through it.

"Vivian?"

"Here," she says next to me, sliding into view as she drops the spell hiding her.

"What happened?"

She doesn't have to answer. Ellis steps out of the room, IV and catheter lines trailing behind him. Wild eyed, unfocused. There's a pulse of light that I'm not sure anyone else can see and then there they are. Swirling around him are all the hospitals ghosts I should have been sensing since I walked in. And at the center of it I see Boudreau's face flickering over Ellis'. Back and forth and back again.

I can sense the ghosts now, but I'm still not getting a read on Boudreau. Not like I can't see him standing right there, but why can't I feel him?

I don't have time to think about it. He sees Vivian and I, raises his hands. I can feel energy collecting around us. I yank a fire extinguisher off the wall, throw it at his head before he can get a spell off. The blow glances off his head, knocks him down.

I grab Vivian and pull her around the corner. Alex is halfway down the hall, helping somebody to their feet. He sees us. Doesn't need us to tell him what to do.

"I'm going to eat your fucking soul, you sonofabitch," Boudreau screams down the hallway. The voice is a weird synthesis of his and Ellis'. He's shuffling after us, slow and unwieldy. As possessions go Ellis probably wasn't the best choice.

We hit the exit door right after Alex, take two steps down and the door blows off its hinges. It's not heavy, but it's moving fast. It slams into me and Vivian, throwing us ass over teakettle down the stairs. I feel a crack in my chest. That rib's never going to heal.

I feel like a cat in a dryer. Tumble down the cement steps. Alex barely manages to jump out of the way. We hit the landing on the next floor down, Vivian half on top of me, the door beneath us.

Alex hangs over the side of the railing, trying to pull himself up. As he scrambles for purchase Boudreau steps through the doorway, grabs him by the wrist, twists.

What Boudreau lacks in speed he makes up for in strength. The snap of bone echoes in the stairwell. Alex screams as Boudreau hoists him up, yanks him back onto the stairs.

I push Vivian off of me so I can draw the Browning. I focus all the gun's hatred into that shot, pull the trigger. But Vivian grabs my arm and the shot goes high. Instead of blowing his head off it tears into Boudreau's shoulder. It's a lot worse than any 9mm should do. Blood erupts from the wound, the shoulder a ragged mess of meat and shattered bone. He almost drops Alex, staggers.

Is that worry on his face?

"What are you doing?" Vivian says.

"Killing him. The fuck does it look like?"

"But he—"

"Wants to kill us, yes."

It occurs to me that she can't see what I see. She doesn't see Boudreau, or all the swirling, screaming ghosts that surround him like a swarm of bees.

She just sees some old man in a hospital gown that she's been treating for years when he comes in off the street looking for something to ease his pain.

"That's not Ellis. Trust me on this, okay? Please?"

I readjust my aim and Boudreau grabs Alex off the floor with his good arm and I don't dare take the shot.

"You want him?" Boudreau says. Blood is pouring out of the shredded wound in his shoulder, the arm hanging limp. "I'll trade. Him for you. I'll even give you some time to think about it."

The ghosts swarming around Ellis' body spin faster, spiral tighter. I can see Boudreau's face over Ellis' pinch, recede into a point. I can't let him get away. But I don't want to hit Alex. I take the shot, anyway.

A blast of light and sound bursts outward from

Boudreau as I pull the trigger filling the room with bright light. When it clears Alex is gone, a bullethole the size of a dinner plate in the wall where he was standing. But Ellis is still there. Or his body is. He lies motionless on the steps. An empty, broken old man.

Vivian yells, pulls herself to her feet, runs up the stairs. "Where is he? Where'd Alex go?"

I limp up after her, holstering the Browning. My ears are still ringing from the gunshots, but I think the overall chaos in the hospital has stopped.

"Boudreau's got him," I say. "I don't know where."

She leans down to check on Ellis while I look at the bullet hole. There's no blood, thank god. If I'd hit Alex on top of the rest of this clusterfuck—

I don't finish the rest of the thought. "How's Ellis?"

Vivian looks up at me shakes her head. "He's gone."

"Probably been gone for a while," I say. I reach under him, hoist him up over my shoulder in a fireman's carry. My chest screams at me and I almost fall over from the pain.

Boudreau probably moved in as he was dying and kept things working in his body long enough to not trip off any monitors. Would I have sensed him if he was hiding in Ellis' body? I don't know.

"We need to get him out of here," I say. "Go downstairs, get a gurney. I'll meet you there. I need to ask Ellis some questions."

"He's dead."

"Never stopped me before."

———

"Do you have a garage?" I say.

"A carport in my building," Vivian says. "Why?"

"That won't work. I need somewhere we won't be disturbed. This could take a while."

We're heading north in an ambulance. I fried the radio and GPS when I stole it. We'll be fine for a while.

Ellis' body is strapped into a gurney in the back. Vivian slapped some gauze bandages over the gunshot wound so he wouldn't leak all over the place. Couldn't find a body bag.

"Alex has a garage. We can go to his place. He's got a place in Hancock Park. Will that work?"

"Yeah, that'll do fine." Hancock Park's old money, big houses. Wilshire Country Club shit. "I need to hit a hardware store first."

"I know one on Robertson," she says. "We can hit it on our way. What do you need?"

Been a while since I've done this. I'm not sure I remember all of it. "Hammer. Iron nails. Pliers. Dropcloth. Hacksaw would be good. Duct tape. Definitely duct tape. Maybe some rope. Couple 2x4s." I'm missing something. "Oh, and razor wire."

She stares at me, horrified. I can feel the gulf between us widening.

"I'm remembering something you said to me last night," she says. "About not knowing the kind of shit you deal with."

"Yeah?"

"You're right. And I don't want to."

———

I find everything but the razor wire. The kind gentlemen at the store directs me to a fencing and lumber place up the street where I'm able to grab a spool. I shouldn't need much. Ellis isn't that big a guy.

"Jesus, this place is huge," I say as we pull into Alex's driveway. Spanish style with terra cotta roof tiles and a jacaranda tree in the yard.

"He got it a few years ago before the market went to hell," Vivian says. "I—"

"What?"

"I was going to move in next month. Now—"

"Hey. We'll get him back."

Before we drag Ellis' body out of the back of the ambulance I pull out a can of Krylon I picked up from the hardware store and spray paint "NOTHING TO SEE HERE" on all four sides of the car, casting a don't-see-me spell as I make each pass. Vivian helps me wheel the gurney into the garage. I flick on the overhead fluorescents, close the door behind us.

I've heard you can tell a lot about a person by looking at their garage. What I can see from this one is that Alex is a neat freak. The cement floor is spotless. What few tools he has are put away in drawers or hanging from pegboards. A few cardboard boxes are stacked neatly in overhead racks. Most importantly, there's plenty of room.

"What can I do?" Vivian says.

I pull out the 2x4s, the hammer, nails and rope. Pull on a pair of painter's coveralls. "Not much at the moment. I have to get this frame set up. Ropes attached. Sling them over the rack up there. Might need your help nailing Ellis up."

"Come again?"

I lay the beams one on top of the other in a crude cross. "We're crucifying him," I say. "Sort of." I stop when

I notice her horrified look. "And then we're going to get him to answer some questions."

"Crucifying him?" She shakes her head. "Jesus, Eric. What kind of sick shit is this? Why don't you just talk to his ghost?"

I throw the hammer and nails down. "You know what, I'm getting fucking tired of this. I can't ask his ghost because he didn't leave one. Ellis has either moved on or Boudreau grabbed him before he could. Either way, there's no ghost for me to talk to. This is what we've got. So either shut up and help me or stay out of my way."

I know she's not squeamish. You don't make it through med school having a problem with corpses. So what gives?

"I'm sorry. This is just really far removed from what I do and—" Vivian swallows hard. "I'm worried about Alex. All right?"

She's been holding it together, but the veneer is starting to crack. "We'll find him," I say.

"Okay. I'll lay down the drop cloth and get Ellis off the gurney."

With her help it doesn't take long to get the old man's ravaged body onto the cross. Positioned upside down, one foot crossed behind the other, hands behind his back nailed and duct taped to the wood. Vivian helps me hold the nails in place as I get them through his wrists.

"Tell me you didn't try this spell when we were dating," Vivian says.

I laugh. It's dry and hollow. "No," I say. "This is old magic. Learned it in New York. Had some help from an old Algonquin spirit. Michabo? I think? Looks like a big rabbit. Kind of like Harvey."

"You know, people like us, we hear stories about these things. I know they exist. I know they're out there. But this still sounds crazy."

"Yeah," I say. I finish wrapping a layer of duct tape around Ellis' left wrist. "I know. I thought so, too. Even with the shit I do. There's so much more out there I didn't know about."

I tape a couple of quarters to his eyes. Rigor's beginning to set in and it takes some work to pry his mouth open. There's a cracking sound as we pry his jaws apart. Vivian's a professional the whole time. I don't know why I thought she might not be. She's a doctor for fuck's sake. She knows dead bodies better than I do. I've never given her enough credit.

By the time we've hoisted Ellis up to the rafters he's a fairly decent approximation of The Hanged Man. A half naked homeless guy with burns and scrapes, face swelling purple from pooling blood. A cut-rate Christ thrown together by mad monks.

I take a second, hang my head and give him a moment of silence. It's not a prayer. What the hell would I pray to? I've met gods. They're nothing special. But I want to give him this one last moment of respect before I turn him into a freak show.

I slide an oil pan under his body, slice a couple wide gashes into his chest to thread the razor wire through. I say a spell of binding as I unspool it around his torso, through the cuts, over his shoulders. Dark blood, dead and beginning to fester, drips into the oil pan. I slice his throat to drain him faster.

Vivian stands at the other end of the garage, watching me, arms wrapped tight around herself. I make a slice in my arm with the straight razor. With the wards Alex has on his home, I've left the ghosts outside. Good thing. Though they won't come in without an intentional summoning, any that are just hanging around would be drooling all over me and I don't need the distraction.

I drip the blood from my arm onto my fingertip, smear it on Ellis' forehead, above his eyes, around his lips. Draw a charm on his chest.

"I hate this bit." I say.

"All that and *this* is the part you hate?" Vivian says.

I flip her the bird, get on my knees, bring in a big gulp of air and clamp my mouth over his. I fill his lungs with air. Gag on the taste of bad teeth, rotting blood and bile. I pull away, force my stomach to stop doing handstands, spit as much of the stink out as I can. I step back, bind all the different pieces of the spell together, snap my fingers.

The razor wire flashes like a magnesium flare, the coins drop from Ellis' eyes and fall into the pan of blood with a dull plop. His body jerks, twists, tries to yank itself off the cross. This goes on for a few seconds then stills. One nail from his wrist falls to the floor.

"Can you hear me?" I ask.

Nothing for a moment, then a labored, "Yes." Voice a reed-thin wheeze that drags its way past decaying vocal chords. I look into Ellis' empty eyes. Okay. Now I've got a dead guy ready to answer questions. So what do I ask him?

"Where's Alex?" Vivian says before I can say anything.

Ellis grunts, but that's pretty much it.

"Why isn't he talking?"

"Probably because he doesn't know. Gotta remember, he's not in there. We're just, I don't know exactly, pulling shit out of his brain? Something like that. And it's probably already starting to rot. So don't expect much."

"Then why are we talking to him?"

"I'm hoping Boudreau left behind some memories or thoughts behind. Happens with possessions some times. Here, let me try." I snap my fingers in front of Ellis' empty eyes a few times to get his attention. They track, after a fashion, and point in my direction.

This isn't reanimation as such. More like hooking a frog leg to a battery to make it twitch. This is all about the right questions to ask. Simple questions give simple answers but they don't always give you what you're looking for.

"Let's start off slow," I say. "Tell me your names."

"Henry Jean Walter Ellis Baptiste Boudreau."

"And there we go."

"What happened?"

"Bits of Boudreau got mixed up with bits of Ellis, I think."

"Why did he possess him, though?"

Good question. "Dunno. Whatta ya say, Sparky? Why'd Boudreau pop his ugly mug in there?"

"Waiting for you," he says. "Saw the woman. Decided to take her to get to you."

Vivian regards the hanging corpse with an uncomfortable intensity. It's not fear. Disgust, maybe? Fascination?

I find myself wondering if Boudreau had grabbed her instead of Alex, would I have traded myself for her? The answer comes immediately. Abso-fucking-lutely. And if I have to I'll do it to save Alex, too.

"What does he want with me?" I ask.

"You're important."

"I don't understand. Important how?"

"He needs you so he can come back. You are bonded."

Takes me a second to connect the dots. "Sonofabitch."

"What does he mean by bonded?" Vivian says. "Or come back?"

"He's looking to come back here. To the side of the living. That's why he was after Griffin. That's why he's after me."

"I'm not following you."

"He wants a body," I say. "He wants mine."

Chapter 22

My head is throbbing. I stand up and start pacing from one side of the garage to the other. I know I'm onto something, I'm just not sure what it is.

"He can manifest here but he's still dead, right? Like in the warehouse?" Vivian says.

"And he can jump into someone else's body."

"Okay," Vivian says. "But why Ellis? He wants you so why didn't he jump into you? Or me?"

Or Griffin for that matter. How was Ellis different? Then I have it. "Boudreau burned him out on purpose." Vivian's looking even more lost. "Ellis told me he lost the ability to cast because Boudreau forced him to channel more and more power until he fried himself."

"Ellis thought Boudreau didn't believe the spell to keep him whole on the other side was working, so he kept making him try. I don't think that was the reason, though."

"It was, what, preparation? To let him take over Ellis' body?"

"I think so," I say. "He was probably going to hang onto Ellis, locked away somewhere as insurance.

Anything happens to him, he's protected by Ellis' spell long enough to move his soul into the guy."

"You kind of screwed that plan up, didn't you?" she says.

"Yeah. I don't think he was expecting some punk to crash through his warehouse wall and speed up his time-table. More to the point, I don't think he was expecting his soul to be fed to a bunch of hungry ghosts."

"Otherwise he'd have just jumped right into Ellis when you'd killed him?"

"I think so, yeah. Instead it took him fifteen years to pull himself together. By then he'd lost track of Ellis."

The pieces start falling into place. "He found Griffin at the warehouse, but he was too weak to really hurt him. And once he was strong enough to start casting or becoming solid he found me."

"Nice timing," Vivian says.

"No shit. And then he spots Ellis in the warehouse, his ready-made vessel. And once he's got his scent he doesn't let go. Tracks him to the hospital."

"Probably wasn't expecting to step into a burn victim in the ICU," Vivian says. "That's why he wants you. Ellis' body was a mess. Even without his injuries I honestly don't know if he would have lived another ten years. Is that why he left with Alex?"

"To get me?" I say. "I'm sure of it."

"No, I mean leaving at all. If he hadn't needed to he wouldn't have, right?"

I play the scenario back in my head. That spell to transport him in spirit and Alex physically to wherever the hell they went had to have sucked up a lot of juice. Which means he had plenty to use. He could have swatted all three of us like bugs. But he chose to run instead.

"It was after I shot him," I say. "I tagged his shoulder. Was Ellis alive when that happened?" Sometimes a possession can animate a corpse like a puppet. Kind of like what I did with the headless body in Texas, only from the inside.

"If he wasn't that shoulder wound wouldn't have bled like it did."

So, for a while at least, Boudreau was actually alive. Would explain why I couldn't sense him. He wasn't something I could sense. And if he was alive —

"He was scared he was going to die again."

"But he's already dead."

"But he wasn't just operating Ellis' body, was he? He was actually *alive*. Hadn't moved in the whole way, though, right? He still had an escape hatch."

I tap Ellis on the side of the head. The eyes flutter a little. "Hey, dead guy, how we doin' so far?" He lets out a wheeze of air that sounds more or less positive.

"I'm going to call that a yes," I say.

"So he spooks," Vivian says, "because he thinks you have a real chance to kill him and takes off with Alex." She frowns, brow furrowing. "So if I hadn't screwed up your aim he'd be dead, Alex would be okay and we wouldn't be having this conversation."

"What? Hell no. We just figured this out. You made the right call."

She doesn't look convinced, but shrugs it off. "So now you know how to kill him."

"More or less. Not counting that we need to get him into another body, preferably one that isn't mine and when he's dead again I don't know what'll happen to him."

"Whatever it is it scares him. Would the spell that held him together before still work?"

I shrug. "Fuck if I know. Maybe. He'd probably be pretty jacked up, though. You know, if we can get him into someone else I don't see why I can't kill him the same way I did before. I just need to be more thorough."

"You think he'll fall for that?"

"No, but I don't have a better idea." I don't even know how I would get him into another body. One that he hasn't prepped the way he did with Ellis? And who?

"What did he mean by bonded?" Vivian says, interrupting my thought.

"Sorry?"

She points at the hanging corpse. "He said you and Boudreau are bonded. What did he mean?"

"It's because I killed him, I think. That happens sometimes. Killers and their victims can get linked."

"And Ellis?"

"Don't know. Probably because of what Boudreau did to him. Goes both ways. Torture might do it. Sheer hate can make a bond. Or love. Griffin, well they were with each other a long time." But that wouldn't do it. Shouldn't do it. What did he do to Boudreau that would make a bond?

"Can he find you?" Vivian looks suddenly worried.

I point to the tattoos on my arm. "Don't know. Maybe." There's a thought. It does go both ways, after all. "I don't know how exactly, but if I have a link to him I might be able to follow it back to him." But that might make it easier for him to find me, too. "Let's table that idea for now."

I squat so I'm eye level with Ellis' corpse. "All this leads us to the main question," I tell him. "Where's Boudreau hanging out."

"Hooouuuussss," it says, slow and drawn out, the final S a long hiss like escaping air. Whatever's left there isn't going to last much longer.

"House?" Vivian says.

"Sounded like it. You got an address?"

"Ssssssssuunnnnnnssstttttt."

"Okay, what the fuck was that?" I say.

"Sunset, I think. Maybe Boudreau had a house on Sunset?"

"Well?" I ask the corpse. Slap it on the face a couple times to get its attention. Nothing.

"I think he's done," I say. "But it's a place to start."

"So we find this house on Sunset," Vivian says.

"I don't think it'll be that hard. Boudreau wants me to find him." What he really wants is for me to walk in and grab my ankles. Well, fuck him. I don't know how I'm going to take him down, but I'm going to make goddamn sure he stays down.

Vivian pulls out her cell phone. "Okay. I have a guy who does some research for me for med journal articles. I can have him dig around for an address." She starts punching numbers. "It seems a lot of effort to go to."

"What does?" I say.

"Boudreau. He killed Lucy just to get you to come back to L.A.?"

Before I can say anything the corpse lets out a low, "Nooooo."

"I thought you said he was done?"

"Guess I was wrong." I turn back to the body. Did it

actually say no or was that escaping gas? "If he didn't kill her to get me back then why did he kill her?"

"Nooooo."

I have a thought I don't like. A thought that takes this nicely wrapped package we just put together and tears off all the ribbons and bows. I don't want to ask, but I'll kick myself if I don't.

"Did Boudreau kill Lucy?" I say.

But this time the talking corpse stays quiet.

———

Disposing of a body is never easy. A lot of the ones I've had to deal with haven't been human. If I'm lucky they turn to ash, or dissolve into goo that seeps into the ground.

But sometimes they stick around, and leaving them in the open is begging for questions I don't want to have to answer. That's when power tools are your best friend.

Even then it takes me a couple of hours to hack Ellis' body and wrap up the pieces in the plastic dropcloth. Most of his blood has already drained, so it's a matter of bottling it in old detergent jugs the way you do used oil. Alex has a freezer chest that I put the chunks into until I'm ready to move him. No rush there. If I survive this whole thing I'll scatter the pieces across the Southland. If not I won't really much care.

Vivian sits it out. I don't blame her. Defiling a body to find her boyfriend is one thing, hacking up the pieces is a bit much. Vivian comes in as I'm finishing with the mop. If we get Alex back he probably won't appreciate all the blood spatter. The least I can do is clean up after myself.

"I think I found it," she says. "Boudreau had a place

in Brentwood on Corsica, a block south of Sunset." She hands me a slip of paper with an address on it.

"Who lives there now?"

"A couple bought it in '04. Not sure but I think they have a couple of kids."

"I hope they're on vacation."

She winces. "You think they're dead," she says.

"Easiest for him, I'd imagine." Considering what he was willing to do to my parents I don't think that would be a stretch.

"So what's our next move?"

I've been going over that for the last hour. I have no fucking idea. There's no way I can take Boudreau on myself. And there's no way in hell I'm letting Vivian go near him.

I've made a decision and she's going to hate me for it. And I kind of hate myself for it, too.

"Getting some dinner and some sleep," I say. "I don't know about you, but I'm barely standing upright."

"But Alex—"

"Isn't going anywhere. We don't even know if he's in that house. We've got time. And we need to be as clear as possible if we're going to get him. Boudreau isn't going to kill him if he thinks he can use him as bait."

I can tell she wants to rip my head off. Wants to jump in the car and run to the rescue, but she's not stupid.

"I know this isn't easy," I say. "But if we just run in there all we're going to do is get all three of us killed."

"Are you sure he won't kill him?"

Fuck no. Probably tear his throat out just out of spite. And if he hasn't I can't imagine what Alex is going through or how he's going to be on the other side of it.

"Absolutely," I say. "He can't kill him. Right now he's hoping we come to rescue him. If we get a whiff that he's been hurt he loses his advantage." It's a steaming pile of utter bullshit, but I say it anyway.

Maybe she knows I'm lying. Maybe she just wants to believe. Either way she closes her eyes, nods once. "You eat. I don't have an appetite."

She turns on her heel and goes back into the house. That's got her for now, but I need her out of the way for a while. After a few minutes I follow her inside, hating myself more with every step.

"Man, and I thought I was living the bachelor life."

His cupboards are almost completely empty. He has an unsliced loaf of French bread, a couple of jars of peanut butter, fifteen different brands of coffee.

"I thought you were living the hobo life?" Vivian says. I know she's trying to make a joke but there's no energy in it. She's sitting on a bar at the kitchen island watching me forage.

"I steal cars for transportation, not ride rails. Subtle but important distinction."

I pull out the peanut butter, the bread. Find some jam tucked in the back of the refrigerator that at least looks like it's from this century.

"Why?"

I sigh. Do we have to get into this now? "Because I'm running, okay? I started running fifteen years ago and I haven't stopped. Yes, you were right. I'm a coward. I'm sorry."

"Me too," she says.

I change the subject. If we keep going down this road I won't have the nerve to follow through with this. "I take it he doesn't cook much."

She gives a weak smile. "Fast food and noodle shops."

"Ah, refined tastes. How about you?"

"About the same. Don't have time for much else." She rubs her temples. "God, I haven't slept in like two days. How about you?"

"Does concussed and unconsciousness count?"

"Not really."

"Then pretty much the same." I slice the bread, make us a couple of sandwiches. Slide one to her on a paper towel.

"Eat," I say, "Doctor's orders."

That gets me a real laugh. "Sure thing, Doctor Kevorkian." As she eats I pour a glass of milk, prick my finger with the end of the knife and let a couple drops go in while muttering a spell over the glass.

It's a small spell and I don't have to tap the pool so she doesn't notice. I shake the glass a little, hiding the drops of blood in the milk.

"Drink," I say in my best Russian accent. "Will make you strong like bull."

"Oh, god, don't do the Russian thing," she says, taking a big gulp of the milk. "You sound like a Norwegian with a head cold."

"I was shooting for Boris from Rocky and Bullwinkle."

She finishes her milk, puts the glass down. Her expression changes. "Your impressions all sound like Norwegians with head colds. That's weird."

"What is it?"

"I feel . . . off." She stands, reels, grabs the table for support. Her expression changes. Confusion, betrayal, anger. "What did you do to me?"

"Sorry, Viv. I'll get Alex back, but I won't have you getting hurt."

"You sonofabitch," she says. I reach for her to keep her from going down ass over teakettle, but she jerks her hands away. "Get the fuck away from me. You bastard. How dare you."

"You're just gonna sleep, Viv. You need rest."

"I need to get my boyfriend away from that fucking psychopath." She lurches away from the island, knocking over her stool. "Where are my keys. I'll get him myse—"

I reach her before she hits the floor. Pick her up and lay her on the couch. Pull a blanket over her. Her breathing is getting shallower. Pretty soon she won't be breathing at all.

It's not sleep so much as it's a simulation of death. She'll be out for about a day and a half and when she wakes up she'll be fine. If anyone finds her and moves her she'll wake up. No worries about her coming to on the morgue slab. And when she wakes up she's going to rip my balls off and I'll deserve it and I'll let her. But at least she'll be alive.

Chapter 23

I pull the ambulance into the parking lot of the nearby Wilshire Country Club, stopping in front of a gawking attendant who rushes in front of the car. Everything's valet in this town.

"Sir, you can't park that here," he says as I roll down the window.

"I'm not going to," I say, giving a little push to my words. "You're going to. And I'd like the keys to a Mercedes, please." I hold out the keys for him.

He blinks a couple of times. "Of course, sir," he says. A few minutes later I'm on the road in somebody's S Class. Kid'll probably lose his job, but who wants to be stuck parking rich assholes' cars, anyway? Doing him a favor.

I can't get Ellis' final hissing word out of my head. What did he mean Boudreau didn't kill Lucy to get me back? If not that, then why did he do it? I've heard stranger noises coming out of corpses.

It could have been gas, the final vestiges of my spell pulling random noise from his brain. I once saw a guy who'd been dead three days sit up, shriek "Eureka," then fall back down, and there wasn't a touch of magic on him that I could find. Dead people just do weird shit sometimes. Chalk it up to a couple of killer burps and move along.

I hit the freeway, head toward Downtown. I have an idea of what to do, but I'm going to need help. A while later I'm standing at the Union Station bathroom wall hoping the door is still there. Dreading the door is still there.

No one has erased my chalk lines and runes, though there have been some creative additions in black marker. Signs and symbols of the city; marking territory, throwing curses, pronouncing love, or at least a good blowjob. Crude, unfocused, but magic nonetheless.

I refresh the lines and symbols, smear a drop of blood onto the wall, wonder if one of these days my brand of magic's going to get me a case of Hep C. I push a little power through it and watch the door slide away. Darius' bar is eerily quiet. Dim lighting, chairs stacked on tables, smell of day-old cigarettes and spilled beer. He sits at the one table still set up. Two chairs, two glasses, a bottle of scotch.

"Am I interrupting a tender moment here?"

"Please," he says. "Been waiting for you for hours now. Have a seat. I know why you're here."

"Then you know I don't have time to dick around."

I take the seat opposite him. He pours a measure from the bottle for each of us. "You got plenty of time here. I just want to make sure you've thought about what you're wanting before you ask for it."

"I have. I'm not crazy about it but unless you got another idea, Santa Muerte's pretty much the only option I got left."

"You could just walk away."

"Little late for that."

"Yeah," Darius says. "Little late for that."

"Why do you care, anyway?" I say.

"You know how many people I let in this place? I mean the ones I let come and go as they please, not the riffraff that I let stumble on in."

"No idea," I say, though I've wondered that before. Darius is lord over his domain. Nobody's getting in unless he wants them to. I know some he lets in out of curiosity. Throw folk together see what kind of trouble they can get up to. But the rest, the ones who know him, who know what he is, that's different. There can't be many of those and I don't know why I rate.

"Damn few, I'll tell you that much. Damn few." He drinks his shot, pours himself another. "I like you, son. I do. Even when you're being a stupid, fuckin' moron."

"Thanks. Not a lot of people see it like you do."

"That's because they don't know you like I do. If I do this thing, if I give you what you want, we're quits. You're no longer welcome here."

"Whoa. What the hell? Why?"

"Balance of power. You don't know your own strength, do you? You been bouncing around from place to place, person to person, you don't know what's what. Settle down a little and maybe you'da figured out you're not like other people."

"Yeah, I know I'm not like other people. I see dead things. I talk to dead things. I make dead things."

"There you go being a stupid, fuckin' moron again. All right, here's how it is. You think you're getting a big gun. Thing is you ARE the big gun. You just don't know how to pull your own trigger. You hook up with that old witch and now she's got the gun, not the other way around."

"And you're afraid she's going to point me at you?"

"Ain't no secret, her dislike of competition," he says. "I'd rather not take the chance."

Darius might be the last actual friend I have in this town. Do I want to throw that away? But how much of a friend is he? I haven't been in here for fifteen years. Will I miss something I've grown so far away from?

Oddly, yeah, I think I will miss it. Out of this entire mess Darius' bar has felt more like home than anywhere else I've been. "You got a better option? Because believe me I don't want to do it."

He shakes his head. "Nope. Wish I could help you, man. Really do. This one's your call and your fight."

"Then I guess we're quits," I say.

———

Sanctuario De La Santa Muerte. Hand painted sign, black on a bright red background, crude painting of her on one side. I look at the card that Darius gave me. The address written on it was easy to find. Wedged between a nail salon and a coin-op laundry in a strip mall south of MacArthur Park. It's a church.

I pull the Mercedes up between a Tercel and a Bondo-patched Mustang. The storefront could just as easily be a donut shop or a taqueria. Mylar covers the glass, throwing back a smoky reflection. A sign in the door proclaims ABIERTO.

I push the door open, an electronic chime sounding off. I don't know what I'm expecting but it's not this. The store is an explosion of color. Bright yellow walls, blue, fuchsia and lime green shelves. Multicolored prayer candles for love, attraction, money, revenge.

Statues and shrines to Santa Muerte line the shelves and sit on the floor. From four-foot-tall resin-cast skeletons down to dashboard models with black plastic gems for eyes. Key chains, jackets, t-shirts. Crazy bitch has her own souvenir shop.

"Can I help you?" A Latino man with heavy-lidded eyes smokes a cigar behind the counter. Thick muscles stand out in his arms, his neck.

"Maybe," I say. "Seeking an audience."

"A believer," he says, nodding slowly. "I thought so." He points at the bruises on my face. "You don't look like a tourist."

"Oh, I believe. I've met her."

"We all have in one form or another. A dying father, a dead wife, a murdered sister."

"No escaping death," I say. "When's Mass?"

"Friday nights at seven," he says. "I'm Eduardo. I lead the congregation." His handshake is like a steel vise.

"Was thinking something a little sooner."

"You don't need to wait if you're giving an offering," he says. "Through there." He gestures to a doorway covered by black, velvet curtains.

"Thanks."

"Don't mention it."

I step through and it's like night and day. Strings of white Christmas lights run along the walls, casting a hazy glow across everything. Wrought iron candelabras every few feet, plastic benches lined up as pews, a podium and a folding table as an altar. And off to one side, her.

At least one of her shrines. This one looks like she did in the cemetery, skeleton in a white wedding dress, the scythe in one hand, globe in the other. Bottles of tequila sit at the skeleton's feet, cigar clenched between crooked teeth. The floor is littered with roses and envelopes stuffed fat with cash.

I sit down on one of the benches. I don't care what church I'm in, I always feel stupid. Gods are petty, pissy children at best. I can't get behind the idea of worshipping them.

I look around the room. "All right," I say, "I'm here. Now what?"

Nothing.

"Helloo." I knock on one of the benches. "You are not gonna make me do this. Seriously?" No response. "Fine." I'm tired and I don't have time for this bullshit. I step up to the shrine, think about kicking it over.

Instead I pluck the cigar from between the skeleton's teeth, bite the end off, stick it in my mouth. Flame from my fingertip and a minute later I'm puffing away, blowing smoke over the altar, whispering her names like a litany; Sagrada Muerte, Poderosa Señora, La Madrina, La Flaca.

I have no idea what I'm doing. I know she likes cigars, I know smoke purifies, I know some of her names. Beyond that for all I know I should be doing this in lederhosen with ABBA playing in the background. I smoke and recite for a good twenty minutes. Nothing happens. Good cigar, though.

This is bullshit. I stub the cigar out in one of her eye

sockets. Crazy bitch doesn't want to talk to me, fine. I push the curtains aside and head back through the storefront. Eduardo's eyes follow me as I stalk past.

"Didn't get the answer you wanted?" he says.

"Didn't get any answer," I say.

"You will. She answers all of us in time."

"Time I don't have," I say and push open the door, the little chime sounding off as I leave.

The 110 Freeway's a parking lot at the best of times, so when my lane opens up and the traffic tapers off I know something's wrong. Cars peel away from me. No matter how many times I move over I'm still in the far right lane.

I pull over to the shoulder and get out of the car. The freeway's empty. No cars, no sounds of traffic. Just the wind whistling past. Below me I can see the city, but there's something off about it. The angles are wrong, details on the architecture somehow off. I turn back toward the road and see the green freeway sign that wasn't there a second ago.

MICTLAN—EXIT ONLY

Guess I'm getting that audience after all.

You'd think by now I'd have been to hell. After all there are so many of them. These are the places the dead end up after they're done hanging around as haunts and wanderers. Gehenna, Tartarus, Valhalla, Duat. The list goes on. Some are punishments, some are rewards.

The Aztecs had Mictlan, a place far to the north

where your spirit would be tried and punished for years before finally coming to rest. Like the Mayan Xibalba most folk need to travel through trials to get to their final reward. From what I hear it's one of the least appealing.

As I take the Mercedes down the off-ramp, I start to see why. The air here is Santa Ana dry, the sun a merciless spotlight that bleaches the landscape. I roll up the windows and crank the air conditioner. The city's still here. Or at least *a* city. The California bungalows, boxy post-war apartment buildings, pre-fab strip malls are all represented. But instead of concrete and stucco, it's bone and sinew, flayed skin, torn muscle. City Hall constructed of femurs and skulls, the L.A. River a thin trickle of blood running through a calcified channel. Palm trees of interlocking skulls span the horizon, their fronds desiccated scraps of flesh.

Los Angeles as a study in bone.

And there are the ghosts. They flicker by, more solid than I'm used to. They aren't playing out their final moments, or wandering around lost and empty. They're just going about their days as though nothing is any different. There aren't a lot of them, which I suppose makes sense. Santa Muerte isn't a huge presence up here in L.A., most of her worshippers are farther south, but she's got a decent following.

And can I really say she's crazy? When it comes down to it she's not human, even if humans created her. And the surroundings might not be the most tasteful, but I'm not seeing tortured spirits hanging over lava pits, or anything.

I look around for a street sign, but I don't find any. If

this place maps onto the real L.A. I should be somewhere around Adams and Figueroa. I have no idea where to go next. I'm not crazy about getting out of the car and asking directions.

Okay, if I were a batshit Aztec death goddess, where would I hang out? It's going to be somewhere symbolic, something that has significance to her.

Or to her followers. Immigrants dealing with death and frustration and injustice. That doesn't narrow it down much. L.A. was Spanish before the U.S. took it over and half the population's Latino. But even then the city has given them a raw deal.

I run through all the local history I can remember looking for something big, something to be pissed off about. The murder at Sleepy Lagoon where nine Hispanic kids got railroaded for a murder they probably didn't commit. The Zoot Suit Riots in '43 that led to four, maybe five hundred arrests and plenty of dead.

Stuff to be pissed about, sure, but neither of those feels right. Would anyone have had to die? Maybe not. Just some kind of big fuck you to Latinos you that she would want to take back, maybe? It takes a second and then I think I have it. I turn the car north and head up the skeletal freeway.

When Mexico lost California things changed. The people who were here had all their power and land stolen or stripped away. Sometimes quickly, sometimes slowly. Demeaned and disenfranchised, they spent the next hundred and fifty years getting the shaft. Still are, and they make up half the population of this city.

Back in the forties Chavez Ravine was a community of Latino families north of Downtown. Had their own schools and churches, grew their own food, kept to themselves. The rest of the city liked it that way. Would have preferred they didn't exist at all, but, hey, you can only do so much without being accused of blatant racism, right? Not that they didn't try or much cared.

And then the money happened. Federal dollars to turn Chavez Ravine into housing projects. Kicked everybody out with false promises of new homes, then sat on the land until a guy cried Socialism and ran on what amounted to a "Kick the Mexicans out" ticket got elected, bought up all the land from the government and plopped a baseball team in the middle of it all.

Fucked-over Hispanic landowners, meet Dodger Stadium.

———

I know I'm in the right spot when I get off the bone freeway and see an Aztec pyramid where the stadium should be. It's the only place I've seen here not made out of bone.

The pyramid is an enormous limestone structure whose size would put Tenochtitlan to shame. From down here the temple at the top looks tiny. I park the Mercedes at the base and make my way up the steps to the top. It seems to take forever. By the time I reach the temple building I'm sweating.

Like the rest of the pyramid the temple building is huge. Carved snakes and jaguars line the entrance and each brick has a scene depicting someone's gruesome death in stunning detail. As shrines go it's a far cry from the back room of a strip mall on Alvarado. Inside, burning braziers cast a golden glow, throw flickering shadows across the stonework, making the carvings dance.

I think about trying to make myself look presentable but toss the thought aside. It'd take a lot more than slicking back my hair and straightening my tie.

Santa Muerte sits on a stone throne at the rear of the building, her scythe in one hand, a globe in the other, her bleached skull hidden behind the veil of her wedding dress. Another throne sits by her side. Empty.

"Talking to you can be a real pain in the ass, you know."

"You are angry," she says. "Hardly the sort of behavior I would expect from a supplicant."

"Damn right I'm angry. But not with you. With Boudreau. You were right. I tracked down his ghost and now he's gunning for me. And he has a friend of mine. I aim to get him back."

She lifts her veil and stares at me with those soulless pits of hers. Not moving, not talking.

"I was wondering if you might give me a hand," I say, finally.

"Why would I do that?" she says. "I've offered you power. I've offered you a place at my side. You've refused my gifts. And now you ask for help. What do you have to offer?"

I take a deep breath, let it out slowly. I know I'm going to regret saying this, know it's going to come back and bite me in the ass. But I don't have the firepower to take on Boudreau myself. I can't see any other way.

"I've reconsidered. If you still have that job open."

Her skull twists to one side. She's looking at me like a

dog that's just seen a particularly unusual bird. "I don't know. Convince me."

Arrogant bitch. "No. You either want me or you don't. I'm not gonna beg for this. I'll take my chances alone with Boudreau before I get on my fucking knees. Sorry I wasted your time, Señora. I'll see myself out." I turn my back on her, head for the exit.

It isn't until I'm stepping over the threshold that she says, "Wait."

"Yeah? Why?"

"Because I need strength and bravery, not a weak willed fool who caves at a little pressure. A test. You passed."

I turn around to face her. She's standing inches behind me. I wish she'd stop doing that. "No more tests."

"No more tests," she says.

"Then it's time to negotiate," I say. "What do you offer for my services?"

"My power added to yours. You will have my command of the dead, you will be known by and safe from my followers. You will have my protection and my help."

"And in return?"

"You will be my red right hand. You will kill in my name. You will carry out my judgment upon my enemies."

"I choose if I carry out your orders. You said you don't want a mindless lackey. I'll decide." She says nothing for a long while. I don't know if she's thinking or just bailed. There's no way to read her. I can't tell if I've pissed her off or made her happy.

"Agreed," she says finally. "But you will not interfere as I carry out a sentence or with whoever I choose as my emissary in your stead."

"Agreed," I say. I can feel her boxing me in already. I can think of a hundred ways that one demand can go wrong. "I will not be at your beck and call. I'm independent and I won't be interfered with. I do a job for you I do it my way."

"Yes. But know that you will be mine and you will be marked as mine."

The noose tightens some more. Am I in? Do I need this that badly? Can I honestly not take Boudreau without this?

"Do you agree to all this?" she says. "Do you swear your oath to me, bind yourself to me, join with me to be by my side and protect me and my interests above all others?" She puts out her hand, fingers stretching out. "Do you agree?" she says again.

I don't want this. Every fiber of my being tells me that this is wrong. Know that I'm fucking myself six ways to Sunday. She knows it, too. But, hey, if I'm going to fuck myself might as well go all in.

I take her hand. The skeletal fingers are dry and cool to the touch. "I do," I say.

And fire burns through me as she brands my soul.

Chapter 24

I wake to the sound of a blaring horn, the smell of smoke and gasoline. I pick myself off the ground, road gravel embedded in my cheek, my hands scraped and raw. The light's too bright, the air too thick. The Mercedes lies in a smashed heap behind me, a small fire in the cab, chunks of cement and metal debris scattered around it. I squint up at the freeway fifty feet above me and see the break where the car went over the side.

I'm lying on the ground in front of the car. Thrown clear? Not possible. Deposited, maybe, just to show me who's boss. I should be dead with a steering column through my chest. Hell, maybe I was. When the sign said EXIT ONLY it had meant it.

The sunlight is too bright. My mouth tastes like smoke and blood. In a week full of headaches and gut punches, this is the worst by far. My left hand feels like it's been slow roasted, the bandages on it tattered and blackened. I peel them off, expecting to see charred skin underneath, but it's no worse than it was the other day.

But the wedding band is new. It would be funny if this were the tail end of a weekend bender in Vegas, but that ring is a hell of a lot scarier than waking up married to a hooker.

Legs are wobbly, hands shaking. I hobble under the freeway to a city maintenance yard through a hole in a chain-link fence.

I stumble out between a row of parked buses, half blind from the glare. The sun feels like it's burning holes in my retinas. I close my eyes, press the heels of my hands against them. When I open them I wish I hadn't. Pain stabs back into my skull like hot needles.

The pain is fading a little. My head's clear enough that I can see where I'm going. Why my eyes are fucked I'll figure out later. Right now I need to get a car and get out of here. I can already hear sirens. I turn back to the maintenance yard, spy a pickup truck on the other side. The light's still painfully bright. Maybe I got a concussion in the crash?

I pop the pickup's lock with a spell, go to open the door and stop short. I can see myself in the glass of the driver's side window and besides the expected wear and tear I'm mostly okay. Except for my eyes.

They're gone.

Pitch black marbles stare out at me from my reflection. No iris, no whites. Well, shit. She did say she'd mark me. Just didn't think it'd be quite so obvious.

———

I'm still having trouble seeing. But it seems to be getting better. I almost crash the truck pulling out onto Figueroa as a fire truck, two cop cars and a paramedic speed by toward the crash I just left behind. I park the pickup on a side street near USC after almost sideswiping a motorcycle and taking out two kids on skateboards.

I press the heels of my hands into my eyes. Take a couple of deep breaths. I can handle this and take control. I don't know what she's done to me, but I've been thrown for loops my whole life. This is just one more thing to add to the pile.

Ten years old, summer day. Walking down an alley after buying a comic book and a pack of Now and Laters at the 7-11. Then gunshots, screaming. Watch a man get taken down in front of me as he runs out a garage.

Then he does it again. And again. And again. I watch in horror as this scene plays out in front of me, pants wet, shaking. My first Echo.

Grow up in my family you hear about magic, you learn what it is, how it works. But dealing with the Dead's a different matter. My parents weren't really the gutting-a-sheep-to-read-the-entrails type. Had an easier time talking to me about sex.

I do now what I did then. Accept it. Work with it. Tease it apart. I check my eyes again in the rearview mirror, but they haven't changed. Something tells me they're not going to. I try to pull off the wedding ring. Doesn't budge. I'm not sure if it's a symbol, an artifact, a reminder of my new status, or just Muerte's fucked up sense of humor.

I lean back in the seat, close my eyes. Exhaustion threatens to overwhelm me. I need sleep and unconsciousness doesn't count. But I don't have time for that. I pull together a spell for wakefulness. At most it'll be like a cup of coffee. Enough to keep me going until I can find a case of Red Bull.

I open myself up to the pool of magic around me and suddenly I'm drinking from a firehose. The shock of that much power slams into me like a 2x4. I push it back, get a handle on the flow. I've never felt this much power before. It's different from when I downed that bottle of demon piss. That was like shoving a hundred gallons into a five-gallon jug. But this is different. It pours into me and I can handle it, hold onto it. Never been able to hold so much.

My brain is buzzing with it. I can feel it in my skin, my bones. Guess I don't need that case of Red Bull after all. I think I might almost be ready to take on Boudreau.

Two hours of traffic later I stand outside Boudreau's old house looking at the curtained-up windows, the Land Rover in the driveway, bills and letters peeking out of the overstuffed mailbox.

There's magic here. Similar to the spells I put on the ambulance and on the name tags I use to disguise myself. Less "Don't look at me" than "Everything's fine, move along." Without it the cops would be swarming over this house. The smell alone would have the neighbors running.

I can feel him in there. And I can feel all of the ghosts he's pulled into himself, too. More than I ever could. I know who they are now, know their names, how they died. How much agony Boudreau's putting them through. That's one power I wish Santa Muerte had kept for herself.

I pull out a prepaid cell phone I bought at the grocery store, dial the number I got off Tabitha's phone. And get ready to lie through my teeth.

"Well, hello sailor," I say when it picks up.

"What do you want?" Griffin says.

"What, no 'How ya doing?' —'How's your head?'—

'Has your soul been ripped apart by a power-mad, psychotic ghost, yet?' I'm hurt."

"I'm hanging up."

"But if you do that, then I won't be able to tell you how I'm about to make your day."

"I'm listening."

"So, I'm standing outside a house," I say. "Nice place. I hear it's got a family with 2.5 kids and 3.2 dogs and everything. Very Americana. Also, and I'm just guessing from the stacked up mail and the stink of rotting flesh, they're kinda dead."

"So you found him. Good for you," he says. "Why don't you charge on in there? I'll try to remember to thank him when he kills you."

"Oh, I like my plan better. I've got two options. Option one is that I take him down, but I need some help to pull that off."

"L.A.'s full of day laborers. Try a street corner."

"Or," I say, "I can go with option two. See, I've been talking to Ellis."

"Ellis is dead."

"Yeah, the dead are awful talkative around me, in case you hadn't noticed. And boy is he a talker. You know that spell that's kept Boudreau around so long? There's a hole in it. It won't let me kill him, but it will let me get control of him for a while."

"What's your point?"

"I can do that bit all on my own. And if I do you know where I'm gonna send him. It won't last long and he'll tear me apart when I lose him, but so help me I'll have him chew through your soul like a fat man through a Vegas buffet before he does."

"And this is supposed to make my day?"

"Yep. Because if you help me kill him I won't have to have him kill you."

"Hard bargain."

"Take it or leave it."

"All right, say I agree to this. How does it work?"

"First, we have him possess someone."

———

I meet Griffin at a café on Rodeo Drive in Beverly Hills full of what pass for socialites in L.A. Impeccable hair, designer labels, conspicuous shopping bags. The hostess looks at me like she's about to call the cops. At first I think it's my eyes, but I'm wearing mirrored sunglasses. So it's either my roguish good looks or the fact that I look like I've been through a mulcher.

"I'm here to see him," I say, pointing at Griffin sitting alone at a nearby table. I push the sunglasses a little higher up on my nose to better hide my eyes. Griffin stands, nods his head. The hostess isn't convinced, but walks me over to the table, anyway.

"I didn't think it was possible," Griffin says, "but you actually look worse today."

Griffin had suggested we meet at his house. I told him to go fuck himself. I wanted public and busy. He'd either shoot me to get me out of the way or try to beat how to control Boudreau out of me. And after he figured out I was blowing smoke up his ass then he'd shoot me. Pretty much a lose-lose situation all the way around.

"Been burning the midnight oil," I say.

"So I gathered," he says. "Tell me."

Time to start dancing. I tell him what's happened.

Most of it, anyway. The hospital, Ellis being possessed. I leave Alex and Vivian out of it.

I keep the story as wide and vague as I can. Enough room, I hope, to slide some whopper lies in here and there.

"When we got there Ellis was still just Ellis. Conscious, but just barely. Then Boudreau popped up. Tried to possess him."

"Did he succeed?"

I nod. "Funny thing about that, though. Right before he moved in, all those ghosts he'd been piling onto himself did a runner."

"Really." He leans forward, hooked.

While I'm shoveling bullshit like I'm fertilizing crops, I catch a glimpse out of the corner of my eye of two of Griffin's men I hadn't seen when I came in. Booth in the back. Clear line of fire. Either to protect him or shoot me. I'll know in a little while, I guess.

"Yeah. Even if I'd been ready for it, I don't think I could have taken him. But you and me together? I think we have a shot."

He leans back. Thinking. "What happened to Ellis?"

"I shot him," I say.

"You killed him?" Griffin says, somewhere between impressed and appalled.

"He was gone already. You think Boudreau was going to move in and let the previous owner hang around? No, he kicked Ellis out, but he bailed when he realized he was in possession of a corpse. By the time I could react he'd already gotten his ghost swarm back."

"So if he possesses someone and leaves he's just as powerful."

"That's my thinking," I say. "If we want to hit him we need to hit him as he's possessing a body. And killing whoever he grabs doesn't do any good."

"So what's your plan, exactly?"

"We get him to come after someone and when he lets his guard down we hit him."

"That simple?"

"That simple. Look, so far he's been at places that are important to him. The warehouse, for example."

"What about the hospital?"

"He was going after Ellis. And you said yourself he'd been attacking you."

"Feeble attempts, yes."

"But still attempts. And he's getting stronger. He can't pop up just anywhere. He has to have a link to the place or something in it. That's why he showed up at the hospital. He had a link to Ellis."

"Why go after a dying man?" he asks. "Why not you or me?" A spear of anger flashes through me. I want to jump on the table and scream, "Just go with it, goddammit," but kill the impulse before it fucks everything up.

"Ellis was prepped. All that time he was down in that hole? It wasn't just to get the spell right. It was to make him a receptacle. He went after Ellis because he was the only one who he could go after."

Griffin leans back in his chair. Eyes clouded over in thought. "That's a lot of supposition. And even if it's true this has been a waste of time," he says.

"What are you talking about?" I say. "We can get him."

"How? Harsh language?"

"The same way I took him out the last time. He'll be

weakened as he's moving into a new body and I can pull him out and shred him."

It's bullshit and I can tell he's not buying it. I try to keep my cool.

"So do it yourself. You don't need me for this. You need bait. You need a body prepped like Ellis for him to move into."

"I already have that. I've figured out how he prepped Ellis and I've got that all handled. But I'll need you to distract him."

"What stupid sonofabitch did you get to sign up?"

I lower my sunglasses, give him a full look at my new, pitch black eyeballs. He startles, taken aback.

"Me," I say. "The ritual leaves a bit of a mark." Please believe this. Please don't ask how I really got these eyeballs.

I push the sunglasses back up. "But just because I'm going to look like a lamb at the slaughter doesn't mean I am one. I have no intention of letting him take over. But I can't kick him out of me and take him out at the same time."

"So what, I run interference? How exactly? Shoot you? I'd be happy to."

"I was thinking more along the lines of an attack dog." I pull out the bottle of Stoli with the drunk ghost I got from Darius' bar in it. He squints at it.

"There's something in there. What is it?"

"Nature spirit," I lie. "Let it loose as he's trying to take me over and it'll go after him like a Doberman. Won't hurt him much but it'll give the chance to take him down. Between that and you and," I nod at the men in the corner, "a couple of your goons sucking up some of the local magic pool, he won't get a chance to fight back."

I can almost see the gears turning in his head. Wondering if I'm telling the truth, maybe figuring out how to fuck me over, get rid of Boudreau and me at the same time.

"I don't like this," he says. "There are too many variables. And I don't trust you."

"I don't trust you, either. But we both want him gone. We have a shot if we do it together."

"And if we don't you take control of him and send him after me?"

"More or less."

"I don't believe you can do that."

"Want to find out if I'm bluffing?"

"I'm tempted, but you're right. We have a better chance working together than against each other. It's a deal. When and where?"

"Give me a few hours. I'll call you with the address. Be ready." I slide out of the booth.

"Why not give it to me now?"

"Because I think you'll go over there without me and get yourself killed and then where will I be? That and if I don't tell you now it's an extra incentive to not have your thugs over there try to shoot me."

"Point," he says. "I'll wait for your call."

Chapter 25

It's a horrible plan. Even if it weren't all lies it's a horrible plan. The only reason I can think Griffin bought it is because he wants it to work. I don't know what kind of crap Boudreau's been throwing at him, but it's been enough that he's worried.

I need to get a better handle on these powers Muerte's given me. I haven't seen or heard from her since the temple. If I've read her right I'm not going to. This is a test. See how I handle things. I know I can see the Dead better. I know I can pull in a hell of a lot more power than I'm used to. Can I do anything else?

I think about the toughest spell I've had to pull off recently. Cost a lot of money and took a lot of prep. I want to see if I can do it on my own. I drive out to a cemetery in east L.A. off the 110 Freeway. Gentle slopes with teetering gravestones encrusted with grime, pitted from smog and acid rain.

I stop at the gates, engine idling. Do I really want to do this? It's not what I'm about to do that gives me pause, it's the venue. It's the people.

If things work the way I hope, at best there will be

screaming. I can't see any way around it. I put the car in gear and drive into the cemetery.

Two funerals going on at opposite ends of the grounds. One is a massive affair. A crowd of mourners, wailing relatives. A wreath next to the casket shows the picture of a kid. High school football uniform, big smiles. The future so goddamn full of opportunity he doesn't know where to start. I drive past, leave them alone in their grief. I'm a bastard, but I'm not that big a bastard.

The other funeral is a small, somber affair. A handful of bored looking mourners, a droning preacher. Far off in a corner of the cemetery. Perfect.

I park the car a little ways off and walk to a grave far enough from the funeral to be unobtrusive, but not so far that I can't see what's going on. The spell I have in mind would normally cost me a small fortune in precious stones, energy and time. The work on the front end is exacting and takes a toll. I used something like it in Texas to make a corpse my puppet.

Now to see if I can do it cold.

I close my eyes, reach out with my senses. I can pick up some wanderers, a few haunts, but they're pretty far away. Nobody dies in a cemetery. It's just a place to bury meat. But some of who we are lingers. It's hard to find, harder to grab hold of. Like talking to Ellis last night, only a lot more complicated. Doing it on my own is impossible.

Well, yesterday it was impossible.

The tiny glimmers of personality hanging onto the corpses in the cemetery flare in my mind. A few already underground. The strongest are the boy across the way and the man in the coffin nearby. I can feel the edges of him, like handprints left in sand, blowing away with each passing moment. Little more than an imprint of dust. I tease at the threads, pull them apart, strengthen them with my own power.

A loud thumping comes from the casket. I open my eyes to see it shake as I make the grisly puppet inside dance. The mourners back away, appalled, unsure what to do. I flail the body around some more, make the casket bounce, rock back and forth on the stand, tilt. It falls over with a crash. The latches locking it shut pop open, the corpse barreling out to roll on the ground.

Like I said there's screaming. Some of the mourners scatter, a couple of men rush forward to stuff him back into his coffin. So I make him stand, stiff on legs like wood, joints cracking. It's grotesque and tragic. Without the ritual I used in Texas the corpse feels like a numb extension of myself. But the fact that I can move it at all is amazing.

One of the men who rushed to the body when it fell out of the casket runs up, beats it over the head with a tire iron. He's not screaming. He's crying. And suddenly I realize what I'm doing to these people. I give up control, let the body fall to the ground, sick at my own power. Why did I do that? I didn't have to make such a display out of it.

I leave the mourners terrified, walk back to the car, start it with shaking hands. Jesus, what am I turning into?

———

I stop at Alex's house and check on Vivian. She's still out. I check the house wards for any cracks, add my own to the mix, strengthen the barriers. My spells lock in place with barely a thought. I could get used to this.

But even with all this power I'm still worried. I have a plan, sure. Sort of.

Okay, not really.

Here's the idea. I get Boudreau and Griffin together, Boudreau takes Griffin and I take them both out at the same time. And maybe unicorns will fly out of my ass.

I sit on the floor next to Vivian, head in my hands. I can't fuck this up. There's too much riding on it. The minute I let my guard down Griffin's going to take a swing at me. And he'll probably do it while Boudreau's doing the same. Griffin was right. There are too many variables. But I can't think of a better idea.

"I'll get Alex back," I say and kiss Vivian's cheek. I don't much care if I make it at this point, but goddamn it I'll keep that promise.

———

Griffin pulls up in a Lincoln Town Car across the street from Boudreau's old house. He and two of his thugs step out of the car, a buzzcut Latino who looks like he just got out of the army and a hook-nosed guy with glasses.

Two was the absolute minimum I figured Griffin would show up with. I half-expected a platoon. I don't need twenty guys to take out on top of everything else.

"I should have known," Griffin says. "His old house." All three of them are wearing black tactical gear. Seriously. Holsters, buckles, the whole nine yards. Considering what we're up against I don't think the guns are for Boudreau.

"You bring your gas masks, too?" I ask.

Buzzcut looks worried. "You think we'll need them?"

Jesus. "We're going into a haunted house, not taking Afghanistan."

"Your fashion advice is noted," Griffin says. "I want to make something very clear."

"I'm all ears."

"I know you're lying to me. About which parts I'm not sure, but your story is so full of holes I can't tell where the truth ends and the bullshit begins."

"And yet you're here."

"And yet I'm here. I want Boudreau gone as much as you do, maybe more. But if this is a trick I'm going to skin you alive."

"You're almost scary when you get all domineering like that. You're going to try to skin me alive, anyway. So I really don't see how I have much to lose. Now that we're all on the same page, are we going to stand out here like idiots waving our dicks at each other or are we going to go do this?"

He gives Buzzcut and Glasses an almost imperceptible nod. They double-time it across the street. Griffin and I follow. The house is a two-story Tudor with a couple heavy chimneys, half-timbering and cross gables. I can feel Boudreau's presence inside.

It occurs to me that, though I know Boudreau's there, I have no way of knowing if Alex is in there, too. I falter for a moment at that thought, but I don't have time for that now.

Griffin nods at Buzzcut. "If you would?" Buzzcut checks the door, whispers a spell and the lock pops. A glow surrounds his fingers as he gets ready for Christ only knows what on the other side. He nudges the door open. A deep smell of rot rolls over us like a tide.

"Maybe we should have brought gas masks," Glasses says.

Buzzcut leans into the doorway, looks around. "It's clear," he says. Except it's not. I can feel Boudreau welling up like a geyser.

"Get away from the door," I say, but it's too late. Boudreau's swarm of ghosts fill the doorway. He's found a new use for them. Hazy tendrils shoot out, yank Buzzcut inside, slam the door in our faces. Griffin gets a spell off, a jagged tongue of lightning and shadow that blows the door off its hinges. I stagger, my vision going double, as a backwash of energy that I can feel down into my soul hits me.

"What the hell did you do?" I say. My sight comes back into focus.

"Something I cooked up that should at least destroy some of the ghosts around him," Griffin says. "It can be a little disorienting to be around if you're not used to it. I guarantee if you felt it, Boudreau felt it more." Yeah, no shit. I feel like a bell that's been rung with a sledge-hammer.

"Well, we know he's home," I say.

"And we're down a man."

"Try another entrance?" Glasses says.

Griffin turns to me. "But you can sense him, can't you? You knew he was there before he hit."

"Yeah, by like a second and a half. When he pops up I won't get much warning. It'll be like playing a game of Whack-A-Mole. This door, another door. I don't see how it matters."

I push my way past them and enter the house.

"Remember to wipe your feet," I say.

"I don't think the owners are going to mind," Griffin says. He points through a pair of double doors across from a staircase. I can see the family piled like rotting cordwood on the dining table.

"Boudreau's not one for sharing, is he?" I say.

"Some things never change."

There's a noise upstairs that grabs all our attention. Something heavy coming down the stairs. Buzzcut's head rolls off the last step and lands with a wet thump on the floor. Glasses nudges it with a toe.

"Looks like an invitation to me," I say and head up the stairs. "You guys coming?"

I follow the blood spatter Buzzcut's head left as it bounced its way down. Dark red blotches on the carpeted steps, splashes on the banister. They stop at the second floor landing where Buzzcut's body is slowly draining into the carpet. One less asshole I have to worry about. I step over him onto the landing, look over the hallway, wondering when Boudreau's going to make another move.

Every time I try to get a bead on him he fuzzes out. He's actively hiding himself. The harder I push the harder it gets. Maybe I can't find him, but if he's here I can find Alex. I go to the nearest door, wonder what's waiting for me on the other side. Do I open it and crouch, lean to the side, hope nothing jumps out at me? Fuck it. I throw it open. A bedroom, drawn curtains, dusty surfaces, an unmade bed.

"Master suite," Griffin says behind me. "I've been here before."

He points at three other closed doors and a short hallway that corners away from us. "Two other bedrooms, bathroom, and down there are a den and a game room."

A sound from down the hallways catches our attention. "Sounded like a cough," Glasses says. "Ghosts don't cough, do they?"

I rush down the hall, ignoring Griffin's warnings, hit the den and stop in my tracks. Alex is lying in a heap on the floor at the far side of the room between a coffee table and a leather easy chair. Heavy bruises mottle his face, one eye so swollen and black he can't open it.

"Is that who I think it is?" Griffin says. "You knew he was here?"

"Yeah. Guess I left that bit out."

"It's a trap," he says.

"No shit it's a trap." I walk into it, anyway. Alex is pale, barely conscious. His skin dry as parchment.

"Eric?"

"Yeah, man, it's me. Come to take you home."

He starts to cry. "Is he gone? Tell me he's gone."

"No," I say. "He's not gone, but I'm not going to let him hurt you, anymore. Can you walk?"

"I think so."

I help him to his feet. He's in bad shape. Beaten, tortured, dehydrated. A feeling of emptiness about him. Like he's been hollowed out. He's leaning on me for support, hobbling across the floor. It's about as vulnerable a position as I can be in without having my pants around my ankles so I'm not surprised when Boudreau picks that moment to hit me.

But I am surprised when he tears the floor out from under me.

Chapter 26

The carpet rips as floorboards splinter and crack. We're more than halfway across the floor. I hold Alex tight, and jump for the door. The floor bucks underneath me, a hole ripping through the area we were just standing on. Splinters and dust blow out in a cloud and I can see the smoky tendrils of Boudreau's ghosts tearing more chunks away, making a larger hole.

I get Alex and I to the door, forgetting that I've got other things to worry about than just Boudreau. I see the glow of Griffin's ghost blasting spell form around him. He doesn't care if I'm in the way.

I duck, pulling Alex down with me, barrel into Griffin as he lets loose. The air around me fills with light and dark, a searing pain running through me. The blast fills the room, bursting from Griffin's hands, raking the ceiling as I knock him over.

Momentum carries me forward. The pain is blinding, but I push past it, keep moving. I have to get Alex out of the house. Boudreau is trying to tear it down around us. He'll follow us outside if we get that far. But if I can get

Alex into the car, maybe the wards I've placed on it will offer some protection.

Smoke flows past us to the end of the hallway. Glasses tries to track it, his own spell ready to fly. Griffin's between him and the den. If he lets it off now he'll fry all of us. The smoke gets behind him before he can turn to face it. I can see Boudreau's form inside it, the ghosts orbiting in a mad dance around him.

He's noticeably diminished, many of the ghosts stripped away. Griffin's spell didn't kill him, but it hurt him. By the time Glasses can face him, tentacles of smoke lash out, spear through him. There's a loud crack, a sharp smell of ozone. Power lashes through Glasses' body, cooking him from the inside. He falls to the floor, smoke drifting off of him.

"I'll kill both you fuckers," Griffin says behind me. I turn to see him covered in plaster dust, propping himself up against the wall, the glow of his spell building around his clenched fist. They've got me trapped in the hallway. Boxed in, nowhere to go. Scylla and Charybdis would be a cakewalk compared to these two assholes.

Before I can call up a shield or even duck, Boudreau pulls back the writhing ghosts like a whip and brings them down at me. I drop Alex, hoping that they'll at least miss him. Maybe he can make it out on his own.

They tear through me, come out the other side and hit Griffin in the chest.

I can feel Boudreau's energy coursing through me, electricity running along the spears punched through my body. I hear Griffin scream behind me as his flesh cooks from the inside out, fire ripping through his eye sockets, smoke pouring from his mouth, his ears. I hear a loud snap as his skull cracks open, boiling blood and steam escaping.

But nothing happens to me. I don't burst into flame. I don't die on the spot. Boudreau's spell passed right through me and did nothing to me. I'm not sure which of us is more surprised.

I have a split second of clarity as the ghosts start to pull back from inside me. I see their lives in a starburst flash of knowledge. And somewhere in that I can see Boudreau. I can feel him. And I know how to hurt him.

I don't know what it is I'm calling up. Distilled death, maybe. Pure hatred. Rage. Maybe it's mine. Maybe it's Santa Muerte's. Whatever it is I channel it through the lines of retreating ghosts, shove it through them like a high-pressure hose. And let it all loose into Boudreau's tattered soul.

He burns. Bright and livid. Pieces of him flaring like tissue paper in a bonfire. The ghosts around him vaporizing. I keep it up until there's nothing left of him to burn.

———

Smoke drifts from the bodies, smelling like Hell's own barbeque. I kneel by Alex. He's unconscious, covered in plaster dust, face lacerated from shrapnel. But he's breathing. Right now that's all I care about. I'll get him to Vivian. She'll know what to do. I throw him over my shoulder in a fireman's carry, arms wrapped around his legs. My muscles are screaming at me.

With Boudreau gone the spell keeping the neighbors away from the house isn't going to last long. I have to get him out of here quickly. He comes to at the top of the stairs as I'm stepping over Buzzcut's body.

"Hey," he says, his voice choked with dust. He coughs, a racking sound like his lungs are tearing.

"We're almost out of here, man. I got him. Boudreau's gone."

"No," he says, voice stronger. "I'm not."

He rams an elbow hard into my kidney. My knee buckles, my feet get tangled up in Buzzcut's headless corpse and all three of us go tumbling down the stairs. I land hard on my back, the wind knocked out of me. Alex picks himself up off the floor and then I get it.

I don't know when it happened. Maybe as I was frying him, probably before. Maybe the thing I killed upstairs was only a piece he left behind for me. At some point, Boudreau moved into Alex.

"Oh, I knew I was going to enjoy this," he says. He kicks me in the chest. "Have to admit I figured you'd be dead by now. I don't know why you didn't go up like Griffin did. Not that I much care." Another kick. Spots swim before my eyes. Can't get a breath.

I finally get a gasp of air. I pull myself away, but not fast enough. His foot glances off my forehead and I see stars. I roll backward to avoid the next kick. Find my voice.

"You sonofabitch. Let him go."

"Nope. I like it here. Thanks for taking your time getting here, by the way. Gave me enough to get this boy prepped and ready to go."

So I was right. He couldn't just go anywhere, take over anyone. He needed to prepare them first. Jesus. He'd had months with Ellis. What did he do to Alex in, what, less than two days? To get it so fast it must have been brutal.

"I said let him go." I reach out, looking for that thread of Boudreau I had hold of earlier, try to find him. Grab him. Tear him apart. But it's not there. He's firmly embedded. Just like when he took over Ellis.

On impulse I pull the Browning out of the shoulder holster under my jacket. I don't know what else to do. He kicks it out of my hand before I can bring it to bear. Just as well. I couldn't pull the trigger, anyway.

It's Alex. The man who raised my sister when I was running away. Who picked up the broken pieces I left behind and helped make them whole again. He's the man I never was, never could be. I'm the one who should be in his place. I'm the one who should be suffering. I'm the one who should be paying this price.

If anyone's going to come out of this alive it has to be him.

Boudreau waves Alex's hand and I feel myself picked up off the floor and thrown against the banister like a ragdoll. "Oh, god this feels good." He flexes the fingers, rolls the shoulders. "You have no idea. It was like being numb all the time. You can't feel anything, can't taste anything. You know what I'm going to do when I'm done killing you? I'm gonna get a burger. Then I'm gonna get laid."

He tries to throw me again, but I'm ready and meet his magic with my own, blocking him. I still can't get hold of him in there and I don't dare do anything that will hurt Alex. Well, not permanently. I try to push him back, but he's got his defenses up as much as I do. So instead of moving him, I yank the rug he's standing on.

He topples onto his back and I'm on him. "Get out of there, goddammit." I wrap my hands around his throat.

If I choke Alex hard enough to knock him out and not kill him, maybe I can scare Boudreau into leaving. It's not tight enough and he breaks out of my hold, kneeing my in the gut and throwing me off.

"You don't get it," he says, giving me another kick to the head. "He's gone. I broke him. Broke him, moved in, kicked his ass out."

"He's not—"

"Oh, yes he is," Boudreau says. "He's not just dead. He's gone."

I lurch to my feet, wrapping my arms around him in a tackle, drive him to the floor. "Bullshit. I know he's in there." He's grinning at me like a maniac. That's Alex's face but it's not at the same time. The expression's all wrong, the way he's laughing and smiling. This isn't like when Boudreau took Ellis. I can't see him the way I saw him at the hospital, his ghost overlaid onto the body. He's in there hard and he's not coming out. But it doesn't mean Alex isn't in there, too. I look into his eyes, trying to find any shred of Alex that might be left. There has to be something there.

And then something weird happens. Maybe it's some newfound gift from Santa Muerte, maybe it's something I'd just never tapped into before. I see Boudreau in there, see his soul taking root like invading kudzu, tendrils seething inside. An infection that won't stop. It flows through empty channels, takes up residence like a squatter in an evacuated house.

And that's when I know. He's not lying. Alex's body has been hollowed out, left empty for this new host. There's nothing of him left.

I feel the air pick me up, slam me against the wall.

Compress around me, hold me in place. I can't move. Can't breathe. He's going to crush me. I try to break his hold, but it's like arm wrestling a bear. It won't work. Brute force won't work. I need to do something he doesn't expect.

I had practiced these moves in my mind for days before I tried it in Texas. That feels like years ago, a lifetime ago. But I remember them. I reach out, find what I'm looking for. Boudreau's laughing. Good. He's not paying attention to what's behind him.

At least until Buzzcut's headless body shoves the Browning against the back of his head and pulls the trigger. Alex's head explodes. His body falls to the floor, spasming as it dies.

Alex might be dead, but Boudreau isn't. He scatters like dust, reforms in front of me. Raging, screaming wordlessly. His shock is so overwhelming he loses control of his spell. I fall to the ground, gasping like a fish. My vision is going black around the edges.

I can feel him now, get hold of him. I pull out all the stops. Every ounce of power I can draw in, every bit of my own. All the rage, hatred and hurt.

I learned something when I destroyed what I thought was all of him upstairs. Understood another power Santa Muerte had given me. Tearing him apart, having the Dead eat him, neither one of those stuck.

So this time I eat him myself.

Chapter 27

I hear the memorial service was closed casket. After all, nobody wants to see a body lying there with a ravaged stump where his head used to be.

The police investigation was a mess. Took weeks to get Alex's body released to Vivian. Some anonymous tips, a little misdirection and a couple of Obi-Wan "These aren't the droids you're looking for" tricks later and the police closed things up with a story of a mafia hit gone horribly wrong.

Explaining things to Vivian was a lot harder. I stand by the mausoleum a long way off from the funeral, watching. Alex is going into a plot at Forest Lawn, out on the grass, under the sun.

He's quite the draw. I count almost a hundred people. Of course he would be a pillar of the community. Local boy does good, owns his own business. Some of the people are his customers, some of them are from the magic set. I recognize a few of them.

I haven't spoken with Tabitha since it all happened. The first week she texted or called every few hours, then every couple days. And now I don't hear from her.

A breeze blows past, bringing a smell of roses and smoke. I hear cloth brushing against grass next to me.

"Was wondering when you were going to show up," I say. I haven't seen Santa Muerte since that day in Mictlan. I haven't gone back to her church, either.

"I grieve for you, Eric Carter," she says.

"That's the first thing you said to me when we met," I say.

"It makes it no less true," she says, "husband."

My stomach clenches when she says it. I've been trying to forget that. Trying to scrub that out of my mind. Tried booze, pills. Downed a bottle of Xanax with a fifth of Old Grand-Dad. Should have killed me. Not surprised that it didn't. Muerte's got too much invested in me to let me go that easily. Something tells me I'm going to have a hard time dying.

After that I threw out the rest of the booze I'd bought, the pills I'd gotten my hands on. Suicide's not for me. I know that. I have something to live for now.

"You're a real piece of work, you know that? And good. Holy fuck are you good. I've known grifters, but man, you really take it."

She cocks her head to one side, bone scraping on bone. "What do you mean?"

"You can drop the act," I say. "I know. I saw it in Boudreau. You can learn a lot from a guy when you eat his soul."

I watch the funeral break up, people exchanging hugs, walking off to their cars. I wonder if anyone can see me up here talking to empty space.

"And what did you learn?"

She moves around to face me, blocking my view of the proceedings, her skeletal hand on my shoulder.

"He didn't kill Lucy. Didn't know a goddamn thing about her. I wasn't even on his radar. I would have figured it out eventually. Started to. There were too many holes. He acted all surprised when I first saw him. He didn't know I was even in town."

She says nothing, stares at me with her empty sockets. I pull off my sunglasses and give as good as I get with the pitch black eyes she gave me.

"You killed her. You knew how to brutalize her so badly she'd only leave an Echo. Possessed somebody? One of the ghosts I talked to said the killer had pitch black eyes. One of your followers, maybe? That guy running your church?"

She says nothing so I keep going. "You wanted Boudreau gone because you were worried he would become stronger. Turn into competition."

She doesn't admit to it, but she doesn't deny it, either. She doesn't need to. We both know it's the truth.

"What I don't understand," I say, "is why me?"

"You are more than a pretty plaything, or a useful lapdog," she says after a long pause.

"Good to know I'm held in such high esteem."

"You are. In very high esteem. If it hadn't been me, it would have been someone else. One of the Loa, perhaps. A god less kind than I."

"Kind? This is kind?"

"You don't know your own power," she says. "I have given you some of mine, yes, but you have barely touched the surface of what you can do. I didn't kill

Boudreau, and very little of what you did that night was because of me."

"I'm getting that," I say. "Wish I'd figured that out sooner."

"That's why I did this. It is a gift. My aid unlocked more of your potential. It was a waste what you've been doing with your power."

"A gift? Murdering my sister is a gift? Setting me up as a patsy to do your dirty work is a gift? Horseshit. You wanted to fucking own me. Congratulations, now you do."

"I'm glad you understand that."

"I know what I signed up for. Do you?"

"What do you mean?"

"I can deny any request you make of me. That's part of the contract. You want me to do a job for you, you can go fuck yourself."

"The blade cuts both ways," she says. "Yes, you can deny me, but you cannot interfere should I will it. I wonder how well Vivian can protect herself."

And there you have it. I was wondering when she was going to play that card. I knew it was coming. Knew that it trumps everything I've got in my hand.

"One of these days I'm going to kill you," I say, putting my sunglasses back on. "That's my purpose in life, now. To see you gone."

She reaches up with a hand, caresses my face. Instead of cold bone, it's a feel of soft skin. "Yes," she says. "I think some day you might." The smell of roses and smoke grows as she fades from view in a gray haze.

Vivian steps through her fading form. I manage to get out a surprised, "Viv—" before she hauls off and punches me. She knocks my sunglasses off and I don't want her to see my eyes. I pick them up from the ground and shield my face.

"How dare you," she screams. "How fucking dare you come here."

"Vivian, I—"

"No," she says. "Shut up. You don't get to talk." Tears are streaming down her face, mascara running into the collar of her black dress. "This is all your fault. All of it. You fucking murderer. Alex died because of you. He died for you. Everything you touch turns to shit and you leave everyone else to pick up the pieces."

"Vivian, I'm sorry, I—"

She punches me again. "Stay away from me. Never talk to me again. Never call. Never look me up. Go be with all your dead people, all your corpses. At least you can't hurt them anymore." She turns on her heel and heads back toward the funeral. Surprised onlookers heading to their cars stop to watch this brief exchange.

I watch as she stalks down the hill toward the cars. I wish I could give her what she wants. But that's not possible. Not with Santa Muerte holding that threat over her head. I left before and look what happened.

I won't do that again.

Joe Sunday's dead...

...he just hasn't stopped moving yet.

Sunday's a thug, an enforcer, a leg-breaker for hire.
When his boss sends him to kill a mysterious new business partner, his target strikes back in ways Sunday
could never have imagined. Murdered, brought back to
a twisted half-life, Sunday finds himself stuck in the
middle of a race to find an ancient stone with the power
to grant immortality. With it, he might live forever.
Without it, he's just another rotting extra in a George
Romero flick.

Everyone's got a stake, from a psycho Nazi wizard and
a razor-toothed midget, to a nympho-demon bartender,
a too-powerful witch who just wants to help her homeless vampires, and the one woman who might have all
the answers — if only Sunday can figure out what her
angle is.

Before the week is out he's going to find out just what
lengths people will go to for immortality. And just how
long somebody can hold a grudge.

City of the Lost
by Stephen Blackmoore
978-0-7564-702-5

DAW 209

Diana Rowland

"Rowland's delightful novel jumps genre lines with a little something for everyone—mystery, horror, humor, and even a smattering of romance. Not to be missed—all that's required is a high tolerance for gray matter. For true zombiephiles, of course, that's a no brainer."

— *Library Journal*

"An intriguing mystery and a hilarious mix of the horrific and mundane aspects of zombie life open a promising new series...Humor and gore are balanced by surprisingly touching moments as Angel tries to turn her (un)life around."

— *Publishers Weekly*

My Life as a White Trash Zombie
978-0-7564-0675-2

Even White Trash Zombies Get the Blues
978-0-7564-0750-6

To Order Call: 1-800-788-6262
www.dawbooks.com

DAW 201

Tad Williams

The Dirty Streets of Heaven

"A dark and thrilling story.... Bad-ass smart-mouth Bobby Dollar, an Earth-bound angel advocate for newly departed souls caught between Heaven and Hell, is appalled when a soul goes missing on his watch. Bobby quickly realizes this is 'an actual, honest-to-front-office crisis,' and he sets out to fix it, sparking a chain of hellish events.... Exhilarating action, fascinating characters, and high stakes will leave the reader both satisfied and eager for the next installment." —*Publishers Weekly (starred review)*

"Williams does a brilliant job.... Made me laugh. Made me curious. Impressed me with its cleverness. Made me hungry for the next book. Kept me up late at night when I should have been sleeping."
—Patrick Rothfuss

And watch for the sequel, Happy Hour in Hell, *coming in September 2013!*

The Dirty Streets of Heaven: 978-0-7564-0768-1
Happy Hour in Hell: 978-0-7564-0815-2

To Order Call: 1-800-788-6262
www.dawbooks.com

DAW 207

P.O. 0005208502 202